Vilama
Vila-Matas, Enrique, 1948-
Dublinesque /

34028079018579
FM $16.95   ocn759908618
10/18/12

3 4028 07901 8579
HARRIS COUNTY PUBLIC LIBRARY

Dublinesque

D0874273

DISCARD

ALSO BY ENRIQUE VILA-MATAS
from New Directions

Bartleby & Co.
Montano's Malady
Never Any End to Paris

Enrique Vila-Matas

Dublinesque

Translated from the Spanish
by Anne McLean & Rosalind Harvey

A NEW DIRECTIONS BOOK

Copyright ©2010 by Enrique Vila-Matas
Translation copyright © 2012 by Anne McLean and Rosalind Harvey

All rights reserved. Except for brief passages quoted in a newspaper, magazine, radio,
television, or website review, no part of this book may be reproduced in any form
or by any means, electronic or mechanical, including photocopying and record-
ing, or by any information storage and retrieval system, without permission in
writing from the Publisher.

"Dublinesque," "High Windows," and "The Importance of Elsewhere" appear in *Collected Poems of Philip Larkin*, edited by Archie Burnett. Copyright © 2012 by the Estate
of Philip Larkin. Used by permission.

"The Irish Cliffs of Moher" appears in *The Collected Poems of Wallace Stevens* (Alfred A.
Knopf, 1954). Used by permission.

The publication of this work has been made possible through a subsidy received
from the Directorate General for Books, Archives and Libraries of the Spanish
Ministry of Culture.

Manufactured in the United States of America
New Directions Books are printed on acid-free paper.
First published in 2012 as New Directions Paperbook 1234
Published simultaneously in Canada by Penguin Books Ltd.

Library of Congress Cataloging-in-Publication Data
Vila-Matas, Enrique, 1948–
[Dublinesca. English]
Dublinesque / Enrique Vila-Matas ; translated from the Spanish by Anne McLean
and Rosalind Harvey.
p. cm.
ISBN 978-0-8112-1961-7 (acid-free paper)
1. Literary historians—Fiction. 2. Spanish—Ireland—Fiction. 3. Dublin (Ireland)—
Fiction. I. McLean, Anne, 1962– II. Harvey, Rosalind, 1982– III. Title.
PQ6672.I37D8313 2012
863'.64--dc23

                    2012008681

10 9 8 7 6 5 4 3 2 1

New Directions Books are published for James Laughlin
by New Directions Publishing Corporation
80 Eighth Avenue, New York 10011

For Paula de Parma

Dublinesque

MAY

He belongs to an increasingly rare breed of sophisticated, literary publishers. And every day, since the beginning of this century, he has watched in despair the spectacle of the noble branch of his trade—publishers who still read and who have always been drawn to literature—gradually, surreptitiously dying out. He had financial trouble two years ago, but managed to shut the publishing house down without having to declare bankruptcy, toward which it had been heading with terrifying obstinacy, despite its prestige. In over thirty years as an independent he has seen it all, successes but also huge failures. He attributes the loss of direction in the end to his resistance to publishing the gothic vampire tales and other nonsense now in fashion, and so forgets part of the truth: he was never renowned for good financial management, and what's more, his exaggerated fanaticism for literature was probably harmful.

Samuel Riba—known to everyone as Riba—has published many of the great writers of his time. In some cases only one book, but enough so they appear in his catalog. Sometimes, although aware that in the honorable sector of his trade there are still some valiant Quixotes, he likes to see himself as the last publisher. He has a somewhat romantic image of himself, and spends his life feeling that it's the end of an era, the end of the world, doubtless influenced by the sudden cessation of his activities. He has a remarkable tendency to read his life as a literary text, interpreting it with the distortions befitting the compulsive reader he's been for so many years. Aside from this, he is hoping to sell his assets to a foreign publishing house, but talks have been stalled for some time. He lives in an anxious state of powerful, end-of-everything psychosis. Nothing, and no one, has yet convinced him that getting old has its good points. Does it?

He is visiting his elderly parents, and at this moment, looking them up and down with open curiosity. He has come to tell them how his recent trip to Lyon went. Apart from every Wednesday—a regular engagement—it's a long-standing custom of his to go and see them whenever he gets back from a trip. In the last two years, he hasn't received even a tenth of the offers to travel that he used to, but he's hidden this detail from his parents, as well as the fact that he has closed down the publishing house, since he considers them to be too old for such upsets, and anyway, he's not sure they would really take it in.

He cheers up every time he gets invited somewhere, because, among other things, it allows him to keep up the fiction of his busyness for his parents. Despite the fact that he will soon turn sixty he is, as can be seen, highly dependent on them, perhaps because he has no children, and they, in turn, have only him: an only child. He's even traveled to places that barely interest him, just to be able to tell his parents about the trip afterward and keep them believing—they don't read newspapers or watch television—that he is still publishing and his presence is still sought in many places, and therefore, that things are still going very well for him. But it's not remotely like this. When he was a publisher he used to have a very busy social life, but now he has far less of one, if it counts as a social life at all. On top of the loss of so many false friendships, there is also the problem of the anxiety that has overcome him since he gave up drinking two years ago. It is an anxiety that comes as much from his awareness that, without alcohol, he would have been less daring in what he published, as from his certainty that his social life was forced, not at all natural and perhaps came only from an unhealthy fear of disorder and solitude.

Nothing has gone well for him since he began courting solitude. Despite trying to keep it from falling into the abyss, his marriage is in fact teetering on the edge, although not always, because his relationship passes through the most varied states and goes from euphoria and love to hatred and disaster. Every day he feels more unstable in every way, and he's become grumpy and dislikes most of what he sees. Something to do with getting old, probably. But the fact is that he is starting to feel uncomfortable in the world, and turning sixty makes him feel as if he has a noose around his neck.

His elderly parents always listen to the tales of his travels with great curiosity and attention. At times, they even look like two exact replicas of Kubla Khan listening to Marco Polo's stories. The visits that follow one of his trips take on a special quality; they seem to belong to a higher category than the more monotonous, habitual Wednesday visits. Today's also has that quality of being extraordinary. However, something strange is happening because, despite having been in the house for a while, he still hasn't managed to broach the subject of Lyon. And the thing is he cannot tell his parents anything about his time in that city, because he was so cut off from the world there and his journey so savagely cerebral that he is unable to dredge up a single, minimally human anecdote. Besides, what actually happened to him in Lyon was unpleasant. It was a cold, unfriendly trip, like those hypnotic journeys that lately he so often undertakes in front of his computer.

"So you've been to Lyon," his mother says again, by now even slightly concerned.

His father has slowly begun to light his pipe and looks at him in surprise, as if also wondering why he doesn't tell them anything about Lyon. But what can he tell them? He's not going to start talking about the general theory of the novel he managed to concoct all by himself, there in the hotel. They wouldn't be at all interested in how he elaborated this theory, and moreover, he doesn't think they really know what a "literary theory" might be. And supposing they did know, he's sure they would find the subject profoundly boring. They might even come to the same conclusion as Celia: that he has been too isolated recently, too disconnected from the real world and seduced by his computer or, in its absence—as in Lyon—by his own mental journeys.

In Lyon he spent his time avoiding all contact with Villa Fonde-brider, the organization that had invited him to give a lecture on the grave state of literary publishing in Europe. In revenge, perhaps, for the disdain shown him by the organizers in not sending anyone to meet him either at the airport or the hotel, Riba had shut himself up in his hotel room and managed to realize one of the dreams he'd had when he was in publishing and didn't have time for anything: to write a general theory of the novel.

He'd published lots of important authors, but only in Julien Gracq's novel *The Opposing Shore* did he perceive any spirit of the future. In his room in Lyon, over the course of endless hours spent locked away, he devoted himself to a theory of the novel that, based on the lessons apparent to him the moment he opened *The Opposing Shore*, established five elements he considered essential for the novel of the future. These essential elements were: intertextuality; connection with serious poetry; awareness of a moral landscape in ruins; a slight favoring of style over plot; a view of writing that moves forward like time.

It was a daring theory, given that it put forward Gracq's book, usually considered antiquated, as the most advanced of all novels. He filled a great many pages expanding on his proposal for the novel of the future. But when he had finished this tough job, he remembered the "sacred instinct of having no theories" spoken of by Pessoa, another of his favorite writers and whose book *The Education of the Stoic* he had once had the honor of publishing. He remembered this instinct and thought of how foolish novelists sometimes were, and remembered several Spanish writers he had published whose novels were the ingenuous product of extensive, sophisticated theories. What a huge waste of time, Riba thought, to come up with a theory in order to write a novel. He now had genuine grounds to say this, as he had just written one himself.

Let's see, thought Riba. If one has the theory, why write the novel?

8

And at the same time as he asked himself this, and doubtless in order to avoid the strong sense of having wasted his time, of wasting it even as he asked the question, he understood that the hours spent in his hotel room writing his theory of the novel had basically allowed him to get rid of it. Wasn't this contemptible? No, of course not. His theory would still be what it was, lucid and daring, but he was going to destroy it by throwing it into the wastebasket in his room.

He held a secret, private funeral for his theory and for all the theories that had ever existed, and then left the city of Lyon without once having contacted the people who had invited him to speak about the grave—or maybe not so grave, thought Riba throughout the journey—state of literary publishing in Europe. He slipped quietly out of the hotel and took a train back to Barcelona, twenty-four hours after arriving in Lyon. He didn't even leave a note for the people at Villa Fondebrider justifying his invisibility in Lyon, or his subsequent strange flight. He understood that the whole journey had served only to set out his theory and then hold a private funeral for it. He left totally convinced that his entire theory of what the novel should be was nothing more than a document drawn up with the single aim of liberating himself from its contents. Or, rather, a document with the exclusive aim of confirming that the best thing to do is to travel and to lose theories, lose them all.

"So you've been to Lyon," his mother says, returning to the attack.

It has been a May of changeable weather, amazingly rainy for Barcelona. Today is cold, gray, and sad. For a few minutes, he imagines he's in New York, in a building where you can hear the traffic driving toward the Holland Tunnel: rivers of cars heading home after work. It's pure imagination. He has never heard the sound of the Holland Tunnel. He soon returns to reality, to Barcelona and the depressing ash-gray light. Celia, his wife, expects him home around six. Everything is happening with a certain degree of normality, apart from his parents' growing concern as they realize their son is telling them nothing about Lyon.

But what can he tell them about what happened there? What can he say? That, as they well know, he hasn't had a drink for two years, since his long-suffering kidneys put him in the hospital, and that this has confined him to a permanent state of sobriety, which means that sometimes he dedicates himself to activities as outlandish as elaborating literary theories and never leaving his hotel room, not even to meet the people who invited him? That in Lyon he didn't speak to anyone and that, in short, since he stopped publishing, this is what he does every day in the long hours he spends sitting in front of his computer in Barcelona? That what he finds most regrettable and what saddens him most is that he left publishing without having discovered an unknown writer who turned out to be a genius? That he is still traumatized by the misfortune inherent in his former trade, that most bitter misfortune of having to look for authors, those tiresomely essential beings, since without them the whole business would be impossible? That in the past few weeks he has had pains in his right knee, almost certainly caused by uric acid or arthritis, supposing these are two different things? That he was once talkative thanks to alcohol and now he has become melancholy, which was probably always his true natural state? What can he tell his parents? That everything comes to an end?

His visit is going by with a degree of monotony and his parents even resort to recalling, due in part to the tedium dominating this encounter, the now distant day in 1959 when General Eisenhower deigned to visit Spain and ended the international isolation of Franco's dictatorship. His father spent that day bursting with enthusiasm, not because of the diplomatic battle won by the wretched Galician general, but rather because the United States, the vanquishers of Nazism, had at last approached a moribund Spain. It is one of the first significant memories of Riba's life. He remembers, above all, the moment his mother asked his father why he was so "excessively enthusiastic" about the American president's visit.

"What does enthusiastic mean?" Riba had asked his parents.

He will always remember exactly how he framed this question, because—timid as he was at that age—it was the first one he asked. The second question he remembers asking, although he's not so sure how he framed it. He knows, in any case, that it had to do with his name—Samuel—and with what some teachers and children at school had said to him. His father explained that he was only Jewish on his mother's side and since she had converted to Catholicism a few months after he was born, he should relax—that's what he said, relax—and just consider himself the son of Catholics.

Today his father, as on previous occasions when they've spoken of Eisenhower's visit, denies he was so excited, and says it's a misunderstanding of his mother's, who thought that he got far too worked up about the American president's visit. He also denies that for a while his favorite film was Charles Walters's *High Society* with Bing Crosby, Grace Kelly, and Frank Sinatra. They watched it at least three times, at the end of the fifties, and Riba remembers this film always used to put his father in an excellent mood. He was crazy about everything that came from the United States; the films and the glamour fascinated him; he was drawn to the lives led by human beings who were like them but in a place that seemed as remote as it was inaccessible. And it's very likely Riba inherited from him, from his father, his fascination with the New World, the distant charm of those places that, back then, seemed so unattainable, maybe because the people who lived there seemed like the happiest people on earth.

They talk about Eisenhower's visit and *High Society* and the D-Day landings, but his father continues stubbornly to deny he felt such enthusiasm. Just when it seems as if, to avoid getting stuck on the subject, his parents will soon return to the Lyon question, night falls on Barcelona with unusual speed; it grows dark very quickly, and a violent downpour arrives with a big flash of lightning. It falls just at the moment he is getting ready to leave the house.

The dreadful crash of a solitary clap of thunder. The rain falls on Barcelona with a rage and force never before seen. Suddenly he has the feeling of being trapped and at the same time of being perfectly capable of walking through walls. Somewhere, at the edge of one of his thoughts, he discovers a darkness that chills him to the bone. He isn't too surprised, he's used to this happening to him in his parents' apartment. The most likely explanation is that, a few moments ago, one of the numerous damp ghosts—peaceful ghosts of some ancestor or other who inhabit this dark mezzanine—has slipped inside him.

He wants to forget about the domestic specter chilling him to the bone, so he goes over to the window and there he sees a young man who, with no umbrella in the rain, standing right in the middle of Calle Aribau, seems to be spying on the house. He is perhaps a superior ghost. But in any case, the young man is without a doubt a phantom from outside, not one of the family. Riba exchanges a few glances with him. The young man has an Indian-looking face, and wears an electric-blue Nehru jacket with gold buttons down the front. What can he be doing out there and why is he dressed like that? When the strange young man sees that the traffic lights have changed and the cars are starting to move along the street again, he crosses to the other side. Is it really a Nehru jacket he's wearing? It could just be some kind of fashionable jacket, but it's not at all clear. Only someone like Riba, who has always been such an attentive reader of newspapers and is now of a respectable age, would remember people such as Srî Pandit Jawâharlâl Nehru, a politician from another age, the Indian leader who was spoken of so much forty years ago, and now not at all.

Suddenly his father turns around in his armchair, and in a gloomy tone of voice, as if consumed by a feverish melancholy, says he'd like someone to explain something to him. And he repeats it twice, very anxiously. Riba's never seen him in such a dismal mood: he'd like someone to explain something to him.

"What, Dad?"

Riba thinks he's referring to the great peals of thunder, and patiently starts to explain the origin and cause of certain types of storms. But he soon realizes what he's saying sounds ridiculous, and moreover, his father is looking at him as if he's stupid. He pauses tragically and the pause becomes eternal, he can't carry on talking. Perhaps now he might resolve to tell them something about Lyon. As things stand, it might even be an opportune moment to distract them by describing the literary theory he put together there. He could say he wrote the theory on a cigarette paper and then smoked it. Yes, he should tell them things like that. Or instead, to stir things up even more, ask them that question he hasn't asked for years now: "Why did Mom convert to Catholicism? I need an explanation."

He knows it's useless, that they'll never answer this.

He could also tell them about Julien Gracq and about the day he visited him and went out with the writer onto the balcony of his house in Sion, and Gracq contemplated bolts of lightning, and with particular attention, what he called *the unleashing of erroneous energy*.

His father interrupts the long pause to tell him, with a smug smile, that he is perfectly aware of the existence of altocumulus clouds and so forth, but he isn't asking his son to tell him about things he learned in his long-ago school days.

A new silence follows, this time even longer. Time passes extraordinarily slowly. Mixed with the rain and "the unleashing of erroneous energy" is the ticking of the clock on the wall that, when it was in a different room of this apartment, witnessed his birth, almost sixty years ago. Suddenly all three of them stop moving and stay almost motionless, stiff, exaggeratedly stern—not at all exuberant, very Catalan, expecting who knows what, but definitely waiting. They have just begun the tensest wait of their lives, as if listening for the thunderclap that must arrive. Then suddenly the three of them are totally motionless, more expectant than ever. His parents are shockingly old, this is patently obvious. It's not surprising they haven't found out that he no longer has the publishing house and that he sees far fewer people than he used to.

"I was talking about the mystery," says his father.

Another long pause.

"Of the unfathomable dimension."

An hour later, the rain has stopped. Riba is preparing to escape the trap of the parental home when his mother asks him, almost innocently:

"And what plans do you have now?"

He says nothing, not having expected that question. He has no plans for the immediate future, not even a wretched invitation to some publishers' conference; no book launch to at least show his face at; no new literary theory to write in a hotel room in Lyon; nothing, absolutely nothing at all.

"I can see you don't have any plans," his mother says.

His self-esteem wounded, he lets Dublin come to his rescue. He remembers the strange, striking dream he'd had in the hospital when he fell seriously ill two years ago: a long walk through the streets of the Irish capital, a city he has never been to, but which, in the dream, he knew perfectly well, as if he'd lived there in another life. Nothing astonished him as much as the extraordinary precision of the dream's many details. Were they details from the real Dublin, or did they simply seem real due to the dream's unparalleled intensity? When he woke up, he still knew nothing about Dublin, but he felt totally, strangely certain he had been walking through the streets of this city for a long time, and found it impossible to forget the only difficult part in the dream, the one where reality became strange and upsetting: the moment his wife discovered he had started to drink again, there, in a pub in Dublin. It was a difficult moment, more intense than any other in that dream. Caught by surprise by Celia on his way out of a pub called the Coxwold, in the midst of his latest unwelcome drinking binge, he embraced her sadly, and the two of them ended up crying, sitting on the curb of a Dublin side street. Tears were shed in the most disconsolate situation he had ever experienced in a dream.

"Oh my God, why have you started drinking again?" asked Celia.

A difficult moment, but a strange one too, maybe related to his having recovered from physical collapse and being reborn. A difficult, strange moment, as if there was some kind of message in their pathetic weeping. A singular moment due to how especially intense the dream became—an intensity he had only known before when, on repeated occasions, he dreamt he was happy because he was in New York—and because suddenly, almost brutally, he felt he was linked to Celia beyond this life, an incommunicable feeling it was impossible to demonstrate, but as powerful and personal as it was genuine. A moment like a stab of pain, as if for the first time in his life he felt alive. A very subtle moment, because it seemed to contain—like a puff of air, the dream coming from someone else's mind—a hidden message that placed him just one step away from a great revelation.

"We could go to Cork tomorrow," Celia was saying.

And that's where it all ended. As if the revelation were waiting for him in the port city of Cork, in the south of Ireland.

What revelation?

His mother clears her throat impatiently when she sees him so pensive. And now Riba is worried that she is reading his mind—he has always suspected that, being his mother, she can read it perfectly—and she has discovered that her poor son is destined to fall off the wagon again.

"I'm planning a trip to Dublin," Riba says, this time getting straight to the point.

Up until this precise moment it has rarely, if ever, crossed his mind to go to Dublin. Not speaking English well has always put him off. For business, he always felt it was enough to attend the Frankfurt Book Fair. He used to send his secretary Gauger to the London Book Fair. Gauger was always a huge asset whenever the English language proved essential. But perhaps now the time has come for everything to change. Didn't it change two years ago for Gauger, who took his life savings and a sum of money Riba suspects he stole from him, and left to go and live in a great big hotel in the Tongariro region of New Zealand, where his stepsister was waiting for him? And anyway, didn't Celia's young lover, the one she had before she met Riba, come from Cork?

With charming innocence, his mother asks what he is going to do in Dublin. And he answers with the first thing that comes into his head: that he is going on the sixteenth of June, to give a lecture. Only once he has answered does he realize that this is precisely the day of his parents' sixty-first wedding anniversary. And what is more, he also realizes that "61" and "16" are like heads and tails of the same number. The sixteenth of June, meanwhile, is the day on which Joyce's *Ulysses* takes place, the Dublinesque novel *par excellence* and one of the pinnacles of the age of print, of the Gutenberg galaxy, the twilight of which he is having to live through.

"What's the lecture about?" asks his father.

Brief hesitation.

"It's about James Joyce's novel *Ulysses*, and the Gutenberg constellation giving way to the digital age," he replies.

It was the first thing that occurred to him. Afterward he pauses, and then, as if dictated by an inner voice, he adds:

"They actually want me to speak about the end of the age of print."

Long silence.

"Are the presses closing down?" his mother asks.

His parents, who—as far as he knows—have not the slightest idea who Joyce is and even less what kind of novel lies behind the title *Ulysses* and who, moreover, have been caught off guard by the topic of the end of the age of print, look at him as if it's just been confirmed that, even though it's beneficial for his health, he's been very odd lately, owing to his permanent sobriety since giving up alcohol so radically two years ago. He senses this is what his parents are thinking and fears greatly that they are not entirely in the wrong, since his constant sobriety *is* affecting him, why pretend otherwise? He is too connected to his thoughts and sometimes disconnects fatally for a few seconds and gives answers he should have thought through more, such as the one he has just given them about *Ulysses* and the Gutenberg galaxy.

He ought to have given them a different answer. But as Céline said, "Once you're in, you're in it up to your neck." Now that he's announced he is going to Dublin, he's going to push on into the tangled affair, up to his neck, as far as is necessary. He will go to Dublin. No doubt about it. This will also allow him to verify whether or not the many extraordinarily precise details in his strange dream were real. If, for instance, he sees that in Dublin there is a pub called the Coxwold with a big red and black door, this will mean nothing less than that he really did cry with Celia, in an emotional scene, sitting on the ground, in Dublin, perhaps before he was ever there.

He will go to Dublin, capital of Ireland, a country he doesn't know much about, only that, if he remembers correctly—he tells himself he'll look it up later on Google—it has been an independent state since 1922, the very year—another coincidence—his parents were born. He knows very little about Ireland, although he knows a good deal about its literature. W. B. Yeats, for example, is one of his favorite poets. 1922 is, moreover, the year in which *Ulysses* was published. He could go and hold a funeral for the Gutenberg galaxy in Dublin Cathedral, which is called St. Patrick's, if he remembers rightly; there, on that holy site, Antonin Artaud finally went completely mad when he saw no difference between the saint's cane and the one he was using himself.

His parents are still looking at him as if thinking that his permanent sobriety has led him perilously down the pathways of autism; they seem to be reproaching him for daring to talk about someone called Joyce when he knows perfectly well they have no idea who this gentleman is.

His father turns around in his chair and appears to be about to protest, but finally says only that he would like someone to explain something.

Again? Now it seems like he's parodying himself. Could it be a touch of humor on his part?

"What, Dad? The storm's over. What else do we have to explain to you? The unfathomable dimension?"

Unperturbed, his father continues what he's started, and now he wants to know why exactly they've chosen his son to speak in Dublin about the decline of the Gutenberg constellation. And he also wants to know why his son still hasn't said anything at all about his trip to Lyon. Perhaps he didn't really go there and wants to hide this from his parents. They are used to him telling them about his trips, and his behavior today is alarmingly anomalous.

"I don't know, it could be you've got a lover and you didn't go to Lyon with her, but up Tibidabo," he says. "You're really doing some things badly lately, and as your father I feel obliged to point this out."

Riba is about to tell him that he went to Lyon simply to hold a funeral for all the literary theories still in the world, including the one he himself managed to devise in a hotel room there. He'd like to be able to say something like this to his father, because he doesn't appreciate those last paternal words one bit. But he holds back, he controls himself. He stands up, and begins the ceremony of saying goodbye. After all, it's not raining anymore. And in any case he knows that when his parents start telling him off, it's usually just a trick to keep him in the house a little longer. He can't stay there a minute longer. He realizes that sometimes he lets his father control his life too much. Not having had children and being, moreover, an only child has led to this ongoing state of strange childish submission, but there's a limit to everything. Years ago, he used to fight a lot with his father. Later on, they made peace. But he thinks that, at times like these, he can sense a certain nostalgia for that period of big arguments, great clashes. As if his father enjoyed hand-to-hand combat more than the current haven of peace and mutual comprehension. What's more, it's possible that arguing makes his elderly father feel better, and he unconsciously seeks out confrontation.

Although it's a recent feeling, in some ways he adores his father: his intelligence, his secret goodness, his unexploited writing talent. He would have liked to have published a novel of his. He adores this man, always so strict, so entrenched in his role as a nineteenth-century father, that he has created in his son the need to be a subordinate, to be such an obedient person that he often even finds himself thanking his father for trying to direct his steps.

"Do you really not want to tell us anything about Lyon? It's very strange, son, very strange," says his mother.

They seem determined to keep him there with trifling matters for as long as possible, as if they wanted to delay him from going home, maybe because deep down they have always believed that, even though he is married and a highly respected publisher of almost sixty years of age, when he's here he is still in short trousers.

Marco Polo is leaving, he thinks of saying. But he keeps quiet, he knows this would make it worse. His father looks at him angrily. His mother reproaches him for having spoiled such a firmly established custom as that of telling them about his latest trip. They walk him to the door, but they don't make it easy for him to get to the exit, practically blocking him with their bodies. "You're grown up now," says his father, "and I can't understand why you'd want to go to Dublin just to see this friend of yours from the Ulysses family."

The Ulysses family! This must be another touch of last-minute paternal humor or sarcasm. He calls the elevator which, as always, takes its time arriving, despite only having to come up one floor. His parents have never accepted that, given the short distance to the lobby, he might walk down the stairs, and he, meanwhile, never wished to be the callous son who breaks with the sacred tradition of always leaving in the same clunky old elevator, once so luxurious.

While they wait, he asks his father with childish sarcasm if he doesn't like the fact his son has a friend. And he reminds him that as a child he didn't let him have friends, and was always jealous of them. He is exaggerating, but in a way he is right to do so. Isn't his father exaggerating too? Doesn't his father, in his heart of hearts, want to forbid him to go to Dublin? So he rebels against him, against his father's secret wish to stop him going to Ireland. But really he is acting as a small child would do, unable to seriously hurt his father, let alone kill him, as he thinks he remembers Freud recommended earnestly.

No matter how great his tendency or vocation for patience might be, and no matter how much heroic fiber he might be made of, the wait for the elevator seems to go on forever. Finally the hulking old thing comes, he says goodbye again to his parents, steps into the elevator, presses a button, and goes down. Such a huge relief; he breathes deeply. The descent to the lobby is, as ever, very slow; the elevator is very old. As he descends, he feels like he is leaving behind the whole saga of the patio of this mezzanine apartment on Calle Aribau, where as a child he played soccer, always eternally alone. Later on, this patio became the center of his happiest dream, his dream linked to New York.

Out on Calle Aribau, as he gets into a taxi, he realizes it's about to start raining again. He had thought that after the great storm the rain would ease up. Maybe he could say this to the taxi driver? He hopes he's not like the somewhat Shakespearean Portuguese taxi driver he met in Lyon, the most theatrical taxi driver in the world.

"It's going to rain some more," Riba says.

For a moment, he worries that the taxi driver is going to answer like the character from *Macbeth* and give the famous reply:

"Let it come down."

But he doesn't always—if ever—come across taxi drivers in Barcelona who speak like characters from Shakespeare.

"You said it," replies the man.

In the taxi he finally finds time to glance through the day's newspaper, and comes across some comments by Claudio Magris about *The Infinite Journey*, his latest book. He's interested in whatever Magris writes. Almost too long ago to remember, he published his book *Clarisse's Ring*, and has been good friends with the writer ever since.

The taxi glides along the apparently lifeless streets of Barcelona under a dirty light after the storm. He always worries absurdly that taxi drivers—it's probably a very childish feeling—will see him barricaded behind his newspaper and get a false impression that, despite having already talked about the weather, he is not in the least bit interested in them and in what they might tell him about their lives of drudgery. He doesn't know whether to bury himself in his newspaper and read Magris's comments or talk to the driver and ask him something slightly odd: for example, if he's been through the forest yet today, or if he's played backgammon, or watched much television.

This fear that taxi drivers will think him so very indifferent means he sometimes turns the pages of his newspaper very furtively, but this isn't the case today, since he's just decided that nothing and no one will be able to distract him from Claudio Magris, whose article is about—a very striking double coincidence—*Ulysses* and Joyce and about precisely what he is doing now: going home.

He feels he should read this reappearance of *Ulysses* as a not at all insignificant coded message. As if secret forces—one of them Magris himself with his comments—are nudging him ever closer toward Dublin. He looks up and gazes out of the window; the taxi has just left Calle Aribau and is turning onto Vía Augusta. When they reach the intersection of Avenida Príncipe de Asturias and Rambla de Prat, he sees a young man on a street corner wearing an electric-blue Nehru jacket. He looks a lot like the man he saw earlier, standing in the rain in front of his parents' house. Two Nehru jackets in such a short space of time is surely a coincidence.

He sees the young man only fleetingly because, almost immediately, as if fearing he'd been discovered, the man turns the corner and vanishes with astonishing speed.

How strange, thinks Riba, he's disappeared almost too quickly. Although it's not so strange really, he's used to such things by now. He knows that sometimes people one didn't expect at all can appear.

He goes back to reading the newspaper, he wants to concentrate on the interview with Magris, but ends up calling Celia on his cell phone to tell her he's on his way home. The short conversation calms him down. When he hangs up, he thinks he could have told her that he's seen two Nehru jackets in a short space of time. But no, maybe it was better just to have said he was coming home.

He goes back to the newspaper and reads that Claudio Magris believes Ulysses's circular journey as he returns triumphantly home—Joyce's traditional, classic, Oedipal, conservative journey—was replaced halfway through the twentieth century by a rectilinear journey: a sort of pilgrimage, a journey always moving forward, toward an impossible point in infinity, like a straight line advancing hesitantly into nothingness.

He could see himself now as a rectilinear traveler, but doesn't want to create too many problems for himself, and decides that his journey through life is traditional, classic, Oedipal, conservative. He's going home in a taxi, isn't he? Doesn't he go to his parents' house whenever he comes back from a trip, and on top of that, visit them without fail every Wednesday? Isn't he planning a trip to Dublin and the very center of *Ulysses* to then come home good-naturedly days later to Barcelona and to his parents and tell them about the trip? It's hard to deny his life is following the pattern of a strictly orthodox circular journey.

"After Calle Verdi, you said?" asks the taxi driver.

"Yes, I'll tell you where."

When he finally gets home, he says hello to his wife and gives her a kiss. He smiles happily, like a simpleton. They have known or loved each other for thirty years, and except for very critical moments—such as during the final escalation of his drinking two years ago that ended in physical collapse—they haven't grown too tired of living together. He tells her straight away that his father suffered an attack of melancholy and asked his son to explain the mystery of "the dimension."

What dimension? she asks. He knew she might ask this. Well, the unfathomable dimension no less, he replies. They look at each other, and an air of mystery appears between them as well. The mystery his father was talking about? He can't help but let his attention wander to other questions. Isn't there essentially an unfathomable dimension between him and her?

"*Without asking who you were, | I fell in love. | And whoever you might be, | I will always love you,*" go the ridiculous, naïve lyrics to the song by Les Surfs that was playing when they met, and fell in love. Back then Celia looked more like Catherine Deneuve than anyone he had ever seen. Even the raincoats she wore that made her look sluttish recalled the ones Deneuve wore in *The Umbrellas of Cherbourg*.

And what do we know about ourselves, he wonders. Less and less every day, because on top of everything, Celia has been studying for some time now the possibility of becoming a Buddhist; she's been contemplating for a few months what she calls the *sweet eventuality*. By now she's almost convinced that she has within her the potential for reaching Nirvana, and believes she is close to seeing, with clarity and conviction, the true nature of existence and of life. It hasn't escaped his notice that these first signs of Buddhism could end up being a big problem, in the same way that the escalation in his drinking was, two years ago, leading Celia seriously to consider leaving him. The fact is, he'd be in danger of being left on his own if one day he had the crazy idea of abusing alcohol again.

Now the two of them are motionless, as if both preoccupied with the same four questions, and this has paralyzed them: life, alcohol, Buddhism, and above all, their ignorance of each other.

They have been gripped by an unexpected coldness, as if they have suddenly realized that deep down they are strangers to each other, and to themselves, although—as well he knows—she is confident that Buddhism can lend her a hand and help her to take a spiritual step forward.

They smile nervously, trying to minimize the tension of this odd moment. Maybe he loves her so madly because she is someone he will never know everything about. It has always fascinated him, for example, that Celia is one of those women who never turn off taps properly. Dripping taps have been a constant in his marriage, in the same way—if such a comparison is possible—as his problems with alcohol.

He thinks he has always combined superbly well this relative ignorance about Celia with his total ignorance about himself. As he remarked once in an article for *La Vanguardia*: "I don't know myself. The list of books I have published seems to have obscured forever the person behind the books. My biography is my catalog. But the man who was there before I decided to become a publisher is missing. I, in short, am missing."

"What are you thinking about?" asks Celia.

Being interrupted annoys him and he reacts strangely and tells her he was thinking about the dining-room table and the hall chairs, which are perfectly real, and about the fruit basket that belonged to his grandmother, but that, however, he is also thinking that any madman could step through the door at any point and remark that things aren't so clear.

He is immediately filled with dismay, as he realizes he has muddled things up unnecessarily. Now his wife is indignant.

"What chairs?" says Celia. "What hall? And what madman? You

must be hiding something from me. I'll ask you again. What are you thinking about? You haven't started drinking again, have you?"

"I'm thinking about my catalog," says Riba, lowering his head.

Since he stopped drinking, he barely has any domestic quarrels with Celia. This has been a great step forward in their relationship. Before, they used to have really awful fights, and he never once tried to rule out the thought that he, with his damned drinking, was always the guilty party. When the arguments were really bad, Celia used to pack a few things in her suitcase, which she then took out of the apartment to the landing. Afterward, if she got tired, she went to bed, but left the suitcase out there. In this way the neighbors always knew when they'd had a fight: the suitcase reflected what had gone on the night before. Shortly before he had his collapse, Celia really did leave him and spent two nights away from home. If he hadn't had health problems and been forced to stop drinking, it's more than likely he would have ended up losing his wife.

Suddenly he tells her that he's thinking of going to Dublin on the sixteenth of June.

He tells her about his parents' wedding anniversary and also about Joyce's *Ulysses*, and finally about his dream, his premonition, especially about being drunk outside a pub called the Coxwold, the two of them weeping copiously and inconsolably, sitting on the ground at the end of an Irish side street.

He has tried to tell her too much too quickly. What's more, he has the feeling that Celia is only one step away from telling him that, although the absence of alcohol in his life and his daily fourteen hours of isolation in front of the computer have calmed him down and are without doubt a blessing, they are making him increasingly autistic. Or, to be precise, more *hikikomori*.

"Dublin?" she asks, surprised. "And what are you going to do there? Start drinking again?"

"But Celia—" he makes a gesture as if arming himself with patience, "—the Coxwold is just a pub in a dream."

"And if I've understood correctly, it's also the place of a premonition, dear."

Riba has been interested for days in everything surrounding the subject of the *hikikomori*, young Japanese people who suffer from autism in front of the computer, and who, in order to avoid outside pressures, react by withdrawing completely from society. In fact, the Japanese word *hikikomori* means "isolation." They shut themselves up in a room in their parents' house for prolonged periods of time, usually years. They feel sad and have hardly any friends, and the vast majority spend the day sleeping or lying down, and at night watch television or concentrate on the computer. Riba is very interested in the topic because, since he left publishing and stopped drinking, he has been withdrawing into himself, and in effect, turning into a Japanese misanthrope, a *hikikomori*.

"I'm going to a funeral in Dublin for the age of print, for the golden age of Gutenberg," he tells Celia.

He doesn't know how it happened, but it just came out. Her eyes burrow into him. Silence. Unease. Before she starts shouting, he begins to explain.

"What I mean is the funeral, ever delayed, of literature as an endangered art. Although really the question should be: what danger?"

He notes that he has got himself tied into knots.

"I would understand perfectly," he continues, "if you asked me that question. Because the fact is the thing that interests me most about this danger is its literary nuances."

He thinks that now his wife will unleash her anger; instead the opposite happens, as he starts to sense a sudden warmth, a certain sort of loving intensity. But it's also as if Celia has taken pity on him. Can that be it? Or maybe she's taken pity on the golden age of Gutenberg, which perhaps in this case is the same thing? Or is she fond of danger, seen from a literary point of view?

Celia looks at him, and asks him if he remembers asking her some days ago to rent the only David Cronenberg film he hasn't yet seen. She shows him the DVD of *Spider* she has just got out, and affectionately suggests they watch it before dinner.

He does indeed like Cronenberg, one of cinema's last real directors. But it all seems a little strange to him, because he never asked to watch this film. He glances at the DVD and reads that the film is about "a lonely man failing to communicate in an inhospitable world."

"Is that me?" he asks.

Celia doesn't even answer.

In the opening sequence of the film, a young man called Spider is the last person to get off the train, and it's clear right away that he's different from the other passengers. Something seems to have seriously clouded his brain, and he stumbles as he alights with his small, strange suitcase. He is handsome, but he has all the signs of being highly mentally-disturbed, maybe a lonely man failing entirely to communicate with an inhospitable world.

Celia asks Riba if he's noticed that, in spite of the heat, Spider is wearing four shirts. Well, no, he hadn't noticed this peculiar detail. He excuses this by saying he hasn't yet had time to focus on the film. Besides, he says, he doesn't normally notice those kinds of details.

Now he troubles himself to count the shirts. And he sees it's true. The man is wearing four in the middle of summer. And what about the suitcase? It's very small and old, and when Spider opens it, we see it contains only useless objects and a little notebook where, in minuscule handwriting, he writes down his illegible impressions.

Celia asks him about Spider's handwriting, she wants to know if it doesn't remind him of Robert Walser's when it became microscopic. Well it's true, that is what it's like. The introverted, microscopic calligraphy of the frail young man who answers to the name of Spider makes one think of the days when, before he entered the first lunatic asylum, the handwriting of the author of *Jakob von Gunten* became gradually smaller and smaller, due to his obsession with disappearance and eclipse. Then Celia wants to know if he's noticed that there is scarcely anyone on the streets of London's gloomy, inhospitable East End, through which Spider is wandering.

He notices that Celia hasn't stopped asking him questions since the film began.

"Has someone asked you to find out if I can still concentrate and notice things in the outside world?" he finally asks her.

Celia seems used to him talking to her like this and his answers coming at her from unexpected directions, not necessarily connected to his questions.

"What you have to do is to love me. The rest doesn't matter," she says, emphatically.

Riba makes a mental note of the phrase, jotting everything down this way. He wants to type it up later in a Word document he keeps open on his computer where he collects phrases.

What you have to do is to love me. The rest doesn't matter. This is new, he thinks. Or maybe what's happened is that she used to put it a different way. It may well be a Buddhist saying, who knows.

Soon it seems to him that Spider is listening in and spying on his conversation, even his thoughts. Might he himself be Spider? He can't deny he feels drawn to the character. What's more, deep down, he would like to be Spider, because he completely identifies with him in some aspects. For him, he's not just a poor madman, but also the bearer of a subversive kind of wisdom, the sort of wisdom Riba has found very interesting since closing down the publishing house. Maybe it's an exaggeration to think he's Spider. But hasn't he been accused many times of reading his life as if it were the manuscript of an unknown author? How many times has he had to listen to people tell him he reads his life anomalously, as if it were a literary text?

He sees Spider look at the camera, then close his suitcase, and walk for a while through cold and deserted streets. He sees him act as if he'd come into his living room. He moves around in it as if it were a rundown neighborhood in London. Spider has come from a mental hospital and is headed for a place that is theoretically less harsh, just a little less harsh, to a hospice or a halfway house, coincidentally situated in the same neighborhood of London where he spent his early years; this will be the direct cause of his starting fatally to reconstruct his childhood.

When Riba sees that Spider is reconstructing his childhood with deceptive faithfulness to the facts, he wonders if it might not also be the case that his own tangled mental life never strays far from his childhood neighborhood. Because he himself is now thinking of his early years too, and the blessed innocence he had back then. He sees a straw hat in the sun, a pair of tan shoes, a pair of turned-up trousers. He sees his Latin teacher, who was an Englishman. And then he doesn't see him. Oh, as everyone knows, there are people who, just as they appear, disappear very shortly afterward. The Latin teacher was a consumptive man who had a spittoon next to his blackboard. These are snippets from his childhood in El Eixample, the neighborhood near the center of Barcelona. In those days, he often felt stupid, Riba remembers. He does now, too, but for different reasons: now he feels stupid because it seems he only possesses *moral* intelligence; that is, an intelligence that isn't scientific, or political, or financial, or practical, or philosophical. . . . He could have a more rounded intelligence. He always believed he was intelligent and now he sees he's not.

"Mad people are very strange," says Celia. "But they're interesting, aren't they?"

It seems once again as if his wife is trying to see how he reacts to the figure of Spider, perhaps to measure his own degree of dementia and stupidity. Perhaps she's even reading his mind. Or who knows, perhaps she just wants to know if he identifies in a highly emotional way with this very isolated, engrossed individual, lost in an inhospitable world. The film is a walk around the East End, taken by a disturbed man. We see life just as this madman registers and captures it. We see life just as it is filtered through the wretched mind of this young man with his strange suitcase and his notebook with microscopic handwriting. It is a life that the poor lunatic sees as dreadful and criminal, terribly limited, and horrifyingly sad and gray.

"And have you seen what he's writing in his notebook?" asks Celia, as if she suspects he's so wrapped up in his thoughts that he's not even watching the film.

It occurs to Riba suddenly that he's missing something. A notebook, for example. Like Spider's. Although he soon realizes he actually already has a notebook; it's the Word document where he occasionally writes down random sentences he likes.

If it were up to him, he'd now start adding the music of Bob Dylan to the images from *Spider*. Dylan singing, for example, "Most Likely You Go Your Way (And I'll Go Mine)," a song he's always found encouraging.

"No, I can't see what he's writing in his notebook. Why would I need to?" he finally answers Celia.

She pauses the film so he can see what Spider is writing in his damn notebook. They are primitive signs, bent sticks or little matchsticks, so incomplete they're not even really sticks or matchsticks, and of course, could never form part of any hieroglyphic alphabet. They are genuinely frightening. However you look at them, the only thing those little sticks spell out are the clinical symptoms of the absurdity of madness.

Although only vaguely, Spider reminds him of the character from *A Man Asleep*, by Georges Perec, one of his favorite books on his list. Why is he so drawn to the figure of Spider, this poor, destitute, feeble-minded man who walks around confused and puzzled by a life he doesn't comprehend? Maybe because there is something in Spider, and also in part in Perec's character, which is common to everyone. This means he sometimes identifies with Spider, and at other times with "the man asleep," who in turn reminds him of *Red Desert*, Antonioni's film from 1964, where Monica Vitti plays a stray character, a female version of Spider *avant la lettre*, a woman lost in an inscrutable industrial landscape in which the apparent calm does nothing to help her establish adequate communication with things surrounding her. This constant failure, this emotional collapse, means she is doomed to become a fearful creature who, incapable of confronting a reality that completely escapes her comprehension, moves through empty spaces, through a metaphysical desert.

From what he has seen so far, the moody atmosphere in *Spider* seems to be establishing subtle links—in particular through the cinematography of Peter Suschitzky, which reflects a depressed state of mind—to the style he has always admired in *Red Desert*. Here too, as in the Italian film, one sees proof of how the futility of any attempt rationally to construct the outside world necessarily implies the inability to create an identity for oneself. And once he has arrived at this point, Riba again wonders if he himself might not be Spider. Just like the man in the film, he sometimes has dealings with ghosts.

When, in the most memorable sequence, Spider tries to find out who he is, we see him weave a tangle of string in his bedroom, like a mental spider's web that appears to reproduce the horrific workings of his brain. But it soon becomes clear that these awkward attempts to reconstruct his own personality are ineffective. He walks through the inhospitable streets of London's East End, down the cold, distant pathways of his irretrievable childhood: he has lost every connection to the world, he doesn't know who he is; perhaps he never knew.

Now Riba thinks he can hear strange voices in the darkness, and wonders if it might not be the spirit of childhood that, one day, just seemed to disappear forever. Or maybe the ghost of the brilliant writer who, as a publisher, he always wished he could discover? A profound unease has hung over him for his whole life due to these absences. Nevertheless, the muffled sound of a certain presence is much worse, the murmur of the *writer's malady*, for example, a ceaseless buzzing, a real pest.

It is natural for publishers to suffer from this strange buzzing. Some hear it more than others, but not one escapes from it completely. There are extreme cases, although Riba was never one of those. They are the publishers with the most acute *writer's malady*, who would prefer to publish books written by nobody, since that way they would avoid the buzzing and keep the glory of what they had published for themselves alone.

In the same way that death shelters the *malady of death* inside itself, that is, its own malady, there are publishers whose most intimate tormentor, the *writer's malady*, gnaws away at them, a background noise, whose sound recalls the crunching of dry leaves.

One day in Antwerp, Riba spoke of this crunching sound to Hugo Claus. He spoke of how he was doomed to live with the *writer's malady*, and mentioned that his head was forever pierced with sorrow, due to that persistent, intimate monster and its goddamned buzzing, reminding him constantly that apparently nothing in life could exist without it, without the *malady*, without that background noise, without that savage, relentless crunching; always reminding him that the *malady*, the murmur of dry leaves, was a vital cog in the diabolical mechanism of his mental clockwork.

Hugo Claus, so famous for *The Sorrow of Belgium*, silently sympathized with him and then remarked simply:

"The sorrow of the publisher."

The anguish that gives every sign of being dementia is gradually causing him to feel lost, drifting strangely through that dangerous childlike area on the edges of his mind, where he knows he might lose himself forever at any moment. But at the last second he manages to escape the danger by thinking of something else, remembering, for instance, that he has a *moral* intelligence, even though at times he feels this is not much, though sometimes he feels it's quite a lot. And he escapes from the danger at last by remembering too that next month he'll go to Dublin. And by recalling a line of Monica Vitti's in *Red Desert*, a line that, he now realizes, is almost as dangerous as the most feverish and most obsessively particular wanderings around London's East End might be for anyone:

"My hair is hurting me."

He could say the same thing too. Spider would certainly say it. Spider, who walks through life so lost, doesn't know Riba could imitate him and reconstruct his personality by adapting other people's memories—he could turn into John Vincent Moon, one of Borges's heroes, for example, or into an accumulation of literary quotations; he could become a mental enclave where several personalities could find shelter and coexist, and thus, perhaps without even any real effort, manage to shape a strictly individual voice, an ambiguous support for a nomadic, heteronymous profile....

There's no doubt Riba has a certain facility for going off on mental tangents and making life more complicated than necessary. He is like a follower of the Italian writer, three of whose books he published, Carlo Emilio Gadda, who was a neurotic as admirable as he was phenomenal: Gadda threw himself into the page he was writing, with all his obsessions. And everything he did was incomplete. In a short article about *risotto alla milanese*, he made things so complicated that he ended up describing the grains of rice, one by one—including the moment when each one was still enveloped in its little husk, the pericarp—and naturally, he was unable to ever finish the text.

Riba has a tendency to read life like a literary text and sometimes to see the world like a tangled mess or a ball of wool. So that when Celia interrupts the film and his reflections on Gadda and the risotto, and his digression about John Vincent Moon, so she can say, in the most prosaic tone possible, that afterward she will heat up the left-over potatoes au gratin in the oven, he remembers a Jules Renard quote, a perfect snippet: "A young woman from London left this note the other day: 'I'm going to kill myself, father's dinner is in the oven.'"

Celia seems to him to be acting as if she's already a Buddhist, and also as if she's convinced that everything he thinks leads him to get dangerously lost on the edges of his East End.

So as not to get so lost, Riba turns slightly and looks to the left, at the kitchen. The potatoes au gratin are, in effect, already in the oven. But it doesn't escape his notice that this is merely a relative truth, as at any time a madwoman, or Spider himself, could come through the door and dispute this piece of evidence and all others, every single one, including the simple truth of the potatoes au gratin.

When they have finished watching *Spider*, he hurls himself at the computer like a desperate man. The hours of computer abstinence have brought him to the brink of a nervous breakdown. And a serious hairache. On the other hand, not sitting in front of the computer has meant that the pain in his right knee has abated slightly, pain he attributes to an excess of uric acid, although in reality it might simply be arthritis, the onset of old age, why kid himself?

He sits down in front of the computer screen wearing the same expression Spider does that clearly demonstrates his failure to communicate with a world he doesn't understand. First, he searches for the latest news about himself on Google. Within the last few days, there is none. He then spends some time looking at a huge range of websites and finally comes across an article that seems oddly related to his decision to hold a funeral in Dublin. The writer of the article claims we will arrive sooner than expected at the digitalization of all written knowledge and the disappearance of literary authors, in the interests of producing a single universal book, an almost infinite flow of words, which will be reached, naturally, the writer says, by means of the internet.

The disappearance of literary authors is a topic that touches him deeply. This reality that the web announces for the future, becoming clearer every day, never fails to move him. "But perhaps," says the writer, "instead of surprise, the predicted end of the printed book might now provoke rejection in the traditional reader. What to say about the writer who sees in this vertigo a sort of attack on the purpose and the nature of his work? However, it would appear that the course has been set and the die cast for paper and ink. No argument will divert its terrible fate, nor is there any clairvoyant or prophet who can predict its survival. The funeral march has begun, and it is futile for those of us who remain loyal to the printed page to protest and rage in the midst of our despair."

He is struck by the writer saying *the funeral march has begun.* Then, he decides to open his email and finds the email he expected from a friend, Dominique Gonzalez-Foerster, who finally tells him in detail about the installation she is preparing for the end of July in the Turbine Hall of the Tate Modern. They have been good friends since he published a very comprehensive book on Dominique's work five years ago. He feels that amidst the general decline of his life, his friendship with the French artist is one of the few things that hasn't turned into a disaster.

He has always been fascinated by the way Dominique's installations connect literature and cities, films and hotels, architecture and abysses, mental geographies and authors' quotations. She is a great lover of the art of quotation and very specifically of Godard's technique from his early period, when he inserted quotations, the words of others—real or invented—into the action of his films.

Recently, Dominique has been filled with passion for other people's phrases and is trying to create an apocalyptic culture of the literary quotation, a culture of the end of the line, and as a matter of fact, of the end of the world. In her installation for the Turbine Hall, Dominique, with her dynamic relationship to quotations, wants in part to situate herself in Godard's wake, while at the same time locating the visitor in a London of 2058, where it has been raining cruelly, without let-up, for years.

The idea—Dominique tells him in her email—is that one sees how a great flood has transformed London, where the incessant rainfall over the last few years has had strange effects; there have been mutations in the urban sculptures, which, invaded by damp, have not just eroded, but have also grown monumentally, as if they were tropical plants or thirsty giants. In order to stop this *tropicalization* or organic growth, they are stored in the Turbine Hall, surrounded by hundreds of metal bunks that, day and night, cradle *men who sleep*, and other vagabonds and refugees from the flood.

Dominique plans to project a strange film, more experimental than futuristic, onto a giant screen, which will bring together scenes from *Alphaville* (Godard), *Toute la mémoire du monde* (Resnais), *Fahrenheit 451* (Truffaut), *The Jetty* (Chris Marker), and *Red Desert* (Antonioni): quite an end-of-the-world aesthetic, very much in keeping with the apocalyptic feeling Riba himself has had for some time now.

On each bunk there will be at least one book, a volume that, with modern corrective treatments, will have survived the excessive dampness caused by the rains. There will be English editions of books by authors almost all published in Spanish by Riba: books by Philip K. Dick, Robert Walser, Stanislaw Lem, James Joyce, Fleur Jaeggy, Jean Echenoz, Philip Larkin, Georges Perec, Marguerite Duras, W. G. Sebald …

And playing an undefined sort of music between the metallic bunks, there will be musicians who will be like an echo of the orchestra that went down with the *Titanic* but playing acoustic string instruments along with electric guitars. Maybe what they play will be the distorted jazz of the future, perhaps a hybrid style that, one day, will be called *electric Marienbad*.

The coexistence of the music with the rain, the books, the sculptures, the literary quotations, and the metal bunks in the exhibit—where Riba imagines, he doesn't know why, replicas of Spider appearing, phantoms walking everywhere—might produce a strange result, as if—Dominique ends up telling him—the spectral hour had arrived and we were all walking lost among the ruins of a great disaster, in an unmistakable apocalyptic state.

He sits absorbed in front of the computer when suddenly he remembers that terrible day last week when, simultaneously sweet and ridiculous, he went for a walk at dusk, in a light rainstorm, wearing his old raincoat, his shirt with its torn collar turned up, his hideous short trousers, his hair completely plastered to his head. Car headlights were blinding him, but he carried on walking through the streets of the neighborhood, focusing on his thoughts. He was aware how strange his appearance was in the rain—mainly due to the short trousers—but also that there was no longer any solution, that it was too late now to try to put things right. He had spent hours hypnotized in front of the computer, and in a fit of lucidity, had decided to dash out into the street to get some air no matter what. He went out just as he was, in exactly the same clothes he wore around the house. Seven whole hours he had spent shut up in his study. It was actually not so much time, considering that his daily ration of confinement was usually much more extreme. But that day he had felt especially sensitive to being confined. Worried about himself and his excessive isolation, he had launched himself into the street carrying his old raincoat, but he had made the mistake of forgetting his umbrella, and then it was too late to go home, to go back upstairs to get it, and while he was at it change his trousers, so short and ridiculous under the raincoat. He must have presented a forlorn image to the neighbors, one he couldn't even justify by explaining that, as a publisher fallen on hard times, he had an understandable touch of madness to him. For a while, as if indifferent to the rain, he could be seen advancing, phantom-like, like one of those guys who showed up in so many of the most celebrated novels he used to publish: those desperate men with a romantic air, always alone, sleepwalking in the rain, walking always along lost highways.

He has always admired writers who each day begin a journey toward the unknown, and who nevertheless spend all their time sitting in a room. The doors to their rooms are closed, they never move, and yet the confinement provides them with absolute freedom to be who they want to be, to go wherever their thoughts take them. Sometimes he links this image of solitary writers in their writing rooms with one that has been his lifelong obsession: the need to catch a genius, a young man highly superior to the others and who travels in his room better than anyone. He would've liked to have discovered and published him, but he didn't find him, and it seems less and less likely he will do so now. He has never doubted the existence of this young genius. It's just that, Riba thinks, he remains in the shadows: in solitude, in doubt, in question; that's why I can't find him.

Celia is sitting right beside him, and when she sees with a certain degree of alarm how completely he has sunk into self-absorption, she decides to intervene, to bring him back—as far as possible—into the real world.

"Let's return, if you don't mind," she says, "to this requiem in Dublin. A requiem in honor of whom did you say?"

He is going to repeat that it is a requiem for the age of print, a funeral for one of the pinnacles of the Gutenberg galaxy, when suddenly from *Ulysses*, the funeral Bloom attends in Dublin on June 16, 1904, springs to mind, and he recalls the sixth episode in the book, when at eleven in the morning Bloom joins a group on its way to the cemetery to bid farewell to the dead man, Paddy Dignam, crossing the city to Prospect Cemetery in a carriage with Simon Dedalus, Martin Cunningham, and John Power. Bloom is still an outsider. Bloom, for his part, joins the group quite reluctantly, because he is aware they don't trust him, because they know of his freemasonry and Jewishness. After all Dignam was a patriotic Catholic who boasted of his own past and that of Ireland. And moreover, he was such a good man he let alcohol kill him.

— *Liquor, what?*
— *Many a good man's fault, Mr Dedalus said with a sigh.*

He remembers when they stop in front of the mortuary chapel. It is a sad chapel, a meditation on death, the saddest he has seen in his life. This is the gray burial of a working-class alcoholic. All the details of the cortège are described and one expects that at any moment happiness will appear in the form of a rose, an unending rose, as Borges would have said. But this happiness is a long time coming, in fact it never arrives. The process of burying the dead man is long and complex. And the grave is deep and endless, as the rose. Nothing is truer than that he has never read anything so sad as that perfectly gray chapter of Joyce's book. In the end, tin wreaths are left hung on knobs, garlands of bronzefoil. Roses would have been better, the narrator remarks, flowers are more poetical.

"A requiem for whom?" repeats Celia.

He wants to avoid at all costs her seeing him as still alienated, or as a now permanently unhinged *hikikomori*, but his reply doesn't let her see him any other way.

"For Paddy Dignam," he says.

"For Paddy who?"

"Dignam, Paddy Dignam, the one with the red nose."

It would have been better if he'd said nothing at all.

Before going to bed, they watch TV for a while. They catch the end of an American film, in which there is a rainy burial. Lots of umbrellas. With great satisfaction, he recognizes Woodlawn Cemetery, in the Bronx, where he went on his second and most recent trip to New York. He went to this cemetery to see Herman Melville's grave. He recognizes it by the style of the tombstones and because the place etched itself deeply on his memory, and also because visible in the background is the elevated train station he disembarked from to visit the place. Although he sees Celia is very absorbed in the burial scene, he intervenes to say he has been to that cemetery, that he recognizes it by the train station in the background and that it is very familiar to him. Celia doesn't know what to say.

"Are you impressed that you're seeing somewhere I've been, or is the funeral scene making more of an impression?" he asks her in a somewhat provocative tone of voice.

Celia chooses to remain absorbed in the film.

He doesn't know why he wants to go to Dublin. He doesn't think it's just because he's fascinated by the idea of waiting around until June 16 to travel to a place where no one has invited him. He doesn't believe it's only because he thinks he should go there and then tell his parents about it, to make it up to them for not having said anything about Lyon. And nor does he believe he wants to go to Dublin simply because, if the premonition is true, it might be that he will find himself at the gateway to a great revelation about the secret of the world, a revelation that will be waiting for him in Cork. Nor does he think it's simply because, if he goes to Dublin he will somehow get a little closer to his beloved New York, although this is another reason he wants to go there. He doesn't even believe he wants to go to Dublin because he wishes to say a requiem for the culture of the Gutenberg age and at the same time say a requiem for himself, literary publisher very much in decline.

Maybe he wants to go to Dublin for all these reasons and also for others that escape him and will go on escaping him forever.

Why do I want to go to Dublin?

He asks himself silently twice in a row. It's possible there is an answer to this question, but also possible that he may never find out exactly what it is.

And it is even possible that the very fact of not knowing the reasons he is going to Dublin in their entirety forms part of the meaning of the journey, in the same way that still not knowing the exact number of words of his requiem may help him to deliver a good eulogy in Dublin.

He will go to Dublin.

The following morning, an hour after waking up and with her time already minutely planned out, Celia is getting ready to go to her office at the museum where she works. Her face radiates peace, serenity, tranquility. It might be that these are a consequence of her imminent conversion to Buddhism.

Celia always goes about things enthusiastically, with enviable drive. She appears helpless and at the same time possesses a frightening strength—both extremes are necessary. Occasionally, he is reminded of what his grandfather Jacobo used to say: "Nothing important was ever achieved without enthusiasm!" Celia is enthusiasm itself and always has an air of giving importance to what she does, whatever it might be, and at the same time of denying all this importance with a simple smile. She says she learned all this from the Oklahoma Theater, that theater whose stage, according to her, was directly connected to the void.

Oklahoma and Celia seem to be inseparable. Buddha will be the third side to the triangle. Celia often says there is no better place for enthusiasm than the United States. And that life there—she once went to Chicago—is pure theater to her, permanently connected to the void. But she wouldn't mind going to live in New York if he would only stop obsessing about it and finally decide to move to that place he so yearns for, to the supposed center of the world.

Celia is going to work, but first she drops a hint by means of a terrifying piece of information. Sensing that it won't be long before her dear autistic husband goes and sits in front of the computer, she tells him that people who regularly use Google gradually lose the ability to read literary works with any kind of depth, which serves to demonstrate how digital knowledge can be linked to the recent stupidity in the world.

Riba accepts the dig, but prefers not to take it personally. When she leaves, he has his first cappuccino of the morning. Really, coffee was devised as a way of concentrating better on the internet, he thinks. Over the last two years, in the absence of alcohol, coffee has been his only stimulant. Today he drinks it faster than ever, at top speed: standing up in the kitchen, gloriously anxious. Then, in an almost desperate attempt not to let a single effect of the caffeine escape, he turns his back on Celia's words and seats himself at the computer.

For a moment, he considers not spending as many hours as usual in front of the screen, not exactly because of what Celia said, although this has a strong influence, but rather because he has been telling himself for some time now he should set himself life challenges far removed from his recent obsessive tendency to sit motionless at the computer. But he immediately changes his mind. Being almost sixty years old he doesn't really have any ideas for life challenges. So eventually he decides to delve once more into the internet, where he is unable ever to avoid giving free rein to a certain narcissism by typing into Google first his name, and then that of the publishing house. He knows that, aside from being egocentric, all of this is clearly obsessive. But even so, he doesn't want to give up this daily habit. The flesh is weak.

This obsessive activity in fact serves to soothe his nostalgia for the time when he used to go to his office and, with his secretary Gauger, inspect every mention in the press about the books they published. He knows that, as a substitute for what he used to do in his office, his current mania is verging on the grotesque, but he feels it is necessary for his mental health. He looks at lots of blogs to find out what they are saying about the books he published. And if he comes across someone who has written something even slightly unpleasant, he writes an anonymous post calling the author ignorant or an idiot.

Today he spends a long time doing this activity and ends up insulting a guy from Barcelona who says on his blog that he took a Paul Auster book on holiday to Tokyo and feels disappointed. What a bastard this blogger is! Riba only published *The Invention of Solitude* by Auster, and although the book the tourist is putting down is *The Brooklyn Follies*, he feels just as affronted by this mistreatment of Auster, whom he considers a friend. When he finishes insulting the blogger, he feels more refreshed than ever. Recently he has been so very sensitive and had such low morale that he thinks if he had overlooked this unjust comment on Auster's book he would have become even more depressed than he was before.

•

He interrupts the hypnotic state the computer has lulled him into for yet another day and stands up. He goes over to the big window for a few moments and from there looks out at the great view over the city of Barcelona, not as fantastic today as it usually is, due to the alarmingly persistent rain. In fact, the whole city has disappeared from his window, disappeared behind a heavy curtain of water. May rain, although a little excessive for this time of year. It is as if up there, in the clouds, someone has begun to collaborate on Dominique's future installation in the Tate Modern in London.

He senses that this short journey over to the window, this modest, fleeting liberation from the digital world, will turn out to be beneficial. Right away, standing here, even though he's facing the *disappeared* view of Barcelona, his *hikikomori* guilt has diminished. And he starts to see that Celia's words as she left today are having quite an effect on him. In general, he barely takes a break from the computer until she gets home at a quarter to three. Today he makes an exception and devotes part of his time to standing there in front of the window from which, nevertheless, he can see nothing. Perhaps he hasn't picked the best moment. What is certain is that today there is nothing to see, except the rubbed-out city and the mist. He stays there for a while, listening to the almost religious, monotonous murmur of the rain. He somewhat loses track of time.

He hardly ever sets foot on the streets of Barcelona. Recently, he merely contemplates the city from up here, but today, with the rain and the mist, he can't even do this. To think that he used to have a busy social life. Now he has become down in the mouth, melancholy, shy—more than he ever thought—shut up between these four walls. A good drink would liberate him from feeling so misanthropic and timid. But it's not worth his while because it would endanger his health. He wonders if there is a pub called the Coxwold in Dublin. Deep down he has a burning desire to break his own internal rules and have a good slug of whiskey. But he won't do it, he knows better. He is convinced that Celia would be capable of leaving him if she saw he was drinking again. She wouldn't stand for a return to the days of the great alcoholic nightmare.

He won't have even one drink, he'll endure stoically. Nevertheless, there's not a day when he's not seized by an indefinable nostalgia for bygone evenings, when he used to go out to dinner with his authors. Unforgettable dinners with Hrabal, Amis, Michon … Writers are such great drinkers.

He leaves the window and goes back to the computer and googles the words *Coxwold pub Dublin*. It's a way like any other to make him believe he is quenching his great thirst. He searches and soon sees there's no pub with this name there, and again feels like going into one for real. Again, he is holding back. He goes to the kitchen and drinks two glasses of water one after the other. There, by the fridge, suddenly leaning on it, he remembers how he sometimes imagines—only imagines—that, instead of spending all his time shut up in the house, a computer addict, he is a man open to the world and to the city at his feet. It is then he imagines he is not a retired, reclusive publisher and a perfect computer nerd, but a man of the world, one of those guys from 1950s Hollywood movies his father wanted so much to resemble, and did. A sort of Clark Gable or Gary Cooper. That kind of very sociable man who used to be called an "extrovert" and who was friends with hotel porters, waitresses, bank clerks, fruit sellers, taxi drivers, truck drivers, and hairdressers. One of those admirable, uninhibited, really open guys who are constantly reminding us that life is essentially wonderful and should be approached with pure enthusiasm, as there's no better remedy against terrible anguish, such a European disorder.

From the fifties, that time linked to the period of his childhood, he still retains—directly inherited from his father, although much deformed and hidden by his shyness and also by his leftist tendencies and his quite rigorous intellectual veneer—a powerful fascination with the "American way of life." What's more, he never forgets that if there is one place where he might one day find happiness, this place is New York. In fact, on the two occasions he's been there, he came very close to it. This conviction is not at all unconnected to a recurring dream that pursued him for a while. In the dream, everything was as it had been when he used to play soccer eternally alone as a child, out on the family patio of the apartment on Aribau, imagining he was both the visiting and the home team at the same time. The patio was identical to the one at his parents' apartment, and the general atmosphere of desolation, characteristic of the postwar years, was also similar to the one back then. Everything was the same in the dream, apart from the fact that the gray apartment buildings overlooking the patio were replaced by skyscrapers from New York. This New York setting gave him a feeling of being at the center of the world, and transmitted a special emotion to him—the same one he'd later recognize when he dreamt of being at the center of the world on his way out of a pub in Dublin—and the warm sense of experiencing a moment of intense happiness.

The dream always ended up being a strange one about happiness in New York, a dream about a perfect moment at the center of the world, a moment he sometimes related to these lines by Idea Vilariño:

> It was a moment
> A moment
> At the center of the world.

Things being as they are, it isn't at all strange that he started to suspect the recurring dream contained a message telling him how a great, thrilling moment of happiness and extraordinary enthusiasm for the things of this world could only be awaiting him in New York.

One day, already past the age of forty, he was invited to a global conference of publishers in this city he had never set foot in, and naturally the first thing he thought was that he was finally going to travel to the very center of his dream. After the long and tedious flight, he arrived in New York as the day was drawing to a close. He was amazed at once by the great physical extent of American spaces. A taxi sent by the organization dropped him at the hotel, and once in his room, he watched in fascination how the skyscrapers gradually lit up as night fell. He felt deeply uneasy, expectant. He spoke on the phone to Celia, in Barcelona. Afterward, he got in touch with the people who had invited him to the city, and arranged to meet them the following day. Then, he busied himself with his dream. I'm at the center of the world, he thought. And looking out at the skyscrapers, he sat and waited for the sensations of enthusiasm, of emotion, of fulfilment, of happiness. It became clear that the wait, however, was just a wait, nothing more. A straightforward wait, with no surprises, with no enthusiasm at all. The more he looked at the skyscrapers in search of a certain kind of intensity, the clearer it became that he wasn't going to feel any special sensation whatsoever. Everything in his life was still the same, nothing was happening that might seem different or intense. He found himself inside his own dream, and at the same time the dream was real. But that was all.

Even so, he persevered. He looked out at the street again and again, attempting unsuccessfully to feel happy while surrounded by skyscrapers, until he realized it was absurd to behave like the people Proust spoke of: "people who set out on a journey to see with their own eyes some city they've always longed to visit, and imagine they can taste in reality what has charmed their fancy."

When he realized it was useless to carry on waiting to be inside that dream, he decided to go to bed. Tired from the journey, he fell asleep in no time. He dreamed then that he was a child in Barcelona playing soccer on a patio in New York. Total bliss. He had never felt so ebullient in his life. He discovered that the spirit of the dream, in contrast to what he had thought, was not the city, but the child playing. And he'd had to go to New York to find this out.

Today it's raining less than yesterday and Barcelona is more visible through the window. Riba thinks about it: no matter what, at nearly sixty, wherever one looks, one has already been there.

Then he corrects himself and thinks almost the opposite: nothing tells us where we are and each moment is a place we have never been. He oscillates between feeling dejected and excited. Suddenly, he's only interested in how he has managed to bring about this sort of rare calm, this new calmness he seems to be treating with the same level of interest he used to treat new manuscripts that seemed promising.

In the background, on the radio he has just turned on, a Billie Holiday song is playing, melancholy and drowsy, infinitely slowly, while he wonders if one day he'll be able to think like his admired Vilém Vok used to when he reflected on those who lived in a dream-world and then returned unscathed from their long travels.

New York's beauty and greatness lie in the fact that each one of us carries a story that turns immediately into a New York story. Each one of us is able to add a layer to the city, conscious of the fact that it is in New York where the synthesis between a local story and a universal story can be found [Vilém Vok, *The Center*].

He has always been a passionate reader of Vok, although he never managed to publish him due to an absurd misunderstanding he would rather not even remember now. But there was a time when he had an almost ferocious desire to have Vok in his catalog.

With each day that passes, the thought of New York makes him feel more enthusiastic. Under its spell he feels capable of anything. But his daily life doesn't correspond well to his dreams. In this he is not exactly different from most mortals. He struggles along with his local Barcelona story that, when possible, turns from a private performance, into a universal, New York one.

Without New York as a myth and final dream, his life would be much harder. Even Dublin seems like just a stopover on the way to New York. Now, after having summoned up his imagination, he walks away from the window in quite a good mood and goes to the kitchen to drink a second cappuccino, and shortly afterward, goes back to the computer, where the search engine offers him thirty thousand results in Spanish for *Dubliners*, James Joyce's book of short stories. He read it a long time ago, and re-read it years later, and still remembers many details, but he's forgotten, for example, the name of the bridge in Dublin cited in the great story "The Dead"; the bridge on which, if he's not mistaken, one always sees a white horse.

He feels wrapped up in a stimulating atmosphere of preparations for his trip to Dublin. Joyce's book is helping him to open up to other voices and environments. He realizes that, if he wants to verify the name of the bridge, he will have to choose between flicking through the book—that is, remaining, heroically, in the Gutenberg age—or else surfing the net and entering the digital world. For a few moments, he feels he's right in the middle of the imaginary bridge linking the two epochs. And then he thinks in this case it'd be faster to look at the book, as he has it there, in his study. He leaves the computer again and rescues an old copy of *Dubliners* from the bookshelves. Celia bought it in August 1972 from Flynn bookshop, in Palma de Mallorca. Back then, he didn't know her. Possibly Celia read about the white horse appearing in "The Dead" before he did.

> *As the cab drove across O'Connell Bridge Miss O'Callaghan said:*
> *"They say you never cross O'Donnell Bridge without seeing a white horse."*
> *"I see a white man this time," said Gabriel.*
> *"Where?" asked Mr Bartell D'Arcy.*
> *Gabriel pointed to the statue, on which lay patches of snow. Then he nodded familiarly to it and waved his hand.*

This snippet reminds him of a phrase of Cortázar's overheard mysteriously one day on the Paris Metro: "A bridge is a man crossing a bridge." And shortly afterward, he wonders if when he goes to Dublin he wouldn't like to go to see this bridge, where in an imaginary space he's just located the link between the Gutenberg and the digital ages.

He observes that one of the two names of the bridge transcribed in the Spanish translation has to be wrong. It's either O'Connell, or O'Donnell. Anyone who knows Dublin would surely resolve this in a fraction of a second. Yet more proof that he is still very green when it comes to Dublin, which isn't an issue, but a stimulus, and—retired and dull teetotaller that he is—he needs incitements of all kinds. So now he decides that nothing would please him more than going into new subjects in depth; studying places he has yet to visit, and returning from these trips, continuing to study, studying then what has been left behind. He must make choices like this if he is to flee from being a computer nerd, and from the deep social hangover his years as a publisher have left him with.

In terms of finding the name of the bridge, the digital world is more use to him than the print one. He has no choice but to turn to Google, which isn't serious, since it offers him the perfect excuse to hurl himself at the computer again. There he very quickly finds his answer. He searches first for O'Connell and the search result resolves everything straight away: "The walks and places of interest in the north of Dublin are mainly all clustered around the main street, O'Connell Street. It is the widest and busiest road in the city center, although not exactly the longest. It starts at O'Connell Bridge, mentioned in *Dubliners* by James Joyce." He realizes he has another more modern edition of *Dubliners* in the study, which he could now take the trouble to consult and see if it has the same mistake of the bridge's name. He gets up, leaves the computer for a few minutes—this morning he seems condemned to go from Gutenberg to Google, from Google to Gutenberg, moving back and forth between the two, between the world of books and that of the web—and he pounces on this more recent edition. Here the translation is not by Guillermo Cabrera Infante, but María Isabel Butler de Foley, and there is no confusion about the name of the bridge:

As the cab drove across O'Connell Bridge Miss O'Callaghan said:
"They say you never cross O'Connell Bridge without seeing a white horse."

...

Gabriel pointed at the statue of Daniel O'Connell, on which patches of snow had settled. Then he greeted it familiarly waving his hand.

Compare two translations and this sort of thing happens. Mr. Daniel O'Connell, the Dublin statue, has just made a dazzling appearance in Riba's life. Where has he been up till now? Who is he? Who was he? Any excuse to go back to the computer screen, the only place where, without leaving the house, he has a chance of finding the text of "The Dead" in English, and so discover if Daniel O'Connell was there.

He goes back to his *hikikomori* position. He searches, and solves the mystery in no time. Daniel O'Connell does not appear in the original: "Gabriel pointed to the statue, on which lay patches of snow. Then he nodded familiarly to it and waved his hand."

He recalls that someone once suggested that the truly mysterious path always leads within. Was it Celia who said this in a profound Buddhist outburst? He doesn't know. He's here now, in their little apartment, awaiting possible events. He has an aptitude for waiting, and has started waiting for this trip to Dublin to somehow take shape. He considers waiting the essential human condition and sometimes will act accordingly. He knows that from today onward, until the sixteenth of June, he will do nothing but be in a state of waiting to go to Dublin. He will wait conscientiously. He has no doubts about managing to prepare himself for the journey.

Now he's really focused, as if he were a samurai about to go on a long journey. He's in his *hikikomori* pose, but ignoring the screen and heading deeper down an inner path, strolling about through a few memories. The memory of the times he's read *Ulysses* in the past. Dublin is at the end of the path and it's pleasant to recall the old music of this splendid book he read with a mixture of amazement and fascination. He's not quite sure, but he'd say that Bloom, at heart, is very similar to him. He's the personification of the classic outsider. He has some Jewish roots, as does Riba. He's a stranger and a foreigner at the same time. Bloom is too self-critical and not imaginative enough to be successful, but too much of a hard worker and teetotaller to fail completely. Bloom is far too foreign and cosmopolitan to be accepted by the provincial Irish, and too Irish not to worry about his country. Riba likes Bloom a lot.

•

"Downtown Train," by Tom Waits, is playing. He can't understand English, but it seems to him that the lyrics are about a train heading for the city center, a train carrying its passengers away from the remote neighborhood they grew up in and where they've been trapped for their whole lives. The train is going to the center. Of the city. It might be going to the center of the world. To New York. It's the train to the center. He can't even conceive that this song is not about a center.

Believing this is the subject of that Tom Waits song, he has never grown tired of listening to it. Waits's voice has for him the poetry of a local train linking his childhood neighborhood to New York. Every time he listens to the song, he thinks of past trips, of everything he had to leave behind in order to devote himself to publishing. Now, the older he feels, he remembers his old zeal, his initial literary preoccupations, how for years he devoted himself endlessly to the dangerous business of publishing, so often ruinous. He relinquished youth for the honest labor of an imperfect catalog. And what's happening now that everything has come to an end? He is left feeling very puzzled and with an empty wallet. Wondering why. A wild remorse at night. But no one can take away the fact that he toiled, and it took him far. And that is no small thing. In the end, as W. B. Yeats said, in luck or out, the toil has left its mark.

I'm all washed up, he thinks. But it would be worse if someone decided to light the lamps of my existence. It would be no good at all if something happened and everything livened up and the house turned into an exalted sideshow and I turned into the center of a vibrant novel. Nevertheless I can see it coming, something will happen soon, I'm sure of it. Suddenly, someone will burst into my monotonous life as an old man who walks barefoot around the house, without turning on any lights, and stands still sometimes, leaning against some piece of furniture in the dark while listening to the mice scurrying about. Something's going to happen, I'm sure, my life will be turned upside down and my world will turn into a sparkling novel. If that happened, it would be awful. I don't think I'd like to be separated from the unsurpassable charm of my current life. I would be happy only to go and live in New York, but leading a simple existence there too, always in contact with the sedate ordinariness of everyday life.

If he didn't sit in front of the all-consuming computer screen, what else could he do? Well, he could carry on researching Dublin, or go back to scaring the neighbors by walking in the rain in short trousers, or else play dominoes with the retired men in the bar downstairs, or get drunk again like in the old days, supremely, savagely drunk; he could go to Brazil or Martinique, convert to Judaism, reap a wheat field, go and screw a casual girlfriend, jump into a swimming pool of freezing water. Although maybe the most sensible thing to do would be to put all his energy into preparing for a future trip to New York, the first stage of which will be in Dublin.

One day, while traveling through Mexico with José Emilio Pacheco, a book of whose he had just published—he would go on to publish another two—they arrived at the port of Veracruz in a friend's convertible and went straight down to look at the sea. Those shapes I see by the sea, said Pacheco, shapes that immediately give rise to metaphorical associations, are they instruments of inspiration or of false literary quotes?

Riba asked him to repeat the sentence and the question. And when Pacheco did so, he saw he had understood them perfectly. Something similar always happened to him. He made associations between ideas, and always had a remarkable tendency to read his own life like a book. Publishing, and consequently having to read so many manuscripts, contributed still more to this tendency of his to imagine that metaphorical associations and an often highly enigmatic code lay concealed behind any scene in his daily life.

He considers himself as much a reader as he is a publisher. It was basically his health that forced him to retire from publishing, but it seems to him it was also partly the golden calf of the gothic novel, which created the stupid myth of the passive reader. He dreams of the day when the spell of the best-seller will be broken, making way for the reappearance of the talented reader, and for the terms of the moral contract between author and audience to be reconsidered. He dreams of the day when literary publishers can breathe again, those who live for an active reader, for a reader open enough to buy a book and allow a conscience radically different from his own to appear in his mind. He believes that if talent is demanded of a literary publisher or a writer, it must also be demanded of a reader. Because we mustn't deceive ourselves: on the journey of reading we often travel through difficult terrains that demand a capacity for intelligent emotion, a desire to understand the other, and to approach a language distinct from the one of our daily tyrannies. As Vilém Vok says, it's not so simple to feel the world as Kafka felt it, a world in which movement is denied and it becomes impossible even to go from one village to the next. The same skills needed for writing are needed for reading. Writers fail readers, but it also happens the other way around and readers fail writers when all they ask of them is confirmation that the world is how they see it....

The phone rings.

What was he saying to himself? He was thinking about the arrival of a new time that might bring with it this revision of the demanding pact between writers and readers and that the return of the talented reader might be possible. But it could be that this dream is already unrealizable. Better to be realistic and think about the Irish funeral.

He will go to Dublin. Partly to do something. To feel a little busier in his retirement.

On odd-numbered days, and always at this time, Javier calls on the phone, a faithful friend and thoroughly methodical man. Riba still hasn't picked up and he already knows perfectly well it can only be Javier. He turns down the volume on the radio, where Brassens's "Les Copains d'Abord" is playing, coincidental background music he thinks most appropriate to his friend's phone call. He picks up.

"I'm going to Dublin in June, did you know?"

Due to the fact that in the last two years he has stopped drinking and avoids going out at night, he has recently seen little of Javier, a very nocturnal man. Nevertheless, their relationship is still active, although now it's nurtured only by telephone conversations every other day at noon and the occasional lunch date. Maybe over time the absence of nights out together will gradually erode the friendship, but he doesn't think so, because he is one of those who thinks that friendships are strengthened by people seeing one another very infrequently. He's not sure that friends exist, exactly. Javier himself usually says that there are no friends, only moments of friendship.

Javier calls on odd days. And he always does so around midday, thinking, perhaps, that for moments of friendship this time of day might offer more guarantees than others. He's very methodical. But after all, so is Riba. Does he not, for example, systematically visit his parents every Wednesday afternoon? Does he not sit punctually in front of his computer every day?

Now Javier is asking him how the talks about selling his business are going, and Riba is explaining that he feels disheartened and that in the end he might not sell his assets, might leave things as they are, in the hope of better times. There are precedents, he says, for other glorious ruins in the Barcelona publishing industry. The case of Carlos Barral, for example. Javier interrupts him to dispute the idea that Barral was ruined. Riba has no desire to waste his energy arguing, Riba doesn't even bother to pursue the topic. Then they talk about *Spider* and he tells Javier he's come to identify entirely with the main character of this strange film. And Javier, who suddenly remembers he's seen it too, says he doesn't understand what Riba saw in the film, as he remembers it as being terribly depressing, and very dull. By now Riba is used to Javier taking the opposite view to him on everything. Their friendship or, rather, their moments of friendship are based on them differing almost completely on questions of art. Riba published Javier's first five novels, before Javier ran off to more commercial publishers. And although he has always disagreed with some aspects of his literary aesthetic, Riba has always had absolute respect for the power of his friend's realist style.

When the topic of *Spider* wanes, they talk about the incessant, even disturbing rain of the past few days. Then, Riba tells him—he told him before—how he spent an entire day in Lyon without speaking to anyone and set out a general theory of the novel. And Javier ends up getting very nervous. Writers don't put up at all well with publishers taking literary baby steps, and Javier ends up interrupting Riba to say indignantly that he already told him, the other day, that he was glad he'd managed to write something in Lyon, but there's nothing more *French* than a general theory for novels.

"I didn't know theories were just a French thing," says Riba, surprised.

"They are, I'm telling you. What's more, it'd do you good to stop being a café thinker. A French café thinker, I mean. You should forget about Paris. That's my impartial piece of advice for today."

Javier is from Asturias, from a town near Oviedo, although he's lived in Barcelona for over thirty years. He's fifteen years younger than Riba and has a remarkable tendency to give advice and above all to be unequivocal. He's very inclined to use a categorical tone. But today Riba can't understand what he's getting at and asks what he's got against the cafés of Paris.

Riba starts to remembering that his vocation as a publisher began during a trip to Paris after May '68. As he was stealing left-wing essays with unusual happiness from the François Maspero bookshop—where the booksellers looked kindly upon people looting the place—he decided to devote himself to a profession as noble as that of publishing avant-garde novels and rebellious books that later enthusiasts would steal from the Maspero and other left-wing bookshops. Some years afterward, he changed his mind and gave the revolutionary dream up for dead and decided to be reasonable and charge for the books he published.

On the other end of the line, his friend Javier is silent, but he can tell he's still indignant. He'd be even more so if he knew his friend had mentally associated his diatribe against French cafés with his Asturian background.

Riba, to calm him down, changes the subject and talks about his growing interest in Dublin. Javier interrupts him and asks if he's not timidly gravitating toward an English landscape. Or Irish, if he prefers. If he is, there's no doubt he's taking the first step toward the great betrayal.

The music now playing on the radio is Les Rita Mitsouko, "Le Petit Train." The first step toward the great betrayal of everything French, shouts Javier enthusiastically. And Riba has no choice but to hold the telephone away from his ear. Javier is too excited. A betrayal of everything French? Is it possible to betray Rimbaud and Gracq?

It's great you've gone over to England, Javier says just a few minutes later. And as he congratulates him for having taken the leap, he manages to surprise Riba.

What leap?

Javier says nearly everything in a highly unequivocal tone, totally convinced it can be no other way. It's as if he's talking about someone who's swapped soccer teams. But Riba hasn't taken any leap, nor has he gone over to England. Everything indicates that Javier would be pleased if he left French culture behind, maybe because he's never had much contact with it and feels inferior in this respect. Maybe because he never stole anything in the Maspero bookshop, or because his father—this is not something easy to forget about Javier—was the anonymous author of the libelous article "Against the French" published in 1980 by a Valencian press: an amusing collection of swipes at the smugness of much of French culture and which began thus: "Their vanity was always their greatest talent."

"It'd be good for you to lose some weight," Javier says suddenly, "take the English leap. Get out of the Frenchified muddle you've been in for so long. Be lighter, more fun. Become English. Or Irish. Take the leap, my friend."

Javier is methodical and sometimes categorical. But above all he's stubborn, incredibly stubborn. He seems like he's from Aragon in that way. Of course, you could probably say there are the same proportion of stubborn people in Aragon as anywhere else. Today, it seems, Javier is directing all his obstinacy against Riba's French influence in his formative years. And he seems to be advising him to leave his Frenchification behind if he wants to get back his sense of humor and lose weight.

Riba timidly reminds him that, in the end, Paris is the capital of the Republic of Letters. And it still is, says Javier, but that's exactly the problem, that culture has too much weight and can't bear the slightest comparison to English liveliness. What's more, the French don't know how to communicate as well as the British nowadays. You just have to look at the phone booths in London and Paris. It's not just that the English ones are much prettier, but they offer a comfortable and better designed space in which to actually talk, unlike the French ones, which are strange and designed for the outrageously pedantic aesthetics of silence.

Javier's argument doesn't convince him at all, among other things because there are hardly any phone booths left in Europe. But he doesn't want to argue. He makes up his mind now to be agile and take a leap, a light English leap, *to land on the other side*, to start thinking about something else, to turn around, to move. And he ends up thinking to himself of some words of Julian Barnes's, which seem very opportune at this moment: words where Barnes comments that the British have always been obsessed with France, as it represents for them the beginning of difference, the start of the exotic: "It's curious: the English are obsessed with France while the French are merely intrigued by England."

He remembers these words of Julian Barnes's in *Cross Channel* and thinks that for him, on the other hand, it is precisely everything English that is the start of difference, the beginning of the exotic. New York intrigues him and when he thinks of this city he always remembers the words of his friend, the young writer Nietzky, who for years now has had a place there: "I live in the perfect city for dissolving your identity and reinventing yourself. Mobility's hard in Spain: people pigeonhole you for life in the box where they think you belong."

Deep down he'd like nothing more than to escape his pigeonhole of the prestigious retired publisher he's been put in—quite firmly, it seems—by his colleagues and friends in Spain. Perhaps the time has come to take a step forward, to cross the bridge—in this case a metaphorical English Channel—that will lead him to other voices, other environments. Maybe it'd be a good idea to remove French culture from his life for a time: he's so close to it now it almost disgusts him, and so it doesn't even seem foreign anymore, but seems as familiar to him as Spanish culture, the very first culture he fled from.

Riba is starting to think that Englishness is where difference begins, where the exotic starts. It's obvious that at the moment, only what is alien to his familiar world, only what is foreign, can draw him in a different direction. He knows he needs to venture into topographies where strangeness reigns and also the mystery and joy that surround the new: he needs to look at the world with enthusiasm again, as if seeing it for the first time. In short, to take the English leap, or something that looks like the leap that a moment ago, in such an eccentric, British fashion, Javier suggested to him.

A way to be even less Latin occurs to him: to stand in front of the mirror, to lose his instinct for melodrama and exaggeration and become a cold, dispassionate gentleman who doesn't wave his arms around when he gives an opinion. And soon he hears the call of the difficult countries, the places and climates where no one—not even he—ever dreamed they would explore with such interest: places he imagined as inaccessible his whole life or, rather, took it for granted that, if only because of the language barrier, they would never be within his reach. He will look, once again, for the impossible. Nothing will be as good for him as to gravitate once more toward the *foreign*, because only then will he be able to get closer to the center of the world he's looking for. A sentimental center, sought by the traveler from the Laurence Sterne book. He needs to be a *sentimental traveler*, to go to English-speaking countries, where he might regain the strangeness of things, where he might recover that whole special way of *feeling* he never found in the comfort of the intimately familiar: to see a wider range of possibilities opening up, of cultures, of strange signs to decipher. He needs to go to a place where he can regain the intense feeling of euphoria, to hear once more the voice of his grandfather Jacobo when he used to say nothing important was ever achieved without enthusiasm. He needs to take the English leap, although actually, he needs to leap in the opposite direction as that taken by Sterne's *sentimental traveler*, who, being an Irish-born Englishman, left England precisely to take a leap that was French.

He knows that if he goes to Dublin, he'll feel, just as he once felt in France, like an outsider again. The wonderful sensation of being from a different place. In Dublin he'll be an outsider as Bloom was, and be able to travel once more through a place in which he won't have the sensation of that disgusting closeness. Larkin wrote a poem called "The Importance of Elsewhere" that spoke of Ireland and that for a long time Riba liked a lot. He remembers it very well. In it the English poet spoke about how he wasn't allowed to feel like an outsider in England, his own country. And he said that, when he was alone in Ireland, since it wasn't his land, at least there he saw it was possible to be an outsider: *"The salt rebuff of speech, | Insisting so on difference, made me welcome: | Once that was recognized, we were in touch."* Larkin spoke of the draughty streets, end-on to hills. And of the faint archaic smell of the Irish docklands. And of the herring-hawker's cry in the distance, making him feel separate but not overshadowed. *"Living in England has no such excuse: | These are my customs and establishments | It would be much more serious to refuse. | Here no elsewhere underwrites my existence."*

Riba feels a nostalgia for the Protestants. He loves their work ethic. He's commented on this more than once to Javier himself, who, conversely, is fascinated by cold, hard Catholicism. Now that he thinks of it, Javier would be a good person to accompany him on this trip to Catholic Ireland.

Another odd-numbered day comes around and Javier calls at the same time as always. Why not ask him if he fancies coming to Dublin? There's still time. He hesitates, but finally does. He tells him the day he's picked to go to Dublin is June 16, and asks him to look at his diary and see if he can join him on his trip. *He's asking him*, he stresses that, he asks him. Javier is silent, disconcerted. His reply takes a while. Finally he promises he'll think about it, but he doesn't understand why Riba asks him like this, as if he's begging him. He'll come if he can, but it's strange that he's begging him. Before when they used to go out in the evening together, he never asked for anything; instead he used to insult him for being published by houses other than Riba's and for even more trivial things.

"It's so we could be there for Bloomsday," interrupts Riba in a little voice, designed to elicit sympathy that he has no one who wants to go with him. For a moment, he worries that the word "Bloomsday" might have ruined everything and Javier will start sounding off about James Joyce and his novel *Ulysses*, which he has never held in particularly high regard, because he was against Joyce's *intellectualism* and in favor of a more orthodox kind of writing, along the lines of Dickens or Conrad.

But today it seems Javier has nothing against Joyce, he just wants to know if Riba won't want to go out at night in Dublin either. No I won't, Riba says, but I have thought about suggesting the trip to Ricardo too, and as you well know he's a night owl. A long silence. Down the line Javier seems pensive. Finally, he asks if it's just about going for Bloomsday.

Here's danger. The question resounds in Riba's ears for a fraction of a second. It would be complete suicide to tell Javier about the funeral for the Gutenberg galaxy; he wouldn't understand right away and perhaps, not understanding, he'd go back on his decision to travel. Javier asks again.

"Is it just about going for Bloomsday?"

"It's about, first and foremost, going over to the English wavelength," he replies.

He worries he's got it completely wrong saying this, but soon discovers just the opposite, as the phrase has had a surprising effect. He hears Javier cough, enthusiastically. He remembers the other day, when they spoke of taking a leap, a nimble English leap, *landing on the other side.*

On the other end of the line it sounds like a party is going on. He can't remember the last time so few words did so much. Shortly afterward Javier says that clearly he has been able to reflect on how good it would be for him to distance himself from the culture that has dominated his life up to now. Even, he adds, if it's just to go in search of other voices and other environments. And he talks, in a strange fury, about taking away the weight of language until it looks like moonlight. And he also talks about the English language, which he says he's completely sure that in prose as much as in poetry is more malleable and ethereal than French. And as an example he recites a poem by Emily Dickinson, who is certainly aerial and nimble: "*A sepal, petal, and a thorn | Upon a common summer's morn— | A flask of Dew—A Bee or two— | A Breeze—a caper in the trees— | And I'm a Rose!*"

A long pause.

I'm only against the French, says Javier as he breaks the silence. At least this morning, he explains. Do you want me to say it again? No, says Riba, that's not necessary. Fine, says Javier, let's not talk anymore about it, I want to take the English leap with you, I'll come to Dublin and may poor old France be well and truly buried.

Minutes later, they're talking about the endless rain that's starting to become an alarming fact for everyone, when they change, almost without noticing, to talking about Vilém Vok, a writer they both admire so much, each for different reasons. To Riba, Vok is, first and foremost, the author of the fictional essay *The Center*, to the point where he sometimes relates paragraphs from the book to his desire to undertake a third trip to New York very soon, as this city has always held for him the exact magic of the myths some people need to live by. And in turn *The Center* has been like a Bible reinforcing this magic, helping him through the times when he needed the idea of New York, not just to live by but to survive. What would become of him without New York? Javier knows the book well and says he thinks he understands why it exerts such a direct influence over his old friend and editor, but also says he himself has always preferred snippets from Vok's other narrative essay, *Some Returned From Long*

Crossings (*The Quiet Obsession* is the altered, though beautiful and elegant title of the English translation).

As always, they end up talking about soccer. It's a tacit rule between them, but when they start talking about soccer, this just means that the conversation has entered its final stage. They discuss the upcoming European Championship. Javier states categorically that France won't get very far this year. And Riba is about to ask him if he doesn't think he's really got something against the French today, but decides not to complicate things any further. Bye, Javier says suddenly, talk to you soon. And when his friend hangs up, he understands that the Irish trip is no longer an unknown, but rather has started to take shape on the horizon. He goes to the kitchen to drink another coffee and think about it all calmly. A trip with Javier and perhaps with Ricardo—he promised Javier he'd call Ricardo tomorrow—could be just the thing. Ultimately it will help, for example, Celia to stop seeing him as so autistic and closed off, so chained to his computer and indolence. This is one of his main objectives, thinks Riba. That Celia sees he is active, sees he still wants to meet up with people, communicate outside of the web, not live off the memory of the great books he has published, not be content to see himself every day old and stagnant in the mirror.

On the radio, as if the outside world evolves along with his life, "Just Like the Rain," sung by Richard Hawley, is playing. He observes with amused surprise how he's gone from a French song, almost without noticing, to music in English. Outside, as if the radio knew the state of the weather or vice versa, it's still raining, *just like the rain*. He registers the fact that by now he can almost whisper the titles of songs in English, and suddenly feels as if his name is Spider and he's lost weight and is already in a bunk in the great Turbine Hall of the Tate Modern in his friend Dominique's installation. As he gradually approaches, in a way, his sentimental and *Sternean* center, in search of some sort of equilibrium, the rain in Barcelona becomes still heavier.

He goes over to the largest window in the house. Barcelona is below, at his feet, invisible again. The rain's persistence over the last few days is strange. He considers what he'd say to someone who asked him what the *English leap* was. Maybe he'd reply the way St. Augustine did when asked what time was to him: "If no one asks me, I know: If I wish to explain it to one that asks, I know not." But he thinks that, pressed to respond in some other way, he would end up saying that the English leap is *landing on the other side*, a pastime it's up to him to invent on his next trip.

In the Eixample district of Barcelona, like anywhere else, there are many casual encounters. It's a well-known fact: life is governed by coincidences. Although at first glance it might seem so, the encounter Riba just had with Ricardo on Calle Mallorca is not at all casual.

"Well, what do you know. Always someone turns up you never dreamt of," Ricardo says with a broad smile.

No, not a casual encounter, although Ricardo might think it is. They've just practically collided head on and actually bumped into each other, their two umbrellas nearly flying out of their hands. Riba calculated it all so it would happen like this, and now pretends to Ricardo that he was simply heading to La Central, the bookshop a couple of steps from here, on the same street. The truth is different: he's spent over an hour across the street waiting for his friend to come out of his house so he could feign a fortuitous encounter. What he is about to propose could never be achieved over the phone. He knows it will turn out well only if there's a conversation in some café, or in the bookshop itself; a conversation that paves the way so that, when the opportune moment arrives, the proposal of Ricardo coming to Dublin appears quite spontaneous. After all, he's the most ardent Anglophile of all his friends, a tireless reviewer of books from English-speaking countries. Surely it might interest him to attend his first Bloomsday. Ricardo, moreover, is a world authority on writers such as Andrew Breen and Derek Hobbs, modest Irish writers whom Riba, following Ricardo's advice, had translated and published in Spanish when they were—they still are—completely unknown.

Apart from being a reviewer and discoverer of English-speaking talents, Ricardo is also an interesting novelist: ultra postmodern at times, more conventional at others. He likes to have, at least, two literary faces: the avant-garde and the conservative. His best work is *The Exception of My Parents*, an original autobiographical book that Riba published in its day.

They share literary tastes, from Roberto Bolaño (who both of them were friendly with for a time) to Vilém Vok. For this and for a thousand other reasons, Ricardo might be a very suitable person for the trip, even an ideal participant in the funeral for Gutenberg and his galaxy, although Riba doesn't plan on mentioning anything about this requiem for the moment, because he thinks that, just as with Javier, speaking about all that would be total suicide. Whether one likes it or not, a funeral can always cause bad vibes and scare people. And anyway, Ricardo might think it's an event organized by publishers nostalgic for the world of the printing press, or something along those lines.

Better, he thinks, not to mention the funeral, at least for now.

"Is your mother well?" asks Ricardo.

Has he confused him with someone else? It's then that he remembers a month ago he used his mother as an excuse not to attend an evening out Ricardo organized for two English translators of his work.

"My mother is perfectly well," he replies, somewhat uncomfortably.

He doesn't ask Ricardo about his own mother, because he already knows she isn't very well—not in any sense—he's heard him say so in a thousand different ways, including in *The Exception of My Parents*, a book where he tirelessly comments on and analyzes his disaster of a mother. Ricardo is from Bogotá, and has lived with his wife and their three children in Barcelona for eleven years. He feels like a stateless writer, and if it'd been up to him to choose a nationality, he'd undoubtedly have opted for an American one. Just as his admired Cortázar as a child traveled slowly with his finger across the maps of atlases, savoring the heady taste of the incomprehensible, as a child Ricardo traveled rapidly through the poems within his grasp in his grandparents' house in Barranquilla and was eventually drawn to one, which led him to feel an immense desire to grow up and be able to leave Colombia forever, actually to be able to leave behind *everything* that might cross his path, to be constantly leaving everything behind, to be free and on the move, without ever slow-ing down.

Even today Ricardo remembers that poem by William Carlos Williams which says that most artists stop, or adopt a style, and in doing so they establish a convention, and that's the end of them; while, for one who moves, everything always contains an idea, because the one who moves, runs without stopping, the one who moves simply keeps stirring things up.... Leaping in the English way, Riba adds now.

Ricardo is the man in motion par excellence. He can even give the impression he is always on the move, without ever pausing at all. His eldest son, Samuel—named in honor of his father's old publisher—is seven years old, and was born in Barcelona, close to this house, by La Central bookshop. His three sons will be the main obstacle in convincing Ricardo to join them on the Bloomsday trip, but he's got nothing to lose by trying; he'll make the attempt, but not right now, rather when he sees that the most appropriate mo-ment has arrived.

They head for the Bar Belvedere, a place that once upon a time—when he wasn't a *hikikomori* and left the house more often—he fre-quented quite regularly.

"You've been really reclusive recently, don't you think?" Ricardo says in a tone of voice that is exquisitely friendly, yet also caustic.

Ricardo's question is too impudent, and Riba falls silent. He likes the shiny orange umbrella, damp with rain, which his friend is carrying today. It's the first time he's seen an umbrella this color. He says this to Ricardo, and then laughs. He stops in front of the window of a men's clothing shop and looks at some suits and shirts he's sure he'd never wear, especially with the rain that's falling now. Ricardo laughs affectionately, making fun of his friend's umbrella, and Riba, in turn, asks him if he happens to be insinuating that his own umbrella doesn't measure up to the orange one.

"No, no," Ricardo excuses himself, "I didn't mean that, but maybe you haven't seen an umbrella for months. You never go out, do you? What does Celia have to say about that?"

No answer. They walk in silence down Calle Mallorca, until

Ricardo asks him if he's read Larry O'Sullivan's poems yet. Riba doesn't even know who this O'Sullivan might be, he's usually only interested in writers he's at least heard of; he always has this feeling that any others are made up.

"I didn't know O'Sullivan wrote poetry," he says to Ricardo.

"But O'Sullivan's always written poetry! You're turning into a badly informed ex-publisher."

As they step onto the terrace of the Belvedere, Ricardo points out a young tree, whose round, firm trunk thrusts itself, almost bodily, into the air with an undulating movement halfway up, sending out young branches in all directions.

"It could be in one of O'Sullivan's poems," says Ricardo, lighting one of his customary Pall Malls.

They are now leaning against the bar in the Belvedere, and Ricardo is still talking about the tree O'Sullivan might have written a poem about. Before long he's just talking about the Boston poet.

"For O'Sullivan, Boston is a city of great extremes," says Ricardo, without anyone having asked for his opinion on the matter. "A city of heat and cold, passion and indifference, wealth and poverty, masses and individuals—" he smokes agitatedly and talks as if he were writing a review of this poet or had just written it and is now reciting it from memory, "—a city to live shut in with double locks on every door or to feel excited by its energy . . . I see you don't know O'Sullivan at all. Later, in La Central, I'll show you something by him. He's very American, you'll see."

Outside, the rain seems to be getting heavier, but it's just an illusion.

Ricardo, too, is very American, however Colombian he may be by birth. Now he's assuring Riba, with admirable conviction, that this O'Sullivan is a master of putting the trivial close to the lyrical, and so that Riba might understand him better, he recites a few lines about walking through downtown Boston: "*I go get a shoeshine | and walk up the muggy street beginning to sun | and have a hamburger and a malted and buy | an ugly NEW WORLD WRITING to see what the poets | in Ghana are doing these days.*"

He'd like to ask Ricardo what a *New World Writing* is, but he holds back and merely tries to find out what Ricardo thinks the poets in Ghana might have been doing on that day when O'Sullivan was so inspired. Ricardo looks at him with sudden compassion, almost as if he were looking at a new species of extraterrestrial. But Ricardo is even more Martian-like. At least, his blessed Colombian parents always were, and Ricardo inherited more than a few things from them. Ricardo's taste for being two-faced probably originated in those parents, his constant leaning toward side A of things, but then his tendency to see its coexistence with side B. All their lives his parents were stubborn progressives, who instilled in him a sort of love-hate feeling toward left-wing revolutionary iconography. Even though they were fiercely *gauchistes*, his parents were friends—in flagrant, scandalous contradiction—with people as rich as Andrew Sempleton, the investor and philanthropist, known as *the good-humored millionaire*.

"Loads of money and a big laugh. Very American," Ricardo always says when he evokes this outstanding man, who was his magnanimous and affectionate godfather. Riba has always suspected Ricardo will end up writing a novel about Sempleton. Despite managing large sums of money, his rich godfather never fell prey to avarice and was generous with many people, including Ricardo's parents, above all, when they went to jail in Bogotá for political reasons. With parents like that, Ricardo was destined to have a double face and personality, and that's what happened: a heavy pipe smoker (domestically, only at home) and (in public places) smoker of Pall Mall cigarettes; a solemn and frivolous writer, depending on the day; a home-loving man and at the same time dangerously nocturnal; a Hyde who was a most wildly modern Colombian, yet a quietly American Jekyll. It would be magnificent if he could persuade him to come to Dublin. Why hasn't he tried yet?

While he waits for the ideal moment to propose the trip, he recalls some of Ricardo's stories. From his adolescence, the most memorable is the one about Tom Waits and in a hotel room in New York. The daughter of a friend of some friends of his parents had an appointment to interview Waits in his hotel. Ricardo managed to convince her to let him come along. He just wanted to see—he was dying of curiosity to find out—what Waits did when he was alone in a hotel room. They knocked at the door. Waits opened it with a grumpy look on his face. He had black sunglasses on and was wearing a Hawaiian shirt and a pair of very faded jeans.

"Sorry," Waits said, "but there's no room for anyone else."

Ricardo experienced his own particular and somewhat unfortunate great moment there. He experienced it in the center of Waits's world, a place he was ejected from by a slamming door. There was no interview. His friend cried and blamed him for Waits having acted that way.

The fact is, the most avant-garde poetics in Ricardo's work, as he himself has always acknowledged, is nourished from the same sources as Waits's: the lyrics of Irish ballads, the blues of the cotton fields, the rhythms of New Orleans, the lyrics of German cabaret from the 1930s, rock and roll, and country music. It's a poetics that always fails, although with dignity, in its attempt to imitate, to put down on paper no more than the barroom register of Waits's voice.

This phrase of the singer's, spoken in the doorway to his hotel room, really stuck in Ricardo's head. The phrase stuck in his memory, but so did the Hawaiian shirt and the dark glasses. And more than once he used this phrase to get rid of someone.

It's what Ricardo uses now in his attempt to leave the Belvedere to go to La Central to buy some books. He says he's sorry, but there's no room for anyone else.

"Eh?"

Ricardo always needs movement. He's monstrously frenetic. Something must be done quickly to detain him. Riba still hasn't proposed going to Dublin. Why not, for God's sake? When does he plan on doing it? Not now, because Ricardo is physically trying to project himself toward the street to flee from the Belvedere, where there really is *no room for anyone else*.

Half an hour later, Ricardo finally gets the proposal. And he claims to have only one question before he accepts the invitation to travel with Javier and Riba to Dublin. He wants to know if it's just to be there for Bloomsday, or if there's some dark motive he sould be warned about beforehand.

He still thinks it would be suicide to give Ricardo any kind of clue about his intentions to hold a requiem for the Gutenberg galaxy. Ricardo might think, and he wouldn't be far off either, that Riba wanted to hold the funeral for himself: a funeral ceremony for his current unemployed state of half-failed publisher, embarrassing idler and computer nerd.

"Look, Ricardo. There is another motive, in fact. I want to take the English leap."

After agreeing to travel with them, Ricardo is quiet for a long time at first and then starts telling him—almost in passing and without giving it the slightest importance—that he was in New York not long ago, where he interviewed Paul Auster in his house for the magazine *Gentleman*. He says it as if it's nothing. At first, Riba can't even believe it.

"You were in Auster's house? And how was it? When did you go to New York?"

His eyes have become like saucers and he's genuinely stunned just by the idea that Ricardo has also managed to visit this three-story brownstone in Park Slope that he once went to and that has since become so legendary in his mind. Straight away he asks Ricardo, doesn't he think the house was really nice and weren't Paul and Siri very likeable, pleasant people? He says it with almost childlike wonder and in the belief he has shared a similar experience.

Ricardo practically shrugs. He has not the slightest opinion on the neighborhood, or the Austers' hospitality, or the house or even the red bricks of the façade. In fact, he has nothing to tell about his visit to the old neighborhood of Park Slope. He hadn't given his foray into Auster's house a second thought. For him, it was just another interview. He had more fun the other day, he says, interviewing John Banville in London.

Could it be that having grown up in New York has left Ricardo immune to have any sense of fascination for this city? Quite likely. For him, walking around there is natural, inconsequential.

How different two people can be, even though they're friends. The city of New York, the Austers, the English wavelength, for Ricardo all this is the most normal thing in the world, it holds no secrets and no special attraction for him. It's something he's had ever since he was a child.

Quite easily, Ricardo changes the subject, and above all the character, and tells Riba that in Boston, the day after his visit to Auster, he interviewed O'Sullivan. And then he starts talking about Brendan Behan, who he says was one of the most tremendous Irishmen who passed through New York back in the day.

He doesn't want to point out to Ricardo it's useless to tell him things about Behan, as he already knows everything about the man. He lets him talk about the Irishman, until, in a brief lapse of concentration, he brings up the topic of Auster again.

"Do you think Paul Auster's considered a good novelist in Ghana?" he asks Ricardo provocatively.

"Oh, how should I know?" He looks at him strangely. "You're behaving really oddly today. You never go out, do you? It's not that you don't go out much, you just don't go out, you're not used to talking to people. It's good you're going to get some fresh air in Dublin. Believe me, you're a bit unhinged. You should start up the publishing house again. You can't just do nothing. Auster in Ghana! Well, let's go to La Central."

They leave the Belvedere. There's a strong wind. Water's flooding everything. They're out in the open. They walk slowly. The rain grows more and more violent. The wind bends their umbrellas. They've heard a few apocalyptic voices speaking of a universal flood. Reality is becoming more and more like the installation Dominique is preparing in London.

In the end it'll turn out to be true that the end of the world isn't far off. In fact it's always been clear that the end couldn't be too far off. While they wait for the end, human beings amuse themselves holding funerals, little imitations of *the great end* that is to come.

As they're about to go into La Central, Ricardo throws away his Pall Mall and doesn't even bother to stamp it out, because the downpour instantly takes care of the butt. As they close their respective umbrellas, a gust of wind hits them with such force that they're pushed forward and burst into the bookshop, falling comically on their butts on the doormat, just at the moment when a young man is leaving La Central wearing round tortoiseshell glasses, a blue Nehru jacket beneath an old raincoat, and with the collar of his white shirt quite torn.

Riba thinks he knows him by sight, although he can't manage to place him. Who is it? The man walks insolently past them, indifferent to their ridiculous fall. An unflappable guy. He acts with astonishing coldness, as if he hadn't noticed that Ricardo and Riba have just fallen over. Or as if he thinks they are two comedians from a silent film. A strange guy. Although he's come from inside the bookshop, his hair is plastered to his head from the rain.

"We nearly killed ourselves," comments Riba, still on the floor.

Ricardo doesn't even reply, perhaps dazed by what's happened.

It's quite striking. The indifferent young man looks like the same one who was spying outside his parents' house the other day, and also the same one he saw from a taxi at the intersection of Rambla de Prat and Avenida Príncipe de Asturias. He tells Ricardo that recently he's seen the guy with the Nehru jacket everywhere, and for a minute fears his friend won't even know who he's talking about. Who knows, maybe he didn't even notice the young man with the round glasses who walked passed them so indifferently. But this isn't the case, he soon realizes he saw him perfectly well.

"Well, you know," Ricardo says. "Always someone turns up you never dreamt of."

JUNE

If one day he were to find this much-searched-for author, this phantom, this genius, it would be difficult for such a person to improve on what's already been said by so many others, about the rifts between the expectations of youth and the reality of one's later years, what's been said about the illusory nature of our choices, about how our search for success culminates in disappointment, about the present as fragile and the future as representing a need for control over old age and death. And what's more, it will always be an annoyance, a malaise of the soul for every perceptive publisher, to have to go out in search of those phantoms, those damned authors. He's thinking of all this now lying on a beach in front of blue water, surrounded by towels, red bathing caps, gentle waves lapping the warm yellow sand, near the center of the world. A strange beach in a corner of New York's harbor.

When he wakes up, still embarrassed as much as for having believed he really was on this beach, as for having unconsciously revived the sickness hidden inside every publisher, he dresses at top speed—he doesn't want to waste time—and goes to his regular branch of the Bilbao Vizcaya bank, knowing there'll be hardly any customers at this hour and he'll be able to resolve a tiresome matter as quickly as possible. He's seen by the smiling bank manager, whom he abruptly informs that he wishes to transfer half the money he has in an investment fund to another account in the same bank, one called External Cash Fund. First he confirms with the bank manager that the bonded capital in this new account is fully guaranteed. Then he carries out the transaction. Then he instructs her to transfer some of the money in his current account to another bank, the Santander. The manager knows she can't ask him to explain this treacherous gesture, but it's very likely she's wondering what they've done wrong to make him undertake it. Finally, he signs some more forms and asks for the checkbook they forgot to give him on his last visit. He takes his leave very politely and cynically. Out on the street, he hails a taxi and goes to the other end of the city, to the neighborhood of Sants, to a branch of the Santander bank where Celia's younger brother, who has worked there for a while, has offered him a pension plan with an excellent seven percent return. Having a pension plan already depresses him, as he'd never imagined growing old, but he prefers to be practical about it.

In the branch of Santander, with the money he's transferred from Bilbao Vizcaya, he takes out the plan and also signs a good number of forms. The bank manager appears, Celia's brother's immediate boss, and shows polite interest in Riba's longstanding, famous, and now finished publishing work. Riba distrusts so much politeness and suspects it is actually because the manager is on the verge of asking him straight out if the whole book trade is going really badly now. He looks at him almost rudely, and then abruptly starts to talk about New York and about how much he'd like to live there. His excessive praise of this city ends up irritating even the phlegmatic manager, who interrupts him:

"Listen, just one question, and forgive me, sir, but I'm dying to know.... Couldn't you be happy living in Toro, in the province of Zamora? What is Toro or Benavente lacking to make you not want to go and live there? And sorry for asking—it's probably because I'm from Toro."

Riba thinks for just a few seconds, and finally embarks upon the rocky Zamoran path of his answer. He replies in a deliberately gentle, poetic, anti-banking, vindictive tone of voice considering the financial space in which he finds himself.

"It's a difficult question, but I'll answer it. I've always thought that, when it gets dark, we all need somebody."

A formidable silence.

"I get the impression," Riba goes on, "that in New York, for instance, if it gets dark and you're all alone, the loneliness would always be less dramatic than in Toro or Benavente. Now do you see what I mean?"

The bank manager looks at him, his face almost expressionless, as if he hasn't understood a thing. He slides some more forms across for Riba to sign. Riba signs and signs. And then, in the same soft voice as a moment ago, Riba requests that tomorrow they withdraw the amount still in the Bilbao Vizcaya fund, and transfer it to one in Santander itself.

An hour later, and he's carried out all the transfers. It's better this way, he thinks. Better to have the money spread about than all in one place. He gets into another taxi and goes home. He finds he's rather exhausted, because it's been two years since he's carried out financial transactions or set foot in a bank. It seems to him he's made a superhuman effort this morning. He starts noticing how incredibly thirsty he is. He's tired and incredibly thirsty. He has a thirst for evil, for alcohol—well, for water, for calm, for being home again—but above all a thirst for doing wrong, for alcohol. He'd like to have a drink and launch back into his evil ways. After two years of abstinence, he's confirming an old suspicion: the world is very dull, or—and this is the same—what happens to him is devoid of interest if not told by a good writer. But it was a real drag having to go out and hunt for all those writers, and on top of that never finding one who was truly great.

What logic is there in things? None really. We're the ones who look for links between one segment of our lives and another. But this attempt to give form to that which has none, to give form to chaos, is something only good writers know how to do successfully. Luckily, Riba's still friends with a few, although it's also true he's had to organize this trip to Dublin in order not to lose them. In terms of friends and creativity, he's been in a critical situation ever since he closed his business. Deep down he misses the continuous contact with writers, such strange, ludicrous beings, so self-centered and complicated, and such idiots, most of them. Ah, writers. Yes, it's true he misses them, although they were such a pain. All so obsessive. But it can't be denied they've always amused and entertained him a lot, above all when—here he smiles maliciously—he paid them lower advances than he could have afforded and contributed to their being ever poorer. Ungrateful wretches.

Now he needs them even more than he used to. He'd like one or two of them to think to call and invite him to a book launch, or a conference on the future of the book, or simply show a bit of interest in him. Last year several of them still took the trouble to call (Eduardo Lago, Rodrigo Fresán, Eduardo Mendoza), but this year no one has. He'll be really careful never to beg one of them, it would be the last thing he'd ever do in his life. Beg to be allowed to take part in some launch, or yet another swansong for the book! But he thinks there are a lot of people who owe part of their success to him and might remember him for some event of this sort or for anything. Although it's a well-known fact: writers are resentful, jealous to the point of sickness, always penniless, and finally a load of ungrateful wretches, whether they're poor or completely poverty-stricken.

As he doesn't drink anymore, there's no danger of him turning into a blabbermouth and going around letting one of his secrets slip. The best-kept one of all is about how much he enjoyed feeling like a real bastard every time he bragged about the number of reduced advances he paid to novelists, who are by far the most unbearable— more than poets or essayists—when they become truly insufferable. Of course, if he reduced their advances it was because he thought that, as he wasn't very gifted in financial matters, if he didn't haggle and earn himself a reputation for being stingy, he would have been ruined even sooner. If he hadn't put a stop to his alcohol consumption and his business, he undoubtedly would have been well on his way to ending up like Brendan Behan: totally impoverished and an eternal drunk. He thinks about this Irish writer and the New York bars he used to visit. And he thinks again that today, after so much banking activity, if it wasn't for the fact he himself has prohibited it, he'd knock back a glass of the strongest liquor right now.

"*Strong liquors / like molten metal,*" said Rimbaud, probably his favorite writer.

It's a suicidal impulse, but what can he do? His thirst is great and the shadow of temptation long. And long too this life that's so brief.

Riba imagines that Nietzky actually has something of the fleeting spirit that accompanied him in his childhood of continuous sessions of soccer on the Aribau patio. Those early years, the shadow of the spirit was always with him, but he soon lost sight of it, and has only seen it again in that dream he had the day he arrived in New York for the first time. He imagines Nietzky is a kind of guardian angel, this *angelo custode.* And he also imagines that now he's speaking to this sort of relative of that lost spirit and that he's doing so in a joyous realm of white cricket trousers, tartan socks, binoculars slung over one's shoulder, and English languages.

You should lead a more healthy life, says Nietzky, you should go for walks in the fresh air. I'd like to see you walking around your neighborhood, or else out in the countryside. Tire yourself out in the natural world. Or else try to have other goals, instead of devoting yourself to your computer, or spending all your time thinking now you're old and washed-up, that you've become very boring. But do something. Action, action. I have nothing else to say.

It seems to him that thinking about Brendan Behan is a more than suitable way of preparing for his trip to Dublin. For a time—long ago now—this Irish writer was an enigma to him, a mystery from the moment Augusto Monterroso said in *Journey to the Center of the Fable* that "travel writing such as *Brendan Behan's New York* is the greatest happiness."

For a long time he asked himself who the hell this Behan could be, but without going so far as actually looking him up. And now he remembers that whenever he saw Monterroso, he forgot to ask him. And he remembers too that, one day, when he least expected it, he found the name of Brendan Behan in an article about famous guests of the Chelsea Hotel in New York. All it said was that he had been a brilliant Irish writer who used to describe himself as "a drinker with writing problems."

This last was etched into his mind; at the same time, an intensity yet scarcity of information made the enigma of this drinking saint still greater, until one day, many years later, he discovered Behan camouflaged behind the character of the garrulous Barney Boyle at a bar in *Christine Falls*, a novel written by John Banville under his pseudonym Benjamin Black. Still surprised by this discovery, he devoted himself to spying on the environment of this Boyle, Behan's counterpart: an atmosphere of fog, coal fires, whiskey vapors, and stale cigarette smoke. And he began to think that each day he found himself ever closer to the authentic Behan. He wasn't wrong. A few weeks ago, he went into a bookshop, and as if it had been there waiting for him his whole life, he suddenly came across the Spanish edition of *Brendan Behan's New York*. The first thing he regretted was not having published it himself. And he regretted it more when he discovered that Behan's book was a wonderful monologue about the city of New York, which he considered "the greatest city on the face of God's earth." To Behan, nothing compared to the electric city of New York, the center of the universe. The rest was silence, glaring darkness. After having been in New York, everything else was awful. And so London, for instance, must seem to a Londoner returning from New York like "a wide flat pie of redbrick suburbs with the West End stuck in the middle like a currant."

Brendan Behan's New York, the book he wrote at the end of his life, turned out to be a tour of the infinite genius of a city's human landscape, a city with a lucky star. What's more, *Behan's New York* confirmed that this city and happiness were the same thing. Behan wrote his book in the Chelsea Hotel, when he was already a total alcoholic, at the start of the sixties. They were days of great parties, where people were always dancing the recently invented twist and the Madison, but also days of incipient revolutions. Some years earlier, the Welshman Dylan Thomas had turned up at the Chelsea

Hotel on the night of November 3, 1953, announcing he'd drunk eighteen straight whiskeys and thought this was probably a record (he died six days later).

Ten years later, as if he were the very same "drunken boat" from Rimbaud's poem, "hurled by the hurricane into the birdless ether," the Irishman Behan turned up at that hotel too in as inebriated a state as the Welshman had been; he was assisted by Stanley Bard, the owner of the Chelsea, who put him and his wife up, even though he knew that the writer, who was always drunk, had been thrown out of every other hotel. The great Stanley Bard knew that if there was one place where Behan might start writing again it was the Chelsea. And so it was. The hotel on 23rd Street, which had always been considered a place conducive to creativity, turned out to be crucial to Behan, whose book was composed on the same floor where Dylan Thomas had lived.

The book speaks of the euphoria induced in Behan by this energetic city in which, as evening fell—probably the eve of his own life—it always became clear to him that in the end the only important thing to do is "to get something to eat and something to drink and someone to love you." In terms of the book's style, it could be summarized as follows: to write and to forget. The two verbs sound like an echo of the well-known relationship between drinking and forgetting. Behan himself used to say that he had decided this: "I will have forgotten this book long before you have paid your money for it."

Although he was Irish, Behan was never an administrator, perhaps the exception to Vilém Vok's rule that New York belongs to the Jews, is administered by the Irish, and enjoyed by the Negroes. Because the last thing Brendan Behan wanted was to have to administer anything in his beloved city. Maybe this is why the style in *Brendan Behan's New York* is made up of opinions that are shots with no intention of reaching beyond that shot itself, of deliberately furtive volleys, judgments about, all the humans he had within his reach: blacks, the Scottish, waiters, homosexuals, Jews, taxi drivers, beggars, beatniks, bankers, Latinos, Chinese, and of course, the

Irish, who went around the entire city in family clans keeping an eye on each other and creating their own culture; it's as if this were just a ballad about their rainy native land.

Throughout *New York*, at no point does Behan forget the inspiration of his literary masters. "Shakespeare said pretty well everything, and what he left out, James Joyce put in." For example, Behan's way of approaching each of New York's bars recalls Joyce's *Ulysses* when the day is drawing to a close and the people and scenery around Stephen start to disappear from his sight, perhaps because the drinks he's consumed over lunch and the intellectual excitement of the conversation in the library—actually trivial and stultifying—are gradually making them sometimes clearer or sometimes more blurred. In the same way, the bars of early sixties New York gradually appear in Behan's book, with transparent or hazy alternative names according to the level of his private enthusiasm. And the names, like some fascinating and disquieting litany, fall one after the other, inexorable, Irish, legendary: McSorley's Old Ale House, Ma O'Brien's, Oasis, Costello's, Kearney's, Four Seasons, and the Metropole on Broadway, where the twist was born.

An essential and secular litany. Riba thinks that remembering Behan's book has been a good way to continue preparing for his trip to Dublin, to move further away each day from the interior space that's holding him hostage, and so slowly approach wider horizons. He devoured Behan's book on the train from Lyon back to Barcelona, imagining many times that he was reading it at a table by the iron door of the amazing Oakland Bar, the one on the corner of Hicks and Atlantic from *When You Wound Brooklyn*, the beautiful novel by his young friend Nietzky.

And he remembers too that in the last few minutes of reading this book of Behan's, as evening fell, still imagining himself to be in the Oakland, he even thought he shared with the author this dark, unrepeatable moment, this moment, somewhere between Joycean and elegiac, when Behan's daydreams gradually absorb the world around him. Daylight fades and the impressions of the day are gathered together in a harmony of urban sounds and a touching blend of feelings and dying light that reaches the very doors of the Chelsea Hotel, where they never turn out the lights.

Without New York he would be nothing. Like eau de vie, he needs the happiness he feels whenever he remembers that this city is out there, waiting for him. Right now, thinking about the Chelsea Hotel and Behan has made him slowly sink into a state of happy New York melancholy, a sort of strange nostalgia for something unlived. Thinking about the Chelsea Hotel and Behan is a way of feeling closer to the magic and warmth of New York and to certain moments from an unlived past and to everything that, for reasons that usually escape him, brings a happiness as mysterious as it is necessary to his continued existence.

When it gets dark we all need someone. That's just as true as that when dawn breaks, we always need to remember that we still have some goal in life. New York fulfills all the requirements for being a real driving force for staying in the world. The most agreeable and also the strangest memory of this city he's visited twice—and where he thinks he should go and live soon—that night in the Brooklyn house of Siri Hustvedt and Paul Auster. He turned up there in the company of young Nietzky. He'll always remember this night out, among many other things because he hasn't had an evening out since; he's banned himself from going out at night, to not feel too tempted by alcohol and to preserve his health. For the Austers he made an exception that he's not repeated. Now he remembers perfectly how on that day when he made that great exception, at around six o'clock in the evening, he and Nietzky left the bar of the Morgan Museum, on Madison Avenue, and walked slowly all the way to the Brooklyn Bridge, which they crossed on foot over the course of an unforgettable half hour. While crossing it, he was able to confirm what some friends in Barcelona had told him, that *feeling* the city from the bridge during the time it takes to cross it on foot is an intense experience.

"Going from Manhattan to Brooklyn over the bridge," said Nietzky, "is like entering another world. I really like this bridge. And I also like the great poem Hart Crane wrote about it before he committed suicide. Every time I cross over this bridge I feel happy. It's a route that does me good."

Marching over the bridge, it was impossible not to remember that, when he was young and dreamed of one day traveling to New York, he had wished a thousand times he could walk over this bridge, which he associated with Saul Bellow. When he was a new arrival to the city, Bellow felt like master of the world there. This story was told many years later by one of his friends, who actually witnessed this moment of great imaginary might and narrated it years later thus: "He looked over the city from the bridge with astonishing generosity and seemed to be measuring the hidden strength of all things in the universe, measuring the world's power to resist *him*: he expected the world to come to him. He had pledged himself a great destiny."

"You know, I feel really good walking across this bridge too," he said to Nietzky.

And then, without mentioning Bellow, he said that for him, walking to Brooklyn meant seeking out again old hidden strengths, and evoking certain days of his youth when he still expected the world to come to meet him.

"Did you think the world would come to you?" asked young Nietzky. And he burst out laughing. Nietzky had lived in the city for years and nothing like this had ever occurred to him.

Later, walking down tranquil streets, they headed further into the historic neighborhood of Park Slope. And Brooklyn slowly revealed itself as a place with a very special atmosphere. As they walked, Nietzky explained to him that this mysterious neighborhood gets under one's skin and stays there forever. Brooklyn, Nietzky said, is a bit like an inventory of the universe and one of its particular characteristics is that, whereas in many parts of the city ethnic differences are a potential source of conflict, here people live side by side in harmony and with a more human, older rhythm than in, say, Manhattan. It's a great place, Nietzky concludes.

They walked farther and farther into Park Slope, where the redbrick house was, the three-story brownstone belonging to the Austers, very good friends of Nietzky's.

In that house in Brooklyn—and this he couldn't even have suspected—the happiness he'd looked for in vain on his first trip to that city awaited him. It came to him suddenly, at midnight, when he realized he was in the Austers' house in that wonderful city. What more could he ask for? The Austers were the very incarnation of New York. And he was in their house, he was at the very center of the world.

It was a moment of happiness he remembers as very intense, similar to that of his recurring dream. Everything seemed so agreeable; he felt in the best mood at that moment. But something he never expected happened. Because of his jet lag, and despite his fantastically happy state, he couldn't help yawning a few times, which he tried to hide with his hands, and this made it even worse. Body and soul were completely divided, each with their own language. And it was clear that the body, with its own codes, found itself radically disconnected from that moment of his spirit's happiness. "When the spirit soars, the body kneels down," said Georg Christoph Lichtenberg.

He'll never forget the moment that night when he thought about telling Paul Auster that, according to something he'd read in a magazine a while ago, when we yawn it doesn't mean we're bored or sleepy, but rather the opposite, that we want to clear our heads and so manage to be even more awake than the wide-awake and happy people we are. He remembers this moment very clearly and also when he realized afterward it would be better not to say anything and not complicate things even further, and then, without being able to help it, he yawned again and had to cover his wretched mouth with his hands.

"Will you leave something as a deposit?" Auster asked him.

He didn't understand the question at the time, or over the following days. Since they were speaking in French, he started to think he hadn't understood because of the language. But Nietzky has confirmed on several occasions now that that's what happened, that Auster did, in fact, ask him if he was going to leave something as a deposit.

Maybe Auster was asking if he was going to leave the memory of his yawns as a deposit, a supposed advance on the rent. The rent for that brownstone? Did Auster know that his guest that night wanted, more than anything in the world, to live in that house? Maybe Nietzky had told him?

Over the last few months, he's turned over this strange question of Auster's many times in his head, but it remains an unsolved mystery. Sometimes, he's at a bus stop, or sitting at home in front of the TV, and he thinks about this and still hears the question, as if charged with an inexplicable energy.

"Will you leave something as a deposit?"

On YouTube he comes across a very young Bob Dylan singing "That's Alright Mama" with Johnny Cash, and observes, with a mixture of surprise and curiosity, that the acclaimed Cash sings here with a resigned expression, as if he'd had no choice that day but to accept the sudden company of the unknown young genius, who'd jumped up onto the stage without anyone's permission.

Riba observes that the presence of the young Dylan at his side doesn't irritate Cash, but even so he seems to be wondering why he has to sing with this young genius who's latched onto him. Perhaps young Dylan is trying to become Cash's guardian angel? Maybe Dylan is an impromptu guardian of Cash's creations?

He ends up thinking something similar occurred with him and Nietzky, who for months he confused with the genius he was always searching for among young writers. Later, when he realized Nietzky had great talent but wasn't the special writer he would so like to have found, he resigned himself to seeing him just as he was, which was a pretty good writer anyway. He wasn't the giant of literature he'd been looking for as a publisher, but he found traces of a lively, exciting creativity in him, which was more than enough.

Riba published *When You Wound Brooklyn*, Nietzky's only novel, and has always thought it very good. A story about Irish characters in modern-day New York. A splendid piece in which his young friend had managed to give a new and unexpected turn of the screw, offering a world of heteronyms, a world of characters unable to be unified, compact, or perfectly outlined subjects. An amusing, strange book, in which the New York Irish seem like Lisboans who have just awoken from one of Pessoa's highly anxious siestas. There were never stranger Irish people in a novel.

Because of all this and many other things, because of his ever-increasing admiration for Nietzky, a young man of indisputable talent, he doesn't give it another thought and fires off an email, one he hopes will be as direct as a bolt of lightning, filled with energy like the tormented psyche of this promising Spanish New York writer. An email to Nietzky's apartment on West 84th Street and Riverside Drive. In it he asks him to be the fourth member of the Bloomsday expedition. He ends up saying: "After all, you went there last year— and other times, I think—I know you flew from New York to go to the Bloomsday celebrations, and so it wouldn't be at all strange for you to want to repeat the experience. Come on!"

This "come on!" has a special power, because suddenly, as if he too were given the fleeting ownership of a certain neurotic energy, he feels as if he's penetrating the essence of the wind that's blowing outside with the rainwater spreading throughout Barcelona: he believes for a few moments—a sensation without a doubt totally unknown to him—that he's inside the wind's thoughts, until he understands that the wind's mind could never be his or anyone else's, and then he contents himself—a sad fate—with a deeply ridiculous thought: the world always feels more spacious in the spring.

For years now he's led his life through his catalog. And in fact he now finds it very hard to know who he really is. And above all, what's even harder: to know who he really might have been. Who was the man who was there before he began publishing? Where is this person who gradually became hidden behind the brilliant catalog and the systematic identification with the most interesting voices contained within it? Now some words of Maurice Blanchot spring to mind, words he's known well for a long time: "Would writing be to become, in the book, legible for everyone, and indecipherable for oneself?"

In his work as a publisher, he recalls the day he read these words of Blanchot's as a turning point, and from that moment on, began to observe how, with each book published, his authors gradually became more and more dramatically indecipherable to themselves at the same time as they shadily became very visible and legible to the rest of the world, starting with him, their publisher, who saw in the drama of his authors one more consequence of the occupational hazards of his job, in this case, the hazards of publishing.

"Oh," he said very cynically one day during a meeting with four of his best Spanish writers, "your problem has been getting published. You've been very foolish to do so. I don't understand how you didn't sense that publishing was going to make you all indecipherable to yourselves, and what's more, would place you on the path of a writer's fate, which in the best of cases always contains the strange seeds of a sinister adventure."

Riba was hiding his own drama behind these cynical words. Leading a publisher's life kept him from finding out who the person gradually hidden behind the brilliant catalog might have been.

Nietzky might be the perfect companion for the trip to Ireland, and could even be the brains of the expedition, as he always has original ideas, and despite his youth, is a real expert on the work of James Joyce. In Spain the Irish writer's importance tends to be downplayed, and what's more, it's become grotesquely common-place to brag about not having read *Ulysses*, and also to say it's an incomprehensible and boring book. But Nietzky has been out of the country for ten years, and can't exactly be considered a *Spanish* Joyce specialist anymore. Really, Nietzky can now only be seen as a young writer and citizen of New York, a man well versed in local Irish topics as filtered through the color of Lisbon tiles.

He thinks about Nietzky and ends up thinking of Celia. He wouldn't like her to find him, once again, engrossed in front of the computer when she gets back from work at a quarter to three. He doesn't switch it off, but stops looking at it and sits there trying to decide what to do, looking at the ceiling. Then he checks his watch and realizes that it doesn't matter, as Celia will soon be home. He goes to look out the window and then to stare at a stain on the roof, in which he suddenly thinks he can see a map of his native country. He remembers, he remembers quite well the culture of his compatriots that became dangerously oppressive and familiar to him. He remembers his desperate leap to France, his by now so outdated *French* leap. Paris allowed him to flee from Franco's eternal uncultured summer, and later on to meet writers such as Gracq, Philippe Sollers, and Julia Kristeva, or Romain Gary, one of the friendships he feels most proud of. It doesn't escape his notice now that many of those who find *Ulysses* unbearable haven't even bothered to get past the first page of a book they assume is leaden, complicated, foreign, lacking the "authentic and proverbial Spanish wit." But he assumes that this first page of Joyce's book, just the first page, is enough on its own to dazzle. It's an apparently trivial page, which nevertheless presents a complete and extraordinary world. He knows it by heart in the now legendary version by that first translator of the book into Spanish, that translator as brilliant as he was strange, the great adventurer J. Salas Subirat, an Argentine autodidact who worked as an insurance broker and wrote a strange manual, *Life Insurance*, which Riba published as a curiosity, at the start of the '90s.

He leaves the window and goes to the kitchen and as he walks down the hall he thinks about the opening of *Ulysses*, so apparently flat, although really this beginning gives off a harmony rarely forgotten. It takes place up on the gun platform of the Martello tower, built in Sandycove in 1804 by the British army to defend against a possible Napoleonic invasion:

Stately, plump Buck Mulligan came from the stairhead, bearing a bowl of lather on which a mirror and a razor lay crossed. A yellow dressing-gown, ungirdled, was sustained gently behind him by the mild morning air. He held the bowl aloft and intoned:
— Introibo ad altare Dei.
Halted, he peered down the dark winding stairs and called up coarsely:
— Come up, Kinch. Come up, you fearful Jesuit.
Solemnly he came forward and mounted the round gunrest.

He's sure that, when the moment comes, he'll enjoy being up on the circular gun platform, where this legendary scene from *Ulysses* takes place. Moreover, very near to there, in Finnegan's pub in the village of Dalkey, is where his young friend proposes that the first meeting take place of the Order of Knights—to be named the Order of Finnegans after this very pub, and not after Joyce's book of the same name—which his friend wants to found on June 16 itself.

The news that this will take place has just arrived in an instantaneous electronic reply from Nietzky. Simply because it comes from Nietzky, the creation of this kind of *Finnegansean* club strikes him as a good idea. Couldn't he, in his melancholy, stand to be in a few clubs and some meetings? In any case, anything Nietzky comes up with or writes usually seems pertinent. What's more, the email has arrived at just the right time, and has made him very happy because it's arrived in the middle of a series of messages from other people in which—with no change in the trend that's established itself in the messages he's received lately—no one invites him to anything, not one conference or publishers' meeting, nothing at all; they just pester him with trivial matters or ask him for favors. In a way, they're forgetting about him without forgetting him.

He's been prudent with Ricardo and Javier, but with Nietzky he's going to act in a very different way. He will dare to tell Nietzky that in Dublin he wants to hold a requiem for the Gutenberg galaxy, for this galaxy, now a pale fire, of which Joyce's novel was one of the great stellar moments. And it's not just that he plans to tell Nietzky this; he's telling him right now in the email he's writing.

Without any sort of preamble or overly complicated explanation, he tells Nietzky he wants to take the *English leap*—he hopes he gets what he means, and that in the long run, with his particular talent, he might even broaden the expression's meaning—and he explains, moreover, that he's thought of holding a requiem for the end of the Gutenberg era, offering a requiem about which all he knows, for now, is that it should have something to do with the sixth chapter of *Ulysses*. A funeral in Dublin, he says, and stresses this. A funeral not just for the extinct world of literary publishing, but also for the world of genuine writers and talented readers, for everything that's needed nowadays.

He's sure that sooner or later Nietzky will come up with some ideas for the funeral rites, will suggest, for example, where to hold them. St. Patrick's, the cathedral, is a seemingly appropriate place for the ceremony, but there may be others. He's also sure Nietzky will end up telling him which words to use to give a dignified send-off to the Gutenberg era. In any case, it would be good and opportune to link the funeral with *Ulysses'* chapter six. It's the only thing that seems self-evident to Riba, especially when he sees—although he keeps this to himself—how Javier, Ricardo, and young Nietzky have already started to seem like living replicas of the three characters—Simon Dedalus, Martin Cunningham, and John Power—who accompany Bloom in the funeral procession crossing the city to Glasnevin Cemetery on the morning of June 16, 1904.

It doesn't escape Riba that it's characteristic of the imagination always to consider itself to be at the end of an era. For as long as he can remember he's heard it said that we are in a period of maximum crisis, a catastrophic transition toward a new culture. But the apocalyptic has always been there, in every era. We find it, for instance, in the Bible, in the *Aeneid*. It exists in every civilization. Riba understands that in our time the apocalyptic can only be dealt with parodically. If they manage to hold this funeral in Dublin, it can't be anything other than a great parody of the weeping of a few sensitive souls for the end of an era. The apocalyptic demands a lack of excessive seriousness. After all, ever since he was a boy he's been sick and tired of hearing that our historical and cultural situation is uncharacteristically terrible and in a certain way privileged, a cardinal point in time. But is this really true? It seems doubtful that our "terrible" situation is so different from that of our ancestors, as many of them felt the same as we do, and as Vok puts it, if our criteria seem satisfactory to us it would have been the same for them. Any crisis, after all, is just a projection of our existential anxiety. Perhaps our only privilege is to be alive and know we're all going to die together or separately. In the end, thinks Riba, the apocalyptic has a splendid fictional veneer, but it shouldn't be taken too seriously, because actually, if I look at it properly, what it offers me is the joyful, emphatic, and happy paradox of a funeral in Dublin, that is, it offers me what I've been most in need of recently: something to do in the future.

Nietzky doesn't always reply to emails straight away. He soon sees that Nietzky's speedy reply to his previous email was an exception to the rule. The minutes go by and he starts to see that Nietzky isn't prepared to reply so swiftly now.

Two whole days of certain amounts of anxiety.

During those days, moments of intense impatience and bewilderment. Like a good *hikikomori*, Riba believes the emails he sends will always be answered immediately. And it rarely happens. With Nietzky he's been left feeling more disconcerted than he should be, knowing as he does that his young New York friend has never been a man of instantaneous email replies.

He spends two days waiting for the reply. And finally even Celia seems to be waiting for Nietzky to deign to reply, perhaps because she wishes with all her heart that her *hikikomori* husband would take some sort of exercise for once—even if it's only getting onto a plane—and get as much air as possible in Dublin.

From time to time, over these two days of waiting, Celia expresses an interest in knowing if his friend from New York, young Nietzsche—she calls him this by mistake, without malice—has shown any signs of life.

"No, not one, it's as if the earth has swallowed him up. But he's already promised to come to Dublin, and that's enough," Riba replies, hiding from Celia his fear that Nietzky might not like, for instance, the idea of having to come up with ideas about how and where to hold the requiem.

When finally, after two long anxious days, Nietzky's reply arrives, night has fallen in Barcelona, and Celia is asleep. So Riba can't tell her the good news straight away. Nietzky writes from a hotel in

Providence, not too far from New York, and tells him that, just as he said in his previous email, he's really enthusiastic about repeating the trip to Dublin he took last year. Regarding the *English leap*, he says he thinks he knows what it refers to. And he remarks, with neurotic energy, that out of the Protestant and the Catholic religions, he prefers the latter: "Both are false. The first is cold and colorless. The second is forever associated with art; it's a *beautiful lie*, that at least is something." Then comes a disconcerting sentence: "You were Jewish, weren't you?" And immediately afterward, for no real reason whatsoever, he starts talking about New York, and begins a long and unexpected string of personal complaints. He writes of the appalling changes the city is constantly subjected to and says his "own requiem for the days when, wherever you lived, you could always find a few blocks from home a grocery store, a barbershop, a newsstand, a dry cleaner's, a florist, a liquor store, a shoe store ..."

Then there is a P.S. in which he mentions a meeting he's set up with a society of *Finnegans Wake* fans, the strange and, according to Nietzky, not at all unsuccessful last book by James Joyce: "On Wednesday I'm going to a gathering the members of the Finnegans Society of Providence have held on the fourth Wednesday of every month for sixty-one years. They have a website. I rang them up and the guy who answered seemed very surprised by my Hispanic accent. He asked me if I had any experience with the text. I said I did. He said it wasn't necessary. He gave me the address of the place they meet, which isn't on their website: number twenty-seven and a half (that's what he said), Edison Street. When I told him my Polish surname, he started doubting I was Spanish again."

And not a word about the funeral?

Unsettled by this piece of information about the sixty-one years of the Finnegans Society, it takes Riba a while to realize there's a P.S. to Nietzky's P.S., which he doesn't notice until he stops thinking about the curious coincidences between his parents' marriage and that of the Providence *Finnegansean* society: they have the same number of years, sixty-one.

In the P.S. to the P.S., he reads: "There'll be time for everything in

Dublin, even I think to find a good place for our heartfelt eulogy for the glorious, annihilated age of Gutenberg."

Perfect, thinks Riba. I hope that when Nietzky says the "heartfelt eulogy," he's doing so mockingly, as if sensing the most ideal way to handle the funeral is to do it parodically. I await his concrete ideas for the requiem, the ones I need. I couldn't have a better collaborator for Dublin. And now that he's confirmed his complicity he's brightened up my day.

But it's a strange way that Riba feels this happiness. He celebrates by starting to worry that his "there'll be time for everything" might refer to going to lots of pubs in Dublin. If this suspicion is true, he's in real danger. He could end up succumbing to the temptation of alcohol and drinking in a pub called the Coxwold, and then crying dejectedly, hopelessly drunk and full of remorse, sitting on the pavement down an alleyway, maybe consoled by Celia, or by her phantom, since Celia won't be going to Dublin, but her phantom might very well do so....

Enough, he thinks. These are ridiculous fears. And he stops being paranoid. Although his strange way of celebrating Nietzky's reply doesn't stop. Because now he starts to celebrate Nietzky's complicit wink by imagining that it takes the color and weight away from life and strips away almost everything until it seems like a delicate shadow, lit by a distorted light, an imaginary anemic lunar shining. This shadow is Riba himself. And it remains logical that this is what he is. After all, doesn't he now just seem like a poor old man, a simple assistant to Nietzky in this whole story?

On the trip to Dublin, Nietzky sees himself acting solely as his friend's protector over there. Riba has secretly handed command of the trip over to him. It matters little that Nietzky's actually an inexperienced young man. A few weeks ago, in spite of Nietzky's age, Riba secretly named him "his second father." And the thing is that he has a very similar relationship with Nietzky to that which he's had his whole life with any "paternal figure": when he's with him, just as with his father, he's nearly always surprisingly meek, and despite being almost sixty, open to all kinds of instructions and orders.

In fact, he feels a quiet and huge fundamental admiration for his father as well as for Nietzky, and an infinite sense of calm in knowing he's at their service, knowing he's controlled and guided by their ideas. He doesn't know any other father as conscientious as his own. Nietzky, meanwhile, has no idea what it means to act as the head of a family; maybe this is why he seems ideal as a second father. They complement each other: the paternal shortcomings of one are compensated by the excesses of the other.

In any case, it's clear that we're dealing with quite an embarrassment of fathers. Maybe caused, as he comes to think more and more insistently, by the fact that he doesn't know himself. He doesn't know himself at all. Because of his brilliant catalog, he doesn't know who he is, and instinct tells him it's unlikely he ever will. And it's likely that it's due to this self-neglect that the need for protection from certain heights arises, for protection from those summits supposedly inhabited by a warm—and in this case two-headed—father, good-natured at times and at others a talented, constant creator of neurotic excitement in New York.

Maybe he has a vague yearning for a concealed architect of his days, and so is forever on the hunt for him, in the family home or the bright streets of New York. He always walks around as if he were about to run into an almighty omnipotent father, that abstract figure he sometimes imagines as a stranger—maybe just a young man with a ridiculous Nehru jacket—someone who'd be directing everything under a weary light.

At night, he remembers a phrase of Mark Strand's he might add to the Word document where he notes down everything that catches his interest during the day, a document that's growing almost on its own, as if the phrases, slowly crossing paths with each other, are falling like snowflakes, *"as flakes of snow | on Alpine summit, when the wind is hush'd,"* as Dante said in the *Inferno.*

Mark Strand's phrase goes like this: "The search for lightness as a reaction to the weight of living." Does he really seek lightness? He realizes that everything this evening seems to be directed toward a loss of gravity and heading toward the very moment he has decided to get some air and take the nimble English leap once and for all; he understands that he has actually become someone waiting for this leap, which began as just a pleasant image, a rhetorical figure.

He walks down the hall; he's going to consult a book by Italo Calvino, which also mentions lightness. And there he discovers the episode of the poet Cavalcanti's leap. Cavalcanti. In this case, an Italian leap. He's quite struck by the relative coincidence, and is literally rooted to the spot in the study. And when he finally manages to move, he takes the book and sits down in his favorite armchair. Celia is asleep, probably happy, if one goes by the last words she said to him: "You must always love me like you do today."

He'd forgotten this leap the nimble Florentine poet Guido Cavalcanti performs in an episode of the *Decameron* by Boccaccio, and in this casual discovery thinks he's found one more reason, in his furious obsession and need to be *more* foreign every day, to take the English leap. To Calvino, nothing better illustrates his idea that there must be a necessary lightness that can be inserted into life and literature than the story in the *Decameron* by Boccaccio, in which the poet Cavalcanti appears, an austere philosopher who walks around in meditation among the marble tombs of a Florentine church.

Boccaccio tells us that the *jeunesse dorée* of the city—youths who ride around in a group and who have it in for Cavalcanti because he will never go out on a bender with them—they surround him and try to mock him. "Guido, thou wilt be none of our company," they say, "but lo now, when thou hast proved that God does not exist, what wilt thou have achieved?" Cavalcanti, seeing he is surrounded by them, presently answers: "Gentlemen, you may say to me what you please in your own house." And resting his hand on one of the great tombs and being very nimble, he vaults over it, and landing *on the other side*, he evades them, and goes on his way.

He's surprised by this visual image of Cavalcanti freeing himself in one leap "*si come colui che leggerissimo era.*" He's surprised by the image, and what's more, the Boccaccio extract immediately makes *him* want to *land on the other side.* It occurs to him that, if he had to choose an auspicious image for the new rhythms his life is moving to, he would choose that one: the sudden agile leap of the poet-philosopher who raises himself above the weight of the world, showing that with all his gravity he has the secret of lightness, and that what many consider to be the vitality of the times—noisy, aggressive, revving, roaring—belongs to the realm of death—like a cemetery for rusty old cars.

And shortly afterward he remembers a few words from a book which, just as with Calvino's collection of essays, was decisive during his first few years as a reader. This book was *Short Letter, Long Farewell* by Peter Handke. He read it in the seventies, and thinks he remembers finding in it his generation's tone of voice, or at least the one he was looking for when he started publishing, because right from the start he believed it wasn't exclusively writers who had the privilege of choosing a voice, but that the publisher also more than deserved the right to acquire a certain tone and to allow this tone, this style, always to come across in all the books on his list.

And now Riba remembers too that what surprised him most about Handke's book was that, at the end of the novel, the two young protagonists—the narrator and his girlfriend Judith—speak with the filmmaker John Ford, a character who's a real person. So characters such as Ford could appear in fiction, even if they weren't exactly themselves and didn't say exactly what they might have said in real life? It was the first time he realized doing something like that was possible. And he thought it very shocking, almost as much as the fact that in the novel Ford always speaks in the first person plural:

> *We Americans always say "we" even when we're talking about our private affairs. We see everything we do as part of a common effort. . . . We don't take our egos as seriously as you Europeans.*

Whether solemnly or not, the narrator of *Short Letter, Long Farewell* always used his "I," probably because he had studied in Europe. The kind of "I" Handke used was one Riba could immediately imagine influencing him. Since then, in his private life, he has always used a first person singular, although his has been an unnatural "I," probably because he lost his childhood spirit, that *first person* inside him that disappeared so early on. And maybe it's also due to this lamentable absence—because of which he now uses this artificial "I"—that he seems always to be perfectly ready to make the leap *over to the other side*, that is, fully prepared to become a multiple "I," in the style of John Ford in the novel, who speaks in the first person plural.

And the fact is, when Riba thinks, he is simply commenting on the world, something he always does *away from home* mentally and in search of his center. And on these occasions it's not strange that he suddenly feels he's John Ford, and also Spider, Vilém Vok, Borges, and John Vincent Moon, and in short, all the men that all the men in this world have been. Essentially, his plural "I"—adopted because of the circumstances, that is, because he has never been able to find the original spirit again—is not that far from Buddhism. Essentially, his plural "I" was always ideal for the job he did. Isn't a literary publisher a ventriloquist who cultivates the most varied different voices through his catalog?

"Do you dream a lot?" Judith asked.

"We hardly dream at all any more," said John Ford. "And when we do have a dream, we forget it. We talk about everything, so there's nothing left to dream about."

When he was a publisher he never spoke in interviews about the plurality of his first person singular. It would have been good if, for example, he'd said something like this at some point: "You won't understand, but really I'm like an Irishman who lives in New York. I combine the American 'we' with a furiously European 'I.'"

Would it really have been worthwhile to say something like that? He's always weighed down by doubt, never sure of anything. But it's true that with the topic of the plural "I" he could have excelled perfectly. Actually, there were so many things he didn't say in interviews when he was in publishing. He let himself down, for instance, by trying to be diplomatic and not always saying what he thought of certain dreadful authors he didn't publish. He probably let himself down, wasted his life, by his ridiculous desire to be too sensitive. He was let down by this and also, obviously, by having the spirit of a *son* instead of the customary protective *fatherly* temperament that seems so typical in publishers, although it's also true that there are quite a few who pretend to have it when they actually lack the most basic paternal instinct.

He remembers that it has been no time at all since he spent an entire morning going around to branches of two different banks and making changes to his investment funds, and yet he sometimes has the impression that an eternity has gone by since that morning. And he observes that even the time when he used to publish all the great literature he could is starting to drift into the distance.

How old he looks, how old he feels since he retired. And how dull it is not to drink. The world, in itself, is often tedious and lacks true emotion. Without alcohol, one is lost. Although he'd do well not to forget that it's a wise person who monotonizes existence because then each small incident, if one knows how to read it in a literary way, has a wondrous quality. Never to forget this possibility of consciously monotonizing his life is the only or best solution he has left. Drinking might seriously damage his health. What's more, he *never found* anything in alcohol, at the bottom of all those glasses, and nowadays can't very well explain to himself what it was he was looking for there. Because he didn't actually manage to avoid boredom, a feeling that always came back relentlessly. Although in interviews he had at times pretended he led an exciting publisher's life; he used to make things up like crazy back then. Now he wonders what for. What good did it do him to make out that he had an extraordinary occupation and that he enjoyed it so much? Of course it was always better to be a publisher than to do nothing, like now.... Nothing? He's planning a trip to Dublin, an homage, a funeral for a disappearing era. Is that nothing? How boring everything is, except thinking, thinking one is doing something. Or thinking what he's thinking now: that it would be good to monotonize his life and try, wherever possible, to look for those hidden wonders in his daily life that, deep down, if he wants to, he's perfectly capable of finding.

Because isn't he capable of seeing much more than what's there in everything he experiences? At least all those years are worth something, all those years of understanding reading not just as a practice inseparable from his occupation as a publisher, but also as a way of being in the world: an instrument for interpreting, sequence after sequence, his day-to-day life.

He carries on getting ready for Dublin, and as his mind drifts, he ends up thinking about Irish writers. Nothing's truer than the fact that he admires them more every day. He only ever published a couple of them, but it wasn't because he wasn't keen to publish more. For a long time, without success, he went after the rights for John Banville and Flann O'Brien. He thinks Irish writers are the most intelligent in terms of monotonizing and finding wonder in everyday tedium. In the last few days he's read and re-read a few Irish authors—Elizabeth Bowen, Joseph O'Neill, Matthew Sweeney, Colum McCann—and his amazement at their capacity for writing astonishingly well has not diminished.

It's as if the Irish had the gift of literature. He remembers that four years ago he saw one of them at a book fair in Guanajuato, Mexico, and discovered, among other things, that they didn't have the Latin habit of talking about themselves. At a press conference, Claire Keegan replied almost angrily to a journalist who wanted to know what topics she wrote about in her novels: "I'm Irish. I write about dysfunctional families, miserable, loveless lives, illness, old age, winter, the gray weather, boredom, and rain."

And at her side, Colum McCann concluded his colleague's contribution, speaking in an exquisite plural, à la John Ford: "We don't usually talk publicly about ourselves, we prefer to read."

He sits thinking about how much he'd like to speak in the plural like this all the time, like John Ford, like the Irish writers. To say to Celia, for instance:

"We don't think it's a bad idea that you're thinking of becoming a Buddhist. But we also think it might become a point of dispute and rupture."

•

He knows Ricardo once felt like he was at the gates to the center of the world, but that he was ejected from this place by a radical slam of the door by Tom Waits. He doesn't know, meanwhile, what Javier's center might be. He phones him.

"Sorry," he says, "but even though it's not an odd-numbered day I wanted to talk to you, I want you to tell me if you remember any especially great moments in your life, some moment when you felt at the center of the world."

An imposing silence at the other end of the phone. Maybe his sarcastic remark about the odd-numbered day has annoyed his friend. There is a silence that seems as if it might go on forever. Until at last, after a terrible, long sigh, Javier says:

"My first love, Riba, my first love. When I saw her for the first time, it was love at first sight. The center of the universe."

Riba asks him what she was doing, his first love, when he saw her that first time. Was she perhaps walking like Dante's Beatrice down a Florentine street?

"No," Javier says, "I fell in love watching her peeling sweet potatoes in her parents' kitchen, and I remember she was missing a tooth...."

"A tooth?"

Riba decides to take it all tragically seriously, despite the fact that Javier might just be joking. It's not long before he realizes he's made the right choice. His friend isn't joking at all.

"Yes, you heard right," Javier says, his voice quivering. "She wasn't even peeling potatoes, but sweet potatoes, mind you, and the poor girl was missing a tooth."

"Love's like that," Javier adds, faraway and philosophical. "The first sight of the beloved, although it might seem trivial, is capable of leading us to the strongest of passions, and even at times to suicide. Nothing's as irrational as passion, believe you me."

Since Riba has the impression of having inappropriately unearthed a dark drama, he takes the first opportunity in the conversation to say goodbye, thinking it's always better to talk to Javier on odd-numbered days, when it's he, on his own initiative, who calls.

"Have you ever eaten sweet potato?" Javier asks when they've practically already finished their farewells, and were both about to hang up.

Riba doesn't like the thought of not replying. But the fact is he doesn't answer. He hangs up. He pretends the line has been cut off. My god, he thinks, imagine, talking to me about sweet potatoes. Poor Javier. A love affair is always an interesting topic, but mixed with food it's indigestible.

He already knows that, at the center of the world, Ricardo had a door harshly slammed in his face by Tom Waits. And that good old Javier, meanwhile, saw a girl peeling something. As for young Nietzky, in his case it might all be different, and the question of the center of things may not be important, given that, after all—almost without realizing it Riba slips into a torrential inner world at the mere mention of New York—he already lives in this center, lives there without any trouble, lives right in the very center of the world. But who knows what's happening in his mind when young Nietzky's left alone in the center of the center of the center of his world, and thinks. What might go through his head, for example, when the light's purity bathes the windows of the skyscrapers, which are like blue, transparent skies pointing toward a superior sky over there in Central Park? What does he really know about Nietzky? And about the superior sky of Central Park in New York?

He tries to forget all this, because it's complicated and because it's Wednesday and now he's at his parents' house and hasn't properly heard what his mother's just said.

"I asked you if everything's all right," she repeats. "You look distracted."

How fast time goes by, he thinks. It's Wednesday again. Love, illness, old age, gray weather, boredom, rain. All the Irish writers' themes seem to be highly topical in his parents' living room. And outside, the drizzle adds to this impression.

Illness, old age, boredom, unbearable grayness. Nothing that's not common knowledge on the face of the earth. The stark contrast between the wake-like atmosphere in his parents' house and Nietzky's torrential inner world seems enormous.

Thinking of his talented young friend, twenty-seven years his junior, reminds him that, right now, Nietzky must be on his way to number 27 ½ Edison Street in Providence. Although Nietzky is in North America and he's in Europe, at this moment they're both in almost identical parallel situations, situations that are both preludes to the same trip to Ireland.

And he thinks that, when he first met Nietzky, no one could have predicted that one day they'd end up being friends. He can't get the idea out of his head that their meeting fifteen years ago in Paris bore a certain resemblance—mainly in regard to Nietzky's age difference and unpleasant farewell phrase—to the meeting that took place in Dublin between W. B. Yeats and James Joyce.

At that first meeting, after having reproached him for even the most impeccable side of his publishing policy, his future friend Nietzky said to him: "We might have been contemporaries, and perhaps even the best two members of our generation, I as a writer and you as a publisher. But that's not how it turned out. You're pretty old now, and it really shows."

He didn't bear a grudge, just as, the many differences aside, Yeats didn't hold a grudge against the very young Joyce when they met in the smoking room of a restaurant on O'Connell Street in Dublin, and the future author of *Ulysses*, who'd just turned twenty, read the thirty-seven-year-old poet a collection of his own brief and eccentric prose descriptions and meditations, beautiful though immature. He had thrown over metrical form, young Joyce told him, that he might get a form so fluent it would respond to the motions of the spirit.

Yeats praised this endeavor, but the young Joyce said arrogantly: "I really don't care whether you like what I am doing or not. Indeed I don't know why I'm reading to you." And then, putting his book down on the table, he proceeded to set out his objections to everything Yeats had done. Why had he concerned himself with politics, and above all, why had he concentrated on ideas and condescended to make generalizations? These things, he said, were all the sign of the cooling of the iron, of the fading out of inspiration. Yeats was puzzled, but then was confident again. He thought: "He's from the Royal University, and thinks that everything's been settled by

Thomas Aquinas—no need to trouble about it. I have met so many like him. He would probably review my book in the newspaper if I sent it there."

But his cheer disappeared when a minute later the young Joyce spoke badly of Wilde, who was a friend of Yeats's." Presently—although this was later refuted by Joyce who classified it as "café gossip," claiming that, in any case, his parting words were never as disdainful as might be inferred from the anecdote—he got up to go, and as he was going out, said: "I am twenty. How old are you?" Yeats replied saying he was a year younger than he actually was. Joyce said with a sigh: "I thought as much. I have met you too late. You are too old...."

He talks to his parents, while imagining the parallel action that might be unfolding in Providence, near New York: Nietzky walking into the Finnegans Society at that very moment and greeting the Joyceans who welcome him as a new and unexpectedly Spanish member of their society, asking him if it's true that he's read *Finnegans Wake* in its entirety and also if it's true that he's a fan of this work. He can imagine Nietzky smiling and wildly launching into a recital of the whole book from memory: "Riverrun, past Eve and Adam's, from swerve of shore to bend of bay..." And he can also imagine the other members, overcome with horror, having to interrupt him.

"So what the hell happened in Lyon? We still don't know anything about what happened there," asks his mother suddenly.

"Oh, no! Please, Mama! Since very early this morning, until just before coming over here to see you two, I've been sitting at my computer reading all kinds of things about Dublin and studying the core"—brief pause, he swallows—"of all things Irish. And now ..."

He stops in his tracks, suddenly. He's embarrassed to have said *the core*, because he thinks that *the essence* would have been a more suitable, more accurate term. But it doesn't matter. Surely his parents can forgive him this sort of mistake. It's all right. Or is it?

"The core? You're so strange, son," says his mother, who at times really does seem to be able to read his mind.

"The essence of all things Irish," he grumpily corrects himself. "Right now, Mama, right now when I know I'm brimming with facts about Dublin and I wanted to tell you some things about this city, now that I even know what sort of trees I'll find on the highway from the airport to my hotel in Dublin, you go and ask me about Lyon. What do you want me to tell you about Lyon? I said farewell to France there for a long time. I think that was all that happened. I said goodbye to France. I've studied it, tramped around it, looked at it for long enough."

As long as he's been tramping around and looking at *this* place, Riba was going to add, but held back.

"Tramped around France?" his father says.

Today more than ever a wake-like atmosphere can be sensed in this familiar living room. And although very early on in his adolescence he became aware of the strange stagnation of air and even the paralysis of everything alive that seemed to have taken possession of the room, never before has he had such a strong feeling of time being blocked, stopped, absolutely dead.

In this house, which seems more and more Irish to him, everything happens at a snail's pace, and what's more—perhaps so no entrenched custom can be altered in any way, nothing happens at all. It's as if his parents were constantly holding a wake for their ancestors and precisely today, with maximum gravity, this ghostly family tradition falls heavily on the home. Indeed, he'd swear that more than ever, as so many times before, he's seeing the ghosts of some of his ancestors. They are beings as blurry as they are out of place—they're a little short-sighted—who act threateningly and resentfully toward the living. It's important to acknowledge that at least they're quite well mannered. And the proof is in the fact that, as if polite enough not to want to disturb things, some have discreetly left the wake, and are now standing over by the door, smoking and blowing the smoke out into the hallway. Riba wouldn't be surprised if there were even a few of them playing soccer out on the patio right now. What good guys, he thinks suddenly. Today he's taken to seeing them as if they were adorable ghosts. Indeed, they are. He's been accustomed to them his whole life. They're familiar to him in every sense. His childhood was swarming with these ghosts, laden with signs from the past.

"What are you looking at?" his mother says.

The spirits. This is what he should reply. Uncle Javier, Aunt Angelines, Grandpa Jacobo, little Rosa María, Uncle David. This is what he should say to her. But he doesn't want trouble. He falls silent as a dead man, while thinking he's hearing voices coming from the patio, maybe directly connected to that other patio, the one in New York. He amuses himself recalling in his mind wisps of the dead he's seen before in other places. But he stays quiet, as if he himself were just another family apparition.

He tries to hear a conversation between the ghosts closest to him, the ones in the hallway—they seem easier to hear than the ones stirring up a fuss on the patio—and he thinks he hears something, but it's so indistinct it's not really anything at all, and then he remembers that famous description of the ghost to be found in *Ulysses*:

What is a ghost? Stephen said with tingling energy. One who has faded into impalpability through death, through absence, through change of manners.

He remembers one day in this very place his maternal grandfather, Jacobo, saying with slightly forced emphasis: "Nothing important was ever achieved without enthusiasm!"

"Right then. And what have you managed to find out about Ireland?"

He doesn't answer his mother straight away, he's amusing himself too much looking around the living room. Suddenly, the voices start growing softer and considerably lower in tone, as if falling asleep, and finally, after a brief process of almost total disintegration, all that remains is the silence and the hazy smoke from some ghostly straggler's cigarette. He thinks there couldn't be a more opportune moment to tell his mother that Ireland is essentially a country of storytellers, full of *ghosts of its own*. He wants to give a weight to the word ghosts, winking at his mother, but it's useless; for years now she's pretended to ignore the subject of the family ghosts, probably because she's spent so many years living in more than stable harmony with the specters and doesn't want to argue about something as obvious as their gentle existence.

"Imagine," he says to his mother, "that an Irish politician or bishop commits a terrible act. Fine. You'd want to know exactly how things had happened. Isn't that right?"

"I think so."

"Well for the Irish, this is secondary. What they care about is how the politician or the bishop is going to explain himself. If they're able to justify themselves with grace, that is, with a gripping, human story, they'll get out of their predicament without much trouble."

Old age, illness, gray weather, centuries-old silence. Boredom, rain, net curtains cutting them off from the outside. The oh-so familiar ghosts of Calle Aribau. There's no reason to try to play down his parents' drama and his own; growing old is disastrous. The logical response would be for everyone who sees their life waning to shout out in fright, not resign themselves to a future of drooping jaws and hopeless dribbling, still less to this brutal tearing apart that is death, because to die is to be ripped up into a thousand pieces that are scattered dizzily forever, with no witnesses. This would be logical, but it's also true that sometimes he feels pretty good listening to the soft, ghostly murmur of voices and spectral footsteps that lull him and which deep down, being so furiously familiar, even win him over.

"And what else do you know about Ireland?"

He's about to tell his mother that the country is the closest thing there is to this living room. His father gently reproaches his wife for overwhelming their son with so many questions about Ireland. And before long they're embroiled in an argument. "I won't make you your coffee for two days," she says. Senile shouts. The two of them have very different characters, different in every way. They've always loved each other, but for this very reason they hate each other. In reality they hate themselves. His parents remind him of something the poet Gil de Biedma once said to him in the Tuset bar in Barcelona. An intimate relationship between two people is an instrument of torture between them, whether they're people of opposite sexes or the same. Each human being carries within himself a certain amount of self-hatred, and this hatred, this not being able to stand oneself, is something that has to be transferred to another person, and the person you can best transfer it to is the person you love.

When he thinks about it, the same thing happens with him and his wife. There are days when he feels like he's lots of people at the same time, that his brain is peopled with more ghosts than his parents' house. And he can't stand any of these people, he thinks he knows them all.... He hates himself because he has to get older, because he's aged a lot, because he has to die: this is precisely what he remembers very promptly every Wednesday when he visits his parents.

"What are you thinking about?" his mother interrupts him.

Old age, death. And not a single one of these normal net curtains can block the funereal view of a gloomy future, or the present. In the living room mirror, as he looks deep into his own eyes, he's horrified to see, for a fraction of a second, Irish light inside his retinas, and in these, dozens of tiny different insects, moths of many varied species, all dead. It could be said that his eyes are like that mental cobweb seemingly reproduced by the terrifying workings of Spider's brain. He is terrified, and looks away, but he remains petrified, frightened, on the verge of crying out.

He goes over to the window in search of a livelier landscape, and as he looks out at the world, sees a young man walking down the street quite quickly; just as he walks past, under the window, the man looks up at Riba with one irate eye and stares hard, softened only by his comical limp.

Who can this irate, limping man be? Riba feels he's known him all his life. He remembers the same thing happened with the young genius who for so many years he dreamed he'd find one day for his publishing house. He always believed he was out there and that in fact he'd known him all his life, and then it turned out there was no way of finding him, as he either didn't exist or Riba didn't know how to find him. Would having found the genius have justified his whole life? He doesn't know, but nothing would have seemed more glorious than to have been able to announce to the world that it wasn't true that all the greats of literature were dead already. It would have been fantastic, because then he would have been able to abandon his quaint practice of referring to the lack of young geniuses by forever quoting—once drunkenly and now with all the serenity and treachery in the world—the first line of a poem by Henry Vaughan, which he knew full well was really about something else:

"They are all gone."

When he looks back at the one-eyed man, he finds he's no longer out there limping around. Maybe the irate, ethereal man has stepped into a doorway, but in any case the fact is he's no longer there. How strange, Riba thinks. He's sure he saw him a moment ago, but it's also true that some of the people he's come across recently disappear too fast.

He goes back to the living room and feels there's no conversation left here, just a wake-like atmosphere growing ever more profound, the leaden air of a waiting room. Then, he doesn't know how, he remembers something Vilém Vok said in *The Center*: "To have a mother and not to know what to talk about with her!"

He has to leave, he thinks, he can't spend any more time in this house. If he does he'll end up totally mute and buried, and days later he'll be walking around sharing cigarettes with the ghosts.

"They are all gone, Mama," he mumbles, head bowed.

And his mother, who's heard him perfectly well, laughs happily as she nods her head.

The day he said goodbye to his vocation as a publisher seems very far off now. The thing he remembers most perfectly is that, after years of familiar, spectral silence, literature came to him alone, completely alone. How can he say it, how can he describe it? It's not easy. Even if he were a writer it wouldn't be easy to explain. Because it was strange, literature came to him lightly, with a graceful step, in red high heels, a cocked Russian hat and a beige raincoat. Even so, he wasn't interested until he consciously confused literature with Catherine Deneuve, whom he'd recently seen in a trench coat, under an umbrella, in a very rainy movie that took place in Cherbourg.

"I don't think you know anything about Dublin," says his mother, interrupting his thoughts.

He'd forgotten he was at his parents' house. It feels like Wednesday of last week, when, head bowed, he said they are all gone, and his mother nodded in agreement. But this is another Wednesday.

It's undoubtedly regrettable that, in the middle of a great muddle in his head, just as he was recalling how he thought that literature was Catherine Deneuve and afterward was never able to correct the misunderstanding, just as he was imagining her, alone and erotic, with her red shoes, naked underneath the trench coat, and with her cocked hat and her slight despair on a rainy day, his mother left him unable to complete this vision, which, once again, was getting him so excited. Because, in the end, when he met Celia, she too had looked to him like the spitting image of Deneuve in Cherbourg.

"It's true, all I know is that it sometimes rains in Dublin," he says, annoyed. "And then the city fills with trench coats."

Has he been talking about raincoats? His mother reminds him that as a child he always loved them, was always waiting for it to rain so he could put one on. His mother wants to know if he really can't remember this penchant of his. Well no, he doesn't. But now that he thinks about it, it's possible that this penchant for raincoats led to his fascination with Deneuve. No one knows about this great confusion of his between literature and Deneuve, not even Celia. It would be awful if someone found out, especially if the information fell into his enemies' hands. They'd undoubtedly laugh at him. But what can he do if that's how things are, and in reality it's not so terrifying? Since time immemorial he's associated Deneuve with literature itself. So what? Other people associate their lover with some rancid piece of chocolate cake they ate at the office. As long as it remains a secret, nothing will happen. Other people have more ridiculous secrets, and they certainly keep quiet about them. Although it's also true that there are some people who don't keep quiet, whose secrets aren't ridiculous. Samuel Beckett, for example. One March night in Dublin, the Irish writer had a decisive vision, the sort of revelation that causes envy:

At the end of the jetty, in the howling wind, never to be forgotten, I saw the whole. The vision at last.

It was night time, and as he so often did, the young Beckett was wandering around on his own. He found himself at the end of a pier buffeted by a storm. And then it was as if everything found its place again: years of doubt, searching, questions, failures, suddenly made sense and the vision of what he had to carry out established itself like a piece of evidence. He saw that the darkness he'd always striven to reject was in reality his most precious ally, and he glimpsed the world he had to create in order to breathe. A kind of indestructible association with the light of consciousness took shape. An association of storm and night until the last breath.

As far as Riba remembered, this nocturne on the Dublin pier appeared later, a little altered, in *Krapp's Last Tape*:

What will become of all this misery of ours? In the end, only an old whore walking around in an absurd raincoat, on a lonely dike in the rain.

In an essay—probably mistakenly, because he was often mistaken in his essays—Vilém Vok pointed out that this woman in the rain was the same one who appeared in *Murphy* and who was called Celia, the prostitute that the young writer-protagonist lived with, although she was much younger.

He's always thought it quite a coincidence that this prostitute was called Celia, like his wife. Depending on how one looks at it, thanks to a simple rule of three, the old woman in the absurd raincoat from *Krapp's Last Tape* could, due to her Deneuvesque trench coat, be literature and at the same time Celia from *Murphy*, very old by now, and also Celia, his wife, also very old.

All this leaves him quite confused, as if wandering around on a Dublin pier buffeted by a storm, wet with passion and from the waves. Until he remembers the raincoat, the mackintosh that appears in the sixth chapter of *Ulysses*. He remembers it's a stranger attending the burial of Paddy Dignam who wears it. And it's odd. Because nowadays, a Mac would just be a famous computer, but in those days it was a raincoat, a garment invented by Charles Macintosh, a name which somehow had a "k" added to it over the years when it came to refer to the coat.

He can't help thinking that while he's been a privileged witness to the leap from the Gutenberg to the digital age, he's also observed the transition of the mackintosh coat to the Macintosh computer. Should he organize a requiem in Dublin for the age of this brand of raincoat? Immediately he congratulates himself on being able to cruelly satirize his projects, his efforts.

The stranger at Prospect Cemetery is someone we meet eleven times over the course of Joyce's book, but who makes his first mysterious appearance in chapter six. Commentators on *Ulysses* have never been able to agree on his identity.

> *Now who is that lankylooking galoot over there in the macintosh? Now who is he I'd like to know? Now, I'd give a trifle to know who he is. Always someone turns up you never dreamt of* [*Ulysses*, chapter six].

"What are you thinking about?" interrupts his mother.

Once again, in his parents' house, that feeling of forgetting where he is. He's annoyed they've interrupted his journey through the Dublin cemetery. Of course, there isn't much difference between the atmosphere of the Prospect Cemetery and that of his parents' house.

"Dublin has dead people everywhere," he answers angrily.

And it's the beginning of the end. Of today's visit at least.

"What?" his mother almost sobs.

"I said that death and children"—he's growing more and more enraged—"look very similar over there. The gravediggers touch their caps after burying them. And some people still say 'mackintosh' when they're talking about raincoats. It's another world, Mama, another world."

He hails a taxi. There are always lots on Calle Aribau. All you have to do is raise your hand and one stops automatically. Today he's out of luck, inside the taxi it stinks. But it's too late to change and the car is already on its way to his house. It's also too late to put right the falling out with his parents. Maybe he shouldn't stick to this unwavering commitment every Wednesday. Today, once more, the overwhelming impression of a wake and that intimate familiarity with ghosts have made him a nervous wreck. After his inappropriate remark, his apologies did no good.

"What was that shout?"

"I didn't shout, Mama."

He ended up slamming the door on his way out, and then feeling full of anguish and remorse. Now he's trying to get away from his sense of unease and concentrate on this sixth chapter he wants to revive in Dublin, and which starts just after eleven o'clock in the morning, when Bloom gets on the tram at the baths on Leinster Street and goes to the dead man Paddy Dignam's house, number 9 Newbridge Avenue, southeast of the Liffey, from where the funeral procession will leave. Instead of heading directly westward, toward the center of Dublin, and then northwest toward Prospect Cemetery, the cortège goes in the direction of Irishtown, turning northeast and then west. Obeying an old custom, they parade Dignam's body first through Irishtown, toward Tritonville Road, north of Serpentine Avenue, and only after crossing Irishtown do they turn west down Ringsend Road and Brunswick Street, then afterward crossing the River Liffey and carrying on northwest toward Prospect Cemetery.

As the taxi drives down Calle Brusi, he sees a man walking fast. He reminds him of the young man who stormed out of La Central bookshop the other day. Riba looks away for a moment and when he looks back again, the stranger isn't there anymore, he's disappeared. Where can he have gone? Who was he?

A man full of life, he thinks, and at the same time ethereal as a ghost. Who the hell can it be? Could it not be me? No, because I'm not young.

As of today, Celia is a Buddhist. He still hasn't entered the house, but he's already been informed of the news. Fine, he says, somewhat bewildered, resigned. And crosses the threshold. And he thinks: once upon a time, marquises went out at five o'clock in the afternoon, and now they become Buddhists.

He'd like to say to Celia that she's not the only one who can change her personality from one day to the next, to tell her that he feels a little perturbed, as if he were an arrow in a cobwebbed cellar of steel-gray light. But he holds back. "Fine," he repeats, "it's fine. I congratulate you, Celia." He notices the Buddhist decision has affected him more than he thought it would, although he was already convinced that Celia would end up converting to another religion, he saw it coming quite clearly. He lowers his head, goes straight to his study, feeling he needs to take refuge there.

It feels like everything in the house is turning oriental.

He's a *hikikomori*, she's a Buddhist.

"What's the matter? Where are you off to?" Celia asks in her most affectionate voice.

He decides not to let himself feel duped and shuts himself up in his study. Once he's there, he looks out of the window and starts meditating. Outside, the daylight is dying. He's always admired Buddhism, he's got nothing against it. But arriving home has annoyed him. It feels as if his experience has come out of a novel, and if there's anything guaranteed to make him genuinely uncomfortable these days it's things happening in his life that could turn out to be appropriate for a novelist to put in a novel. The way Celia has decided to tell him she's become a Buddhist seems like the start of a classic conflict story: a wife who all at once has a different ideology than her husband, the first fights and serious disagreements after years of happiness.

If he's gained anything from giving up the publishing house it's no longer having to waste hours reading so much garbage: manuscripts with conventional plots, stories that need a conflict in order to be anything. Manuscripts telling the same old pernicious, traditional stories have disappeared from his view, and he doesn't want to feel he's inside one of them now. It's a source of irritation to him that, having been so peaceful for two years—for twenty-six months to be precise—his life has taken this unexpected fictional turn. He loves the daily life he's been leading recently, and more than most things, he loves his daily world, so tranquil and boring. If someone came to examine his day-to-day life they'd find it hard to see anything exciting about it, let alone to tell anyone else, because really it's one of those lives in which scarcely anything happens. He leads an existence like a character in a book by Gracq, the writer he chose as the model for his theory in Lyon. That's why it's so irritating that this melodramatically inclined event has occurred now. He's annoyed that everything has suddenly sped up, as if someone wanted him involved in a less slow novel.

He's fascinated by the charm of everyday life. It's true that at times he's worried about having become so blocked, such a computer nerd, and it's also true that at times he's worried about leading a life lacking the excitement of before. But in general he repeats a daily mantra that the more insignificant the things happening to him are, the better. As a future member of the Order of Finnegans and a supposed expert on Joyce's oeuvre, he knows the world functions through insignificances. After all, Joyce's greatest achievement in *Ulysses* was to have understood that life is made up of trivial things. The glorious trick Joyce put into practice was to take the absolutely mundane and give it a Homeric foundation. It was a good idea, yes, although it's never stopped seeming like a con to him. But that's not enough for him to deprive his Dublin funeral of its symbolism. He doesn't want to deprive it of the grandeur the occasion requires, even if a requiem for the end of an age in which Joyce reigned is nothing over there. What's more, without grandeur, the parody would be incomprehensible. On the other hand, this grandiose, symbolic aspect would coexist—just as happens in *Ulysses* too— with the mundane procession of trivialities that comes with every journey. He can already start to imagine this coexistence: him in Dublin, bidding farewell with a somewhat heroic urge and funereal pomp to a historic period, and at the same time, in contact with the soporific vulgarity of the everyday, that is, buying T-shirts in some big department store, wolfing down a mediocre chicken curry in a restaurant on O'Connell Street and, well, keeping time with the gray rhythm of the prosaic.

Huge contrasts between greatness and the prosaic, between the heroic urge and chicken curry. He laughs. Maybe heroic urges nowadays are something completely vulgar and common. What is a heroic urge anyway? He thinks of it as if it were something very obvious when in fact he doesn't really know what it is.

"Did you know that in Buddhist monasteries one of the exercises is to meet each moment of your life by living it to the full?" asks Celia.

She's come into the study, and it doesn't look like on her first day as a Buddhist she's going to let him be much of a *hikikomori*. Riba is surprised because Celia never comes into his room without knocking.

"In Buddhist monasteries they help you to think," says Celia completely naturally, as if she hasn't infringed one of their house rules by coming into his study.

"I don't know what you're talking about."

"Really? I'll explain. In Buddhist monasteries they help you say to yourself, for instance: now it's noon, now I'm walking across the patio, now I'm going to meet the abbot, and at the same time you have to think that noon, the patio, and the abbot are unreal, they're as unreal as oneself and one's own thoughts. Because Buddhism denies the *I*."

"That's something *I* am not unaware of."

He observes that the conflict he wanted to avoid is about to happen, and thinks again that in no way does he want to live in a novel. But the fact is, what he feared is happening: it won't be easy living with someone who's changed a lot in the last few weeks and who now has a markedly religious world view very different from his own.

Celia thinks she can guess what he's thinking, and calms him down. She says he mustn't worry, because Buddhism is gentle, it's good, and what's more, Buddhism is just a philosophy, a way of life, essentially just a technique for personal improvement.

One of Buddhism's meditation themes, Celia explains, is the idea that there is no subject, but rather a series of mental states. Another theme is that our past life is illusory. He should calm down, Celia tells him. Riba doesn't know what to reply, and says he's prepared to calm down but he's not inside a novel.

"I don't understand," Celia says.

"Nor I you."

"But let's see if you at least understand this. If, for example, you were a Buddhist monk, you'd think at this moment that you've started to live now. Are you listening?"

"I've started to live now?"

"You'd think that all of your life before now, that alcoholic period of yours and the very one you hate so much and feel so proud of having escaped, was a dream. This is what you'd think, do you follow? You'd think this and also that all of universal history is a dream. Are you listening?"

He is, sort of. The irruption of Buddhism into his life has overwhelmed him. The truth is he preferred her when she used to talk to her mother on the phone every evening, or to her siblings, or her work colleagues about the problems at the museum. Buddhism has come to complicate everything.

"You'd gradually liberate yourself by doing mental exercises," Celia continues. "And once you understood for real that the *I* doesn't exist, you wouldn't think that the *I* can be happy, or that your task is to make it happy, you wouldn't think any of that."

He thinks that all that remains for her to say is: And don't get so excited about your trip to Dublin, or your search for enthusiasm and lost genius, or about New York, which represents your hope of abandoning your mediocre life, or about the idea that you're not that old, or about the English leap.

But being a Buddhist, he wonders, would she be able to say something so incredibly cruel? He prefers to think not. Buddhism isn't merciless. Buddhism is gentle, Buddhism is good. Isn't it?

His eyes round as saucers, he's sitting in front of the computer. He doesn't know how many hours he's been here. Relentless insomnia. He gets the impression he's being *observed*. Maybe by someone not visible. By someone who has faded into impalpability, whether through death or through a change of manners.

It's well known that every man shows a different face when he feels he's being spied on, and now Riba, sensing he might be watched, changes even his gestures. He should go to bed, maybe that's all it is. Tiredness. It's almost five o'clock in the morning. He should get some rest, but he's not convinced it's the right thing to do. He turns back to the computer.

He discovers via Google that on February 2, 1922, the day his father was born, other things happened in the world. One of them is astonishingly related to a very important event for Dublin. On this day Sylvia Beach, the publisher of *Ulysses*, was walking restlessly along the platform of the Gare de Lyon in Paris for a long time. Shrouded in the chilly morning air, she awaited the arrival of the train from Dijon. The express arrived at seven o'clock on the dot. And Sylvia Beach ran toward the ticket inspector who was holding a packet and looking for the person to give those first two copies of *Ulysses* to, sent by the printer Maurice Darantière, who had worked his fingers to the very bone on every correction of every paragraph of every galley that had been crossed out, rewritten, and manhandled to ridiculous extremes. There were the first and the second copies of the first edition, with their Greek blue cover and the title and author's name in white lettering. It was James Joyce's birthday, and Sylvia Beach's present to him would be unforgettable. Perhaps this was one of the great secret moments of the age of print, of the Gutenberg galaxy.

That same day, at the same time that Joyce received his first copy of *Ulysses*, at a strange age—he'd been in the world a mere four hours—Riba's father let out a huge resounding grunt, which went right through the walls of the house where he was born.

He writes a really long email to Nietzky to say that every day he feels more predestined to go to Dublin, but in the end he doesn't send it. He goes back to Google and after looking at a few random pages ends up with the paintings of Vilhelm Hammershøi on the screen, which leave him even more wide awake than he was before. He always finds this Danish artist immensely hypnotic, a man who for his entire career limited himself to a few motifs: portraits of his relatives and close friends, paintings of the inside of his home, monumental buildings in Copenhagen and London, and Sjælland landscapes. He likes these canvases where the same motifs appear again and again. And although their creator projects great peace and calm in all of them, Hammershøi might be reproached for being obsessive. But he thinks that in art this is often precisely what matters, unbridled obsession, the fastidiousness behind the work.

In Hammershøi's works the painter is always present, with his persistent images circling around his insistent empty spaces, and nothing apparently happens though nevertheless, a lot does—what happens—unlike a subject in a painting by someone like Edward Hopper for example—would never catch on as material for an orthodox novelist. There is no action in his paintings. And without exception, they are all impregnated with a very solid atmosphere: behind the extreme calm and motionlessness, one senses something indefinable and maybe threatening lying in wait.

His palette is very limited and is dominated by a range of gray tones. He's the painter of what happens when it looks like nothing's happening. All this turns his interiors into places of hypnotic stillness and melancholic introspection. Happily, in these paintings there is no place for fictions, for novels. One can relax comfortably in them, however much an obsessive mind sweeps over all the canvases.

But what's more, Riba likes this painter precisely because, in the midst of the lethargic stillness of his empty spaces, everything in him is obstinate, insistent. Hammershøi lives in a permanent state of *quiet obsession*—to use the title of one of Vok's books, given in English. The peaceful man's universe seems to revolve around his restrained fascination.

He has always liked this expression—*quiet obsession*—coined by Vok's English translator. Riba also believes he has obsessions of a similar style. His quiet passion for New York, for instance. His tranquil obsession with a funeral in Dublin, with bidding farewell—he doesn't yet know whether with a gunfire salute or with tears—to the age of print. His tranquil obsession with experiencing one more moment in the center of the world, traveling to the center of himself, and reaching significant degrees of enthusiasm, and not dying of shame after having lost almost everything.

He's especially gripped by an obsession with *The British Museum*, the strangest, most obsessive Hammershøi painting he knows. A painting of an almost aggravated gray tone and in which a thick morning fog can be seen spreading down a totally deserted street in Bloomsbury. As in so many paintings by this artist, the canvas has no people in it. It belongs to a series of works by Hammershøi in which foggy, deserted streets in this area of London that must have hypnotized the painter appear with marked insistence.

He's only set foot in London once, five years ago, when he was invited to a publishers' conference. He never visited the book fair in this city because he was worried he would feel self-conscious about his non-existent English, so he always used to send Gauger there instead. On this first and only trip to London, he was put up in a little family-hotel in Bloomsbury, next to the British Museum, near the building of the enigmatic Swedenborg Society. The conference meetings took place in a Bloomsbury theater. And during his brief three-day stay he barely had time to look around anywhere other than his hotel and the museum. He got to know the streets of that district so exhaustively that he's been under the impression ever since that he knows it really well, in depth. This has been his way of trying to take possession of the area. Maybe that is why, when he watched the film *Spider*, the rundown streets of the East End surprised him, because he didn't want to accept something as basic as the fact that in London there were areas quite different from Bloomsbury.

On that journey five years ago he took great care not to say to anyone it was the first time he'd visited the city. He knew it would make a terrible impression that a publisher such as himself, with all his prestige, was such a yokel and hadn't set foot in London, and moreover, had not set foot there purely out of embarrassment at having no idea how to speak English.

On that journey five years ago he carefully and meticulously studied the streets around the British Museum. He walked up and down them many times and ended up memorizing them and when he got home was able, almost immediately, to identify the street in any of Hammershøi's London paintings he saw, and even knew, almost by heart, the street's name. This was the case with all the paintings except *The British Museum*. The same thing happens to him today. It's strange, but he still loses himself, gets confused, drowns in this painting. The more he sees the street that features in this painting, the less he knows which one must have served as a model for the painter, and the more he wonders if Hammershøi invented it himself. Nevertheless, the bit of the building that can be seen on the left of the canvas must be one side of the museum, and as such, he should recognize this street, which is probably no great mystery and is very possibly a street that exists and that is there—one more quiet obsession, for when he decides to return to London and see it.

In any case, he has a relationship with the painting *The British Museum* as strange as the one he's always had with London. Because, in actual fact, if he hasn't been to London more than once, it's not just because of his lack of a command of English, but also because for years a strange fear has been growing inside him caused by the fact that on several occasions, having been on the verge of traveling to this city, something odd always prevented him at the last minute. The first time was in Calais, at the start of the seventies. His car was already on the ferry due to drop him on the other side of the Channel, when an unexpected argument with a female friend—a somewhat fatuous argument about Julie Christie's miniskirts—had him backing out of the trip. In the eighties, the plane ticket already bought, a colossal storm blocked his path and ended up stopping him from crossing the English Channel.

He started thinking London was that place to which, for obscure reasons, we know we should never go, because death awaits us there. That's why, five years ago, when the invitation to London he'd always feared arrived, he felt genuine panic. After quite a few doubts, he finally left his house in Barcelona, convinced, however, that before taking the plane, the most unforeseeable event would prevent him from setting foot on English soil. But nothing stood in his way, and he ended up landing at Heathrow, where, with extreme suspicion, he was able to verify that he remained perfectly alive.

Feeling threatened by strange, dark forces, he began walking very apprehensively through the airport. For a moment, he even thought he'd lost his sense of direction. An hour later, when he got to his hotel room, he sat on the bed for a long time, in silence, surprised nothing had happened to him yet and that he hadn't even felt the slightest possibility of a visit from Death. After a short while, seeing that everything remained in a state of normality almost as vulgar as it was obscene, he turned on the television, found the news, and despite not understanding a word of English, very quickly deduced that Marlon Brando had just died.

He was filled with terror, because he understood that, due to an error by a distracted Death, so predisposed to getting muddled, Brando had died in his place. Afterward, he rejected the idea as inconsistent. But he spent quite a while holding a private funeral for poor Brando and at the same time keeping alert for any possible movements in the third-floor corridor outside his room, as he felt enormously afraid that Death might come down that narrow hallway with the aim of paying him a visit.

He was alert to all the building's movements when he heard footsteps: someone was heading for his room. There was a knock at the door. He froze. Four more very sharp knocks. The shock didn't fade until he opened the door and saw that it wasn't the loathsome scythe-bearing figure at the door, but the publisher Roberto Calasso, who was also staying at the hotel, a guest at the conference, and he had simply come to suggest going for a stroll around the neighborhood.

When the two of them went out for that walk at dusk, they couldn't have imagined they'd end up watching Joseph Mankiewicz's film *Julius Caesar*, perhaps as a kind of unexpected and improvised homage to the film's lead actor, the illustrious death of the day. They discovered, by one of those casual coincidences that sometimes occur in life, that the film starring Brando and James Mason was being shown at dusk in the Stevenson Room of the British Museum, a few yards from their hotel. And they decided they couldn't ignore this wink from fate and went in to watch the admirable film that so many times and on so many different occasions they'd seen before.

He remembers that, last night, Celia was telling him, with a marked Buddhist emphasis to her words, that we're all weaving and interweaving every moment of our lives. Not only, said Celia, do we weave our decisions, but also our acts, our dreams, our states of vigilance: we're constantly weaving a tapestry. And in the middle of this tapestry, she concluded, it sometimes rains.

He's started remembering these noteworthy phrases from yesterday, and this doesn't stop him from imagining a tapestry where it can clearly be seen that it's been pouring rain in Barcelona for months, without interruption, and it seems it will never stop raining. It always rains in high fantasy, said Dante. And it's raining, especially now, in his imagination, and in Barcelona too. It's pouring in this city, that's for sure. And it's been doing so, on and off, ever since he decided to go to Dublin. Rain always makes us remember, it brings other times to mind, and maybe this is why he now recalls that, five years ago in Bloomsbury, after having watched James Mason in *Julius Caesar*, he came across this actor again back in his hotel room that night, and there he was quite still on the television screen, in that scene from Kubrick's *Lolita*, in which Humbert Humbert, before going up to his room to sleep with his nymphet, talks to a stranger, another guest at the hotel, a man called Quilty, who seems to know all about his life.

Who is this Quilty? Was he wearing a Nehru jacket in the film? He doesn't know if it's because he's had severe insomnia and hasn't slept for many hours or because he's still got *The British Museum* on his computer screen, but he's acting more and more disturbed. Carried along by the rhymes the rain is gradually spinning in the unknown street of the painting, thinking about the rainy installation his friend Dominique is preparing at the Tate, he's mentally writing phrases and wondering in one of them what London will be like when he and all the people he loves are dead. There will be days—he can be sure of this now—when all his dead will have become pure vapor and will speak from their wild, remote solitude; they'll speak just as the rain in Africa does, and won't remember anything anymore. Everything will have been forgotten. Even the rain beneath which all the dead once fell in love will have faded away. And lost too, the memory of the moon beneath which they once walked along an also forgotten road like lost souls.

And although, once more, things are getting occasionally complicated, he thinks he knows that, as long as everything still depends only on him, as long as he's still in control of the action and can make sure things are pure and exclusively mental, he won't be fazed. This is why he gets lost with a certain amount of calm down the foggy, presumably unknown street, next to the British Museum, and gets trapped at a strange bend, what at first sight had seemed like a street corner. It's not a street corner, it's a blot, and in it there's a shadow that seems to want to escape from the screen.

Alarmed at this threatening shadow, he clicks the mouse and in two moves gets to the page with his emails, where he finds one containing the poem "Dublinesque," by Philip Larkin, which young Nietzky has just sent him from New York. It's a poem that talks of an old Dublin prostitute, who in her last hour is accompanied only by a few co-workers along the city streets. Nietzky says he's sent Riba this poem because there's a funeral in it and it takes place in Dublin: a deliberate wink at the funeral ceremony they're preparing for June 16. A poem that begins:

> Down stucco sidestreets,
> Where light is pewter
> And afternoon mist
> Brings lights on in shops
> Above race-guides and rosaries,
> A funeral passes.

He stops reading to turn on the radio and think about other, less funereal things, and he hears "Partir Quand Même" sung by Françoise Hardy. It's been years since he's heard this song that he's always liked. It looks like it's stopped raining. It must be past seven already. He memorizes the first line of Larkin's poem, *Down stucco sidestreets,* so he can pretend he's starting to know English, so he can say it at the slightest opportunity. His insomnia now seems to be irrepressible. Celia sees this for herself. She's there all of a sudden, standing in the doorway, looking threateningly at him, although at the same time with what might be an air of despair. I didn't know, thinks Riba, that Buddhists could experience anxiety too. But he's wrong, it's not despair, it's just that Celia has to go to work and isn't helped by seeing her husband so outrageously wide-awake. Riba puts his head down and hides in "Dublinesque." He reads the rest of the poem, hoping that this might protect him from the telling-off that could come from Celia at any moment. And as he reads, he wonders what would happen now if that blot were to reappear on the screen, that threatening shadow.

Celia is about to leave and he—so she can see he's not hypnotized—switches off the computer, avoiding several problems at once. Celia still hasn't left and is trying on a new shirt in front of the mirror. He realizes that, as soon as he turned off the computer and lost the possibility of seeing the shadow, he started to feel hugely, strangely, most unexpectedly sad. *Absurdly* sad, because he doesn't think it's the absence of the shadow that's caused his spirits to sink, but still he can't find a better explanation. He decides to evade this odd sadness with one that's more clear; he starts thinking about the sad—but not so sad, because it's associated with a trip with good prospects—funeral ceremony awaiting him in Dublin, this ceremony about which all he knows is that it will have to uphold some sort of connection with the sixth chapter of *Ulysses.*

Now that he thinks about it, his life over the last two days seems to have points of contact with this chapter. He decides to re-read it, to check if what he senses is true. And shortly afterward he's closely examining the pages of Paddy Dignam's burial and in particular the moment when a lanky guy appears at the last moment in the cemetery. He's a man who seems to have come from nowhere at the very minute the coffin drops into the hole in Prospect Cemetery. Bloom is thinking about Dignam, the dead man they've just lowered into the hole, and as his gaze flits among the living, it pauses for a moment on the stranger. Who is he? Who can this man in a mackintosh be?

"Now who is he I'd like to know? Now, I'd give a trifle to know who he is. Always someone turns up you never dreamt of," thinks Bloom, and lets his thoughts drift to other matters. At the end of the ceremony, Joe Hynes, a reporter who's taking the names of everyone attending the burial for the funeral report, asks Bloom if he knows "that fellow in the ..." and just at that moment, as he's asking the question, he realizes the individual he's referring to has vanished, and the sentence goes unfinished. The missing word is raincoat (macintosh). Bloom completes the phrase a moment later: "Macintosh. Yes, I saw him. Where is he now?" Hynes misunderstands and thinks the man's surname is Macintosh, and notes it down for his report of the burial.

Rereading this passage reminds Riba that in *Ulysses* there are ten more allusions to the enigmatic man in the raincoat. One of the last appearances of this mysterious character occurs when, after midnight, Bloom orders a coffee for Stephen in the cabman's shelter and picks up a copy of the evening *Telegraph* and reads the short report on the burial of Paddy Dignam written by Joe Hynes. In it the journalist gives the names of thirteen mourners, and the last of them is ... Macintosh.

Macintosh. This could also be the name of the dark shadow he saw before on his screen. And as he thinks this, perhaps involuntarily, the link between his computer and Paddy Dignam's funeral is strengthened.

He's not exactly the first person in the world to wonder this.

"Who was M'Intosh?" he remembers from the second chapter of

the third part of *Ulysses*, a chapter formed of questions and answers.

One of these questions, intriguing and thorny, has always appealed to him: "What selfinvolved enigma did Bloom risen, going, gathering multicoloured multiform multitudinous garments, voluntarily apprehending, not comprehend?"

He goes over all the debates about who this M'Intosh was. The widest range of interpretations exists. There are those who think that he is Mr. James Duffy, the indecisive companion of Mrs. Sinico in "A Painful Case" from *Dubliners*, who commits suicide overwhelmed by lovelessness and solitude. Duffy, tormented by the consequences of his indecision, wanders around the tomb of the woman he could have loved. And there are those who think he is Charles Stewart Parnell, who's risen from the grave to continue his fight for Ireland. And there are also those who think it might be God, disguised as Jesus Christ, on his way to Emmaus.

Nietzky has always been especially fond of Nabokov's theory. After reading the opinions of so many researchers, Nabokov deduced that the key to the enigma of the stranger was to be found in the fourth chapter of the second part of *Ulysses*, in the library scene. In this scene, Stephen Dedalus is talking about Shakespeare and maintains that he included himself in his plays. Very tensely, Stephen says that Shakespeare "has hidden his own name, a fair name, William, in the plays, a super here, a clown there, as a painter of old Italy set his face in a dark corner of his canvas."

This, according to Nabokov, is what Joyce managed to do in *Ulysses*: to set his face in a dark corner of his canvas. The man in the macintosh who crosses the book's dream is none other than the author himself. Bloom actually sees his creator!

He wonders whether he should make an effort to stay awake, or give in to sleep—he doesn't think that is such a good idea because his insomnia is giving him a special sort of lucidity, although Celia's already gotten seriously annoyed with him because of it. They had a morning argument, so she hasn't gone back to the old days, that is, to the times when she used to get so annoyed she'd end up putting a few things in a suitcase and leaving it on the landing. She hasn't acted like that this time, but it's clear that if things get worse, she might do so later, when she gets home from work at lunch time. It's terrible. Everything's always hanging from a thread with Celia.

He leaves the computer and goes over to the window, looks out at the street. He hears Celia slamming the door loudly as she goes to work. She's gone at last. It's ridiculous, but it seems as if the thing that's really irritated her, that's made her explode with rage, is when a moment ago, he flippantly quoted W. C. Fields at her: "The best cure for insomnia is to get a lot of sleep." This little phrase drove her crazy. "Excuses are worthless," she said.

He went too far with the Fields quote, he thinks now, uselessly repentant. When will he learn to control his words better? When will he realize that there are certain inappropriate remarks that might seem witty in many settings outside the conjugal one? Celia was probably more than justified in slamming the door. For a while, from the big window, he stands and watches what happens when nothing is happening. When he turns his eyes away from the general view of Barcelona and looks down to focus on what's going on nearby, he realizes that a man in a gray Burberry coat is walking down his street, a man who reminds him—who has an air—of the stranger in the raincoat with his hair plastered to his head that Riba and Ricardo saw in La Central bookshop. At first this seems strange and then less so. The fact is he ends up feeling a mysterious emotional affinity with him. Couldn't he have come to tell him to persist in his search for "the unfathomable dimension," the dimension that, in the middle of a storm, his father asked about in a low voice the other day? He feels dizzy. And he remembers the Swedish thinker Swedenborg who, one day, finding himself by the window of his London house, noticed a man walking down the street for whom he felt instant empathy. To his surprise, this man came over to his door and knocked at it. And when he opened it, Swedenborg felt from the first moment absolute trust in this individual, who introduced himself as the son of God. They took tea together, and over the course of the encounter, the man told Swedenborg that he saw in him the most suitable person to explain the right path to the world. Borges always said that lots of mystics could pass as madmen, but that the case of Swedenborg was special, as much for his enormous intellectual capacity and great scientific prestige, as for the radical change in his life and work brought about by the visions that came from the hand of this unexpected visitor, who connected him directly to celestial life.

He watches the footsteps of the man in the gray Burberry and for a moment fears, and at the same time wishes, that this individual will come over to the front door of his building and press the intercom. It might be that the man wants to congratulate him for planning a requiem for the Gutenberg age, but also that he wants, as well as this, to tell him there's no reason to look at things in such a short-term way and that he should intone a funeral song for the digital age too—which one day will disappear—and not be afraid, moreover, of time-traveling and intoning another requiem for everything that will come after the apocalypse of the internet, including not just the end of the world but the end of the world that follows that one. After all, life is an enjoyable and serious journey round the most diverse funerals.

Will the second end of the world include the brilliant blue dress with silver needlework, the white gloves and the little cocked hat his mother used to wear every Saturday night in the fifties when she went out with her husband to dance at the Flamingo? Back then no one in the family asked about the unfathomable dimension.

He looks out of the window again and sees that the man in the gray Burberry isn't on his street anymore. What if it was Swedenborg? No, it wasn't him. Just as it wasn't that guy he one day thought might be directing everything under a weary light. It was someone who's walked right by, although it's strange, because at first that hadn't seemed to be his intention.

His insomnia leads him to sit and read in his armchair. Like in the old days, when the computer didn't limit his time so drastically. The music on the radio is still French, as if the English leap is up against curious domestic resistance from his favorite station.

He's rescued from the shelf a book by W. B. Yeats, one of his favorite poets. It wasn't planned, but reading this book might also contribute perfectly to the preparations for his trip to Dublin. Time goes by very quickly, and his insomnia adds even more to a sensation of time flying, but the fact is there are now only five days left until his trip. Everything has gone by really quickly and it seems like only yesterday when, in order to avoid his mother finding out he had absolutely no plans for the future, it occurred to him to say he had to go to Dublin.

He dives into the Yeats, into a poem where it clearly says that everything is falling apart, and that turns out to be ideal for the bloodshot eyes of a profoundly sleepless reader. Letting the verses carry him along, he imagines that the bright light of day is blinding him and that he's turned into a skilled pilot who flies quickly over the geography of infinite life. A pilot who very soon leaves behind all the stages of humanity—the Iron age, the Silver age, the Gutenberg age, the digital age, the definitive, mortal age—and arrives just in time to witness the universal flood and the grand end, the funeral of the world, although in reality it would be more accurate to say that the world itself had been gradually burning through the ages and traveling toward its grand finale and funeral, previously announced in these lines of Yeats's that carried Riba so far along this morning: *"Things fall apart; the center cannot hold;/ Mere anarchy is loosed upon the world,/ The blood-dimmed tide is loosed, and everywhere / The ceremony of innocence is drowned...."*

There his flight ends. He comes back to reality, which is not so different from where his imagination has transported him. He shuts the book of the great Yeats and looks out of the window and follows the course of a cloud extremely curiously and then his head nods and he feels he might soon fall asleep, and then, to stop this from happening, he reopens the book he'd closed and finds in what he reads traces of the cloud he's just been looking at, he finds it in a fragment of Vilém Vok's prologue to Yeats's book: "The winds that shake the coast and the woods where the *sidhe* talk, emissaries of the fairies, allude to a lost, but recoverable splendor." And later: "It said that the world was once all perfect and kindly, and that still the kindly and perfect world existed, but buried like a mass of roses under many spadefuls of earth." And he suddenly realizes what the real content of his father's words were when he asked, the other day, if someone could explain the mystery to him.

If he hadn't read those lines of Yeats's, he surely wouldn't have thought this just now. But he did read them and he can't help but think that he's just understood what exactly might have been behind those words of his father's. Maybe the winds battering the Catalan coast at that moment disturbed his father's unconscious, until he was driven to ask, indirectly, about a lost splendor. And the thing is that maybe his father wasn't really asking about the mystery of life in general, or about the mystery of the storm, but rather about everything close to his emotional world, everything that, with time, he'd come to see was buried, like a mass of roses under many spadefuls of the dampest earth.

This could have been the true and fundamental cause of his father's worries about the storm. And if this was the cause then Riba can't deny that it was insomnia that helped him realize it, that his insomnia was hiding a visionary power he was previously unaware of, and by leading him to understand the true meaning of those words of his father's, it was able to widen his outlook.

He goes to the kitchen, and lapsing once more into the mundane, makes himself a sandwich with ham and two layers of cheese in it. He wonders if it might not be the case that, when he thinks of New York, really what he's interested in—a worthy successor to his father—is a perfect, kindly world, which as a child he lost very early on, and which he hopes to find again in this city one day. Is it symbolically concentrated in New York—his whole search for that great part of his life buried like a mass of roses under tons of earth? It's possible. He takes a bite from the sandwich, then another one. He hates himself for having base needs, but the cheese is superb. He recalls a quote of Woody Allen's about reality and steak. He's feeling wider and wider awake. Wasn't this what he was after? If so, then he's achieving it, and he's *seeing* more than ever. It's as if he were approaching the experience of Swedenborg, the man who spoke totally naturally to angels. At times it seems to him that insomnia is capable of having the same effect on him as alcohol once did. Alcohol, which he needs so much sometimes. Who's there? He smiles. He detects a presence again, although this time it might be merely wild intuition, provoked by his sleep-deprived state. The presence ends up seeming so obvious and large that he grows sad wondering what would become of him if reality suddenly showed him evidence of a great absence.

He starts reading *The Dalkey Archive* by Flann O'Brien, which is simply another way of conscientiously preparing for the trip to Dublin. What's more, Finnegans pub, where Nietzky is planning to found the Order of Knights, is in Dalkey, a small town some twelve miles south of Dublin, on the coast.

Flann O'Brien says: "It is an unlikely town, huddled, quiet, pretending to be asleep. Its streets are narrow, not quite self-evident as streets and with meetings which seem accidental."

Dalkey, a town of accidental meetings. And also of strange appearances. In *The Dalkey Archive*, St. Augustine appears alive and kicking, talking to an Irish friend. And James Joyce also appears, working as a bartender in a tourist pub outside Dublin and refusing to be associated with *Ulysses*, which he considers "a dirty book, that collection of smut."

A violent wave of exhaustion now jolts his head forward. And again he has the sensation of being *watched*. Has Celia come back without him hearing her? He calls her, but no one answers. Total silence.

"James?"

Well, he doesn't really know why he's asking for James, but he hopes it's not actually Joyce who's now walking around out there.

He's afraid of falling asleep, and if that's true he suspects it's because he'll be assailed by that recurring nightmare where a sightless god with the look of a weary primate wants to shake his hand and so is forced to raise his elbow as high as he can. Riba looks at him from above, but it can't be said he's in a better position, as the two of them are locked in this cage in which they're condemned for all eternity to be eaten away by an intimate Hydra, by a fearsome pain: the author's ache.

Just after eleven o'clock in the morning, he starts to feel overcome by sleepiness. He wavers between going meekly to sleep falling victim to what his friend Hugo Claus called *the sorrow of the publisher*, or resisting a bit longer. He's annoyed that sleep threatens just when, only a few moments ago, he felt most lucid.

In exactly five days, at this very hour, his plane will be landing in Dublin. Javier, Ricardo, and Nietzky will already have been there for a day when he arrives. Javier and Ricardo still don't know that, apart from taking part in Bloomsday and the founding ceremony of the Order of the Knights of Finnegans, they're going to participate in a funeral for the Gutenberg age. They have a tight schedule. Maybe Nietzky will explain it to them over the course of that first day the three of them spend together. Perhaps when he, Riba, gets to Dublin, Nietzky will already have thought of a way to celebrate this funeral and found the ideal place to hold it.

For quite a while, he resists the ravages of tiredness and fatigue by thinking about the imminent Irish trip. He's worried, above all else, that even though he stopped being a *hikikomori* a few hours ago, now he seems more like one than ever. While he's stopped being one in spirit, he knows that when Celia comes home, if she finds him asleep, the first thing she'll think is that he's turned, tragically and once and for all—unjustly, but it's what she'll think—into one of those Japanese people who spend their time in front of the computer all night and sleep all day.

It seems quite clear that if people say that as well as being respectable one must have the appearance of respectability, then it's not enough to stop being a *hikikomori*, he also has to stop acting like one. But what can he do to avoid it? Sooner or later, he'll give in. He's had enough. He'll sleep, he's got no alternative. He leaves the idea of continuing experimenting with reason and madness for another time. But immediately he sees that he can't interrupt them. He makes a huge effort and gets to his feet, he's decided he won't let sleep win, much less let Celia think he's still a stubborn computer nerd.

He gets dressed, picks up his umbrella, hesitates for a few seconds, but finally goes out to the landing, takes the elevator, and goes down into the street. He's spent days lazily avoiding buying some medication he needs. Now he has time to take care of some errands. He goes to the same pharmacy as usual and buys the pills he's nearly run out of and which he's been taking on prescription ever since his physical collapse two years ago. Pills to control high blood pressure: Atenolol, Astudal, Carduran, Tertensif. Then, in the bakery he buys a Roquefort pizza—which he'll eat cold on the way home—and some croutons for the soup Celia made yesterday.

He can be seen all over the neighborhood, in the rain, with a bag from the pharmacy and eating a pizza. His oversized sunglasses hide physical deterioration caused by his insomnia. Comical and touching, from time to time, he glances furtively at the croutons. Today, despite his evident outlandishness, he looks more normal than on other occasions, at least he's on his way from the bakery and the pharmacy, and might seem—indeed he is—just like one more local. The last time he was in this area there were a lot of people who saw him walking around in the rain in his old raincoat, his shirt with its torn collar turned up, those hideous short trousers, his hair completely plastered to his head. It was a strange picture he made, a poor, formerly prestigious publisher, dressed to be taken straight to a psychiatrist. A dreadful picture of an unhinged eccentric. Because of his behavior that day, lots of people in the neighborhood now look at him dubiously, and this despite the fact they've seen him more than once on TV talking sensibly about the books he published and which brought him such great fame.

He walks slowly, with his Roquefort pizza and his croutons and his umbrella held up straight and the pills he's just bought from the pharmacy. I'm normal, look at me, his appearance seems to be saying. Of course the sunglasses give him away, and the raincoat is the same one he wore the other night, and his slightly meandering walk also gives him away, as do his anxious bites of the pizza. Actually, everything puts him in his neighbors' sights. In the glass window of the florist, he studies himself and gives a start as he sees a strange passerby, with short trousers on under his raincoat. But he's not wearing short trousers. Why did he think he was? Who is this fucking old man; who's this comic character reflected in the glass?

He starts to laugh at himself and to walk like a tramp from a silent film. He plays at being his shadow, that comic character he saw in the shop window. He walks in a deliberately erratic way and then, outside the deli, imagines he's not a common tramp—he has a house, a stable home where, it's true, he does trample around. While he carries on walking in a funny way, he imagines it's night time already and that he's in his house, the rain lashing against the windowpanes, where there's a reflection of his shadow, the shadow of another shadow. Because in this imagined house he is an ex-publisher waiting to meet the man he was before he created—with the books he published and the catalog life he's led—a false personality for himself.

He imagines that in his house he's not tired—this last tallies with his own reality—and his old lamp is illuminating him as he starts preparing a report on his situation in life, a report he imagines he must finish before dawn breaks. So as not to feel bored out on the street—he's never bored except when he walks around places as familiar as the ones in his neighborhood—he slowly elaborates mentally, painfully, sentence by sentence, as he advances in a decidedly pathetic way, with his silent cinema actor's air, spitting a tide of garbage from his mind:

"Soon I will turn sixty. For two years now I've been haunted by the reality of death, at the same time as I devote myself to observing how bad things are in the world. As a friend says, it's all over, or coming to an end. There is nothing else left but a great illiterate throng deliberately created by the powers that be, a kind of amorphous crowd that's sunk us all into a general state of mediocrity.

There must be a huge misunderstanding. And a tragic jumble of gothic stories and despicable publishers, guilty of a monumental mess. A funeral is already being prepared in Dublin for the literary publishing I gave my life to. And now all I can do is to devote myself to trying to breathe, to opening as many spaces as possible in the days I have left, to trying to search for an art of my own being, an art that maybe one day I can perfect by making an inventory of my main errors as a publisher. I have the impression—one last project, merely imaginary—that it would be great if other publishers wanted to do the same, and for there to be a book containing the confessions of publishers who described what it was they believe went awry in their publishing policy; independent publishers who told how extraordinary the books were that they dreamed of bringing to light one day; publishers who described their greatest hopes and how it was that these did not materialize (it would be good for a publisher such as the great Sensini to speak on this, someone who only published stories of *brave characters who are adrift*, who ended up standing trial in the United States); literary publishers who described the poverty of literature, now a whole symphony of crows lost in the funereal center of the corrupt jungle of their industry. In short, publishers who would agree to publish the great map of their disappointments and who would confess the truth and say once and for all, to top it all, that not one of them ever discovered a true genius along the way. A map like this would allow us to move deeper into the quicksand of truth. Riba thinks, I'd like one day to have the audacity to go deeper into these sands and to make an inventory of everything I tried to achieve in my catalog and never did. I'd like one day to have the honesty to reveal the great shadows hiding behind the lights of my work that was so absurdly praised...."

He decides to speed up on his way home because he's exhausted, and what's more, realizes his insomniac's lucidity might start to wane at any moment, as even the outline of his laughable but ultimately pathetic silent cinema figure is dissolving and dangerously transforming itself in the shop windows. The only thing that matters to him now is that, when Celia gets home from work, she finds him with lunch made, nicely laid out on the tablecloth, and the TV on so they don't have to talk as they eat. For now, he'll have another coffee. She has to find him awake, as if there were nothing wrong. He must seek a prompt reconciliation. Become a Buddhist, if necessary. He has no faith in people with faith—even if it's a Buddhist faith—but he'll pretend to have it; his relationship with Celia is more important than anything else. Although it is also true he greatly distrusts people with faith. When he thinks of these matters, he always recalls something he heard Juan Carlos Onetti say toward the end of the seventies at the French Institute in Barcelona. Onetti, who seemed enormously, joyously drunk, was saying that Catholics, Freudians, Marxists, and patriots should all be lumped together. Anyone—he said—with faith, it didn't matter in what; anyone who spouted opinions, who believed they knew or acted according to repeated, learned, or inherited thoughts.

Those words lingered for a long time in his mind. He recalls Onetti said, that day, that a faithful man was more dangerous than a hungry beast and that faith should be placed in what is most insignificant and subjective. In the woman you happen to be in love with at the moment, for example. Or a dog, a soccer team, a number on a roulette wheel, a lifelong vocation. This is what he believes Onetti said on that evening now so long ago in Barcelona.

Since the woman, in his case, is Celia and as such not exactly a *woman of the moment*, and since, not so long ago, he gave up publishing, which was always his lifelong vocation, and besides he has no dog or soccer team, it seems more than obvious that all he's got left is a number. A roulette number, if he's got anything left at all, and this number might well be on the wheel of life itself, that is, his destiny.

For a moment and without panicking, he stands in a daze looking at the croutons, as if they were his only true future.

As he walks past the patisserie, standing in the doorway smoking, is the transsexual who works there, the only person in the world who still makes passes at him, at least in such a brazen way. The tragedy of growing old, thinks Riba, leads to these things: nowadays this kindly transsexual is the only woman who still notices him. A man knows he's grown old when age spots appear on his hands and he realizes he's become invisible to women. Celia sometimes talks to this shop assistant, when she goes to buy dessert on Sundays. The patisserie is so bad that she hardly has any work to do and is usually stationed in the doorway, smoking. Since Riba knows she does tarot readings, whenever he sees her he imagines asking her to tell his fortune. He imagines her inside the patisserie, dressed as a gypsy after having made a huge effort to read his future, as if she were Marlene Dietrich in *Touch of Evil*. A very serious laugh. Tell me my future once and for all, please, says Riba. There's barely any light at all in the back of the patisserie. You have no future, she replies. And laughs conclusively.

Back home, the rain lashes against the windows. It's as if he's arrived at his imagined house from earlier, except this is his real house, luckily. Thinking about the character Bloom, he wonders what sort of face he'd have had. Joyce doesn't provide too many clues in this respect. He's the typical modern man, that much is clear. Modern, of course, if one compares him to Homer's Ulysses. (Inner laughter.) Supposedly, Joyce devised him to seem like any provincial European citizen. A man without qualities. Bloom is outstripped by the two other main characters in the book: Stephen Dedalus and Molly Bloom. Stephen, who represents the intellect, the creative imagination, surpasses him, illuminating him from above. And Molly, who represents the body, the earth, supports him. But in the long run Bloom is neither worse nor better than either of them, as Stephen has an excess of intellectual pride, and Molly finds herself at the mercy of the flesh; Bloom, on the other hand, although lacking their robustness, has the power of humility. And what's more, Bloom was certainly—this is certainly true today—more charming than his author.

He looks over his bookshelves and stops here and there; he picks up a volume, flips through it nervously, puts it back. He stands hypnotized looking at the rain. He goes into the kitchen to make lunch. The sound of the rain reminds him of that day in his youth when he walked around without an umbrella, and even so, wasted time staring at the faces of passersby, on the hunt for the unique essence of each one, and ended up very wet. His ridiculous youth could be summed up in this one episode, but he prefers to forget it forever, he's not prepared to be depressed by the rain and his memories.

He stops paying attention to the heavy downpour, and for a moment, it seems as if that strange feeling has come back, as if someone had started walking silently at his side, someone different, obviously, although at times seeming almost familiar. It's a silent walker who has perhaps always been there. He goes back to the window. He sees the silvery gleam of the rain. He thinks he should tell someone, but Celia is clearly not the best person. When she gets in, she'll probably still be annoyed with him. With no one to tell, he decides to note it down in the Word document where he collects phrases. He turns on his computer, opens the document and writes down his impression from a moment ago:

The silvery gleam of the rain.

He can't resist adding something else and writes, in smaller type: *The author's ache, my intimate Hydra.*

Celia gets home and finds him awake, and what's more, euphoric, listening to Liam Clancy singing "Green Fields of France." And she also sees that, as incredible as it seems, he has very helpfully set the table and put lunch out on the checked tablecloth they were given as a wedding present that February day over thirty years ago. He's made a huge effort, he's stayed awake, although his mental acuity is on a steep decline. Luckily, Celia has come in peace. And even better, with mind-blowing remedies for insomnia and stress.

"Relaxation gadgets!" she cries with a smile.

Buddhism seems to be agreeing with her. She's come back with a product someone at the office sold her, a sort of digital machine using audiovisual stimulations, with a pair of multicolored glasses, a mask, and headphones. She tells him that, by way of its twenty-two programs, the machine uses light, color, and sound models to calm the user's brain and create sensations conducive to relaxation.

"Now all we need to do is figure out the frequencies of your brainwaves," Celia says somewhat mischievously.

The what waves? He smiles. He can't help thinking of Spider and his mental cobwebs. She insists on asking what his frequencies are. The salespeople have promised the product will make you mentally sharp, relaxed, and less stressed, leading to a pleasant sleep.

Now Celia asks him to try the digital relaxation machine.

"It's not good for you to get no sleep. This music! Liam Clancy! What is it with you and Liam Clancy?"

"I find it moving, I think it's a patriotic song and it's moving, I'm turning Irish."

"I don't think it's really that patriotic. Come on. You can't go to Dublin on Sunday without having slept," she says in a tender, maternal tone, but one that is also deliberately banal, carnal, provocative.

She shows him her cleavage. She asks him an apparently trivial or, at least, incongruous question.

"Why don't you take the odd Wednesday off from going to your parents' house? Do you feel you owe them something?"

"It's filial duty, a perfectly natural sentiment in the human species."

She ruffles his hair.

"Don't get annoyed," she says.

She moves closer still and caresses him.

They make love, Celia's ass on a red cushion, legs wide open. A tangle of bedsheets. Liam Clancy, still singing. And with a great racket, the digital machine smashing violently onto the floor.

Barcelona, noon on Friday the thirteenth, two days before the plane leaves for Dublin.

From a place where he can't be seen, he carefully observes, with a jolt of astonishment how two pseudo-friends, or rather acquaintances from his generation, prepare to walk very solemnly down La Rambla. Their ceremonial gestures leave little room for doubt:

they are about to begin a ritual they've been performing for years. Indeed, he saw them forty years ago, getting ready to do the very same thing. They are preparing themselves for a conversation about the world and the vicissitudes of their lives as they walk elegantly down La Rambla.

A jolt of astonishment, but also a certain amount of envy. All their gestures and this air of preparing for an old ritual sends him back to the idea that they have all the time ahead of them to talk about the world. And they've probably attracted his attention more than usual because their slow, solemn ritual contrasts with the people rushing about all around them. It seems there's no one else who has the time to think or simply talk about the world, but rather people must walk quickly with barely enough time, people hurrying, but without thought.

He knows them. They went to university at the same time as him and they're from the same social class. He knows they're not particularly intelligent. But the solemnity of their gestures, their good manners—the final flourish in that type of natural Catalan aesthetics. That they've managed to conserve this openness, this sense of time, leaves him thunderstruck. It even looks as if they're going to start thinking. And now he realizes: they are the true representatives of his generation. If he didn't feel like an educated person, if he felt like an intellectual from Barcelona who didn't want to betray his social class, he'd recognize himself immediately in these two acquaintances, who have all the time in the world ahead of them.

It's a shame, but they seem different. He is envious of the ritual his two compatriots have conserved, but also he feels compassion, a deep, endless compassion. And he regrets it greatly: a generation he envies, but also pities; he doesn't want this to be his generation.

He sees them up there at the start of La Rambla, just as he saw them forty years ago, exactly the same as then, getting ready to converse, think, initiating the ritual of the walk. Even back then, seeing them there, so educated and so majestic, preparing for the descent, the time they had was enviable.

Time does not pass for them. They were going to conquer the world and now all they do is comment on it, if that's what they do, confined as they are to their limited ability to think. Yet, it also seems true that time does not pass for them and they're not yet at the gateway to their future of drooping jaws and hopeless dribbling. That will be the end of a generation that might have been his. But it's not, and yet it is, only in a very remote way. Why should "belonging to his generation" be more important than being compassionate or not compassionate, for example? If someone told him he's compassionate he'd know more about his identity than if he were told he's from Barcelona or that he belongs to his generation.

Goodbye to this city, this country, goodbye to all that.

Two old professionals over there at the start of the stately, commercial avenue. They don't seem aware that all life is a process of demolition and that the hardest blows await them. He thinks about all this from a spot where he can't be seen by them. Without them knowing it, he's a traitor, he represents one more blow of the many that will hit them. Here he is now, saying goodbye in his own way to Barcelona, in his shadowy corner, crouching down as he waits for absolute darkness. It will be much better if, at the end of everything, sorrow disappears and silence returns. He'll carry on as he always has done. Alone, without a generation, and without even a modicum of pity.

Time: Just past eleven in the morning.

Day: June 15, 2008, Sunday.

Style: Linear. Everything can be understood, displaying an air similar to that of the sixth chapter of *Ulysses*, in which we find a lucid and logical Joyce, who introduces the occasional thought from Bloom that the reader can easily follow.

Place: Dublin Airport.

Characters: Javier, Ricardo, Nietzky, and Riba.

Action: Javier, Ricardo, and Nietzky, who have already spent a day in Dublin, meet Riba at the airport. The idea is to hold the funeral ceremony for the Gutenberg galaxy at dusk tomorrow before visiting the Martello tower. Where? Riba delegated this decision to Nietzky days ago now, and he, with good judgement, thinks that the Catholic cemetery of Glasnevin—formerly Prospect Cemetery, where Paddy Dignam is buried in *Ulysses*—might be a suitable place. But Ricardo and Javier still know nothing of the funeral. And because they don't know, they don't know it's been included in the informal itinerary Riba and Nietzky have been putting together.

Meanwhile, Riba's friends, the three writers, are already, unbeknownst to them, living replicas of the three characters—Simon Dedalus, Martin Cunningham, and John Power—who accompany Bloom in the funeral procession in the sixth chapter of *Ulysses*. To Riba's secret satisfaction.

Themes: The usual ones. The now unalterable past, the fleeting present, the nonexistent future.

First, the past. This suffering relates to what Riba might have done and what he didn't do and left buried like a mass of roses under many spadefuls of earth, and his need to not look back, to attend to his heroic urges and take the *English leap*, to direct his gaze forward, toward the insatiable quality of his present.

Then, the present, fleeting, but in some way graspable in the shape of a great need to feel *alive* in a *now* that is giving him the gift of feeling joyously free at last, without being criminally hindered by publishing fiction, a task that in the long run became a torment, with the sinister competition of books filled with gothic stories and Holy Grails, holy shrouds, and all the paraphernalia of illiterate modern publishers.

And finally, the question of the future, of course. Dark. You have no future, as the transsexual from the patisserie downstairs would say. The famous future is the main theme, which turns out to be not exactly a unique one: Riba and his destiny. Riba and the destiny of the Gutenberg galaxy. Riba and the heroic urge. Riba and his suspicion a few hours ago that he was being watched by someone who maybe wants to do some sort of experiment on him. Riba and the decline of literary publishing. Riba and the grand old whore of literature, already now out in the rain on the last pier. Riba and the angel of originality. Riba and the croutons. Riba and whatever you like. *As you like it*, as Shakespeare, Dr. Johnson, his friend Boswell, and so many others said.

"Where shall we celebrate?" asks Riba, as soon as he arrives at the terminal and meets up with his friends.

He's referring to the funeral for the Gutenberg world, for the world he knew and idolized and which has worn him out. But he's caused a misunderstanding. As Javier and Ricardo still haven't been informed of the requiem, they think Riba is talking about celebrating the fact that the four of them have just met up in Dublin and is suggesting they go for a few drinks, that is, they assume he's decided to start drinking again. It's odd, but they're excessively thrilled by the idea of their former publisher supposedly having fallen off the wagon. And so they laugh happily.

"In Glasnevin Cemetery itself," Nietzky interrupts tersely.

"Is there a bar in the cemetery?" Javier asks, surprised.

State of the sky: It's not raining like in Barcelona. But a cloud is starting to cover the sun and plunges the land around the airport into a darker shade of green. Riba's memories melt into the dark, refreshing waters of the shadows.

They get into the Chrysler that Walter, a friend of Nietzky's from Dublin, has lent them. Ricardo drives, since he's an expert in driving on the left and the only one of them, moreover, who is dressed as an Irishman, although an Irishman who is, if anything, straight out of the John Ford film *Donovan's Reef*, that is, in a flowery shirt with Polynesian designs, hidden, however, under a very long, old-fashioned raincoat that recalls those used by Sergio Leone in his spaghetti westerns. In comparison, Javier is dressed in a very sober, almost British way. Depending how one looks at it, they make an unwittingly comic pair.

They head for Morgans hotel, the quartet's headquarters. A strange place, as Javier explains to Riba, a place full of solitary executives, individuals in suits and ties whom they've decided to call

"Morgans." It's a place on the road leading from the airport to the city of Dublin and that belongs to the same chain as the sophisticated Morgans hotel in New York, on Madison Avenue. The bar of the Morgan Museum, next to Morgans hotel in New York, was precisely where Nietzky and Riba set out from a few months ago to visit the Austers' house.

"Oh, have you two been to the Austers' house?" asks Javier mockingly, as he's heard Riba tell this story a thousand times.

Ricardo found this Dublin highway hotel on the internet and booked the rooms because of its proximity to the airport, never imagining it would be so hip, especially since it looked like a motel on the website. They all protest, because Ricardo seems to have had no qualms about putting them up in a motel like that.

Riba tells them his wife had been on the verge of coming with him, but luckily she couldn't make it. While Celia's intentions were good, her presence on the trip would have made the unfortunate scene he'd witnessed in his dreams far too likely to come true, a terrible sequence resulting from cold, hard alcoholism on the way out of the Coxwold pub. Perhaps a pub with this name doesn't exist in Dublin, but he believes that, if his wife had come with him, the terrifying, prophetic vision from his dream might have come true: Celia, appalled when she discovers the undesirable fact that he's fallen off the wagon, embracing him emotionally, the two of them crying in the end, sitting on the curb of a Dublin side street.

Everyone is quiet. They're probably thinking malicious thoughts.

Nietzky interrupts the silence to say that no one has noticed it, but the bar of Morgans hotel is called the John Cox Wilde pub, which sounds a lot like Coxwold. At first Riba chooses not to believe him, but when the others confirm that this is, in fact, the name of the bar, he says he'd actually be in favor of staying at a different hotel. He says it quite seriously, because he believes that, in general, dreams come true. Then he changes his mind, just as they get to Morgans and he finds he likes the foyer, decorated with large black and white tiles, and the statuesque receptionists as well. They're extremely tall and look like fashion models, maybe they are. They're also very friendly, although he can't understand what they're saying, or why they're receptionists and not models.

In the large black and white foyer, several strangely tormented guests can be seen, their heads bowed, sad "Morgans" wearing dark glasses and impeccable business suits, thinking of impenetrable matters. Sophisticated background music. It doesn't seem as though they're on the road from the airport, or even near Dublin, you'd think they were in the very center of New York. It seems like Ireland's economic situation has improved recently, thinks Riba, as he notices with some surprise that the foyer of this Dublin Morgans is almost identical to that of the hotel on Madison Avenue.

Javier de Galloy's version of "Walk on the Wild Side" is playing. Whenever Riba hears this song—and especially when the singer pronounces the syllables of the words "New York City"—he thinks he's listening to the background music for his *English leap*, for his great Sternean sentimental journey, his Odyssey in search of his original enthusiasm.

He's not lacking in enthusiasm; although, at the sight of the closed John Cox Wilde, he is momentarily lost down depressing paths, evoking the brutal alcoholic life he led for many years so as to be able to get his independent publishing house off the ground and to have life experiences that would help him create a catalog disconnected from the academic formalism and the reactionary life of the people of his generation.

He needs to see alcohol as something monstrous, something to which he can never go back, because if he does so he'll seriously risk his health. All in all, he needs to remember that he had to drink a lot to make the publishing house a success and that he paid a very high price, his health to be precise, for his alcoholic adventures. In any case, he doesn't regret anything. It's just that he no longer wants or is able to repeat that experience. After his great physical collapse, everything became calm and now he'd like to think that he's come back to life, that he's gradually forgotten this hardened period of alcoholic activity. As he left the hospital a new man, he started to listen in astonishment to what people were saying about his work as a publisher; at first he listened and pretended to believe that it was someone else who had done this work, his double, as if he'd just now inherited it as a surprise. And by pretending like this, he ended up believing, for a while, in his own farce.

Only when he was conscious once more that he had founded the publishing house and it had cost him his health did he start to feel old and washed up and depressed, and he began to sink into melancholy; this is a world where he doubts publishers with a passion for literature like his own will ever exist again. With every day that goes by it seems more and more to him that these kinds of passions have already begun receding into history and will soon fall into oblivion. The world he once knew is ending, and he knows full well that the best novels he published were practically only about this, worlds that would never exist again, apocalyptic situations that were mainly projections of the authors' existential angst and that nowadays raise a smile, because the world has continued on its course despite meeting with an inexhaustible number of grand finales. Riba thinks, if the world doesn't quickly fall into oblivion, it won't be long before the tragedy of the decline of the print age (the decline of a great and brilliant period of human intelligence) will also raise a smile. Distancing oneself from fleeting dramas seems, at the very least, the most sensible option.

Morgans hotel looks different when one starts to explore the long corridors and discovers that the numbering of the floors and rooms is not the slightest bit logical. There is a phenomenal disorder inside the building. What's more, the corridors are full of workers who seem to be adding the final touches to the hotel, as if the place weren't finished yet. An aggressive hammering can be heard everywhere. And there is an exceptional amount of chaos, which has always been a famous source of creativity, and which recalls certain scenes from American films from the years of New York's great economic optimism, when a certain kind of world was under construction and there was a simple, pure enthusiasm everywhere.

Riba wheels his suitcase to his room, and because of the strange numbering system he gets lost several times; he thinks that, among so many workers spread through all the corners of the great building, he wouldn't be surprised if he suddenly came across Harpo Marx with a hammer, ready to bash in a nail then and there. This place, still in the middle of being built, is the ideal place to bump into Harpo, but he wouldn't know how to explain why. It must be the general chaos that's given him this idea.

In his room, next to the telephone, there's a card inviting guests to the John Cox Wilde pub. It opens at six in the evening; in other words, somewhat to Riba's relief, there are still a few hours to go. The room smells of perfume and it looks as if it's been recently tidied, everything is in its place. There's a slightly ridiculous token from the hotel, a lonely chocolate, on the bedside table. Do those businessmen like these little chocolatey gestures? The view from the window is a sad one, but he's fascinated by the gray air, the smoke from the chimneys, the brownish color of the bricks of the houses opposite. He loves the view, because it is not at all Mediterranean, which allows him to feel properly abroad. This is what he's wanted for weeks. He couldn't feel any better. He's got what he came for: to *land on the other side*. Finally he's in an environment where strangeness and also—for him at least—mystery prevail. And he notices the joy surrounding everything new; he is almost looking at the world with enthusiasm again. In countries like this, a person can reinvent himself, mental horizons open up.

He has the impression that absolutely everything is new to him, even the steps he takes, the ground he walks on, the air he breathes. If everyone knew how to see the world like this, he thinks, if everyone understood that maybe everything around us can be new, we wouldn't need to waste time thinking about death.

He thanks himself for being where he is, in this geography of strangeness. He notices that, above the bed, there is a framed photograph of Dublin from 1901. The picture is of a coach and horses, which makes him think of the funeral carriage Bloom got into on June 16, 1904, at eleven o'clock in the morning. He looks carefully, and seeing the atmosphere, he thinks he can sense in this unpaved street down which a black coach drives, it seems to him that in those days the city might have been frankly sinister. And this despite the fact that it was beginning to be a new city. But the atmosphere, given off by this photo is literally funereal. Back then, thinks Riba, maybe all of Dublin was an enormous funeral of funerals. All that was needed now was for some little old woman to look out of one of the windows of those sad houses on the unpaved road: a little old woman like the one who, in chapter six of *Ulysses,* peeps through her blinds and reminds Bloom of the interest old women take in corpses: "Never know who will touch you dead."

Although he stops looking at the photograph, he continues to recall the start of chapter six: "Martin Cunningham, first, poked his silk hatted head into the creaking carriage and, entering deftly, seated himself. Mr Power stepped in after him, curving his height with care."

Full of contradictory feelings toward the novelty of everything, Riba decides to go back down to the foyer, to keep from creating anymore mental spider's webs for himself, and to forget that the character of Spider can sometimes be overly tyrannical and possessive with him. He decides that the most sensible thing to do now is throw himself into discovering Dublin with his friends, with his own personal Martin Cunningham and Mr. Power.

He's already getting ready to leave the room when he sees, next to the curtains, a red suitcase. He stares at it in amazement. What's a suitcase doing there? He can't believe it. He remembers when Celia used to get angry and leave her suitcase out on the landing. He doesn't find it funny when things happen to him that might seem appropriate for a novelist to put in his novel. He doesn't want to be *written* by anyone. Could it be that they wanted to surprise him and it's Celia's luggage? No, surely not. If she said she was staying in Barcelona that was because she was going to stay. Anyway, he's never seen this suitcase at home. He picks it up as if it stank, not wanting to think about it, takes it out into the hallway. It's not his, how awful.

He goes down to reception, planning to tell them he's found a suitcase in his room and has left it in the fourth-floor corridor—actually the fifth, if one goes by the strange numbering—but when he gets down there he remembers he doesn't speak a word of English, and ends up walking right past, saying absolutely nothing. In the brief walk from the foyer to the Chrysler, he puts the incident out of his mind. Any other time, it would have been the first thing he'd have told his friends. I found a red suitcase in my room, he would have said immediately. And he would have told them the story, as if he had a gift for storytelling.

Time: Around two in the afternoon.

Day: Sunday June 15.

Place: The port of Howth, at the north end of Dublin Bay. Less than a mile from here is Ireland's Eye, a rocky seabird sanctuary built on the ruins of a monastery.

Characters: The four travelers in the Chrysler.

Action: They park at the edge of the town, at the foot of the cliffs where Nietzky, who knows the place, has suggested they walk for a while. They stride along a path through the rocks, and once a certain amount of vertigo has been overcome—blue and gray lights in the fishing port, and high up, in the sky, scudding clouds over the Irish Sea—Riba can finally see Dublin. He still hasn't seen the city, despite already having been on the island for some hours.

Even though it's so far off, he finally sees something of Dublin, sees it from high on these cliffs that rise up from the sea. Flocks of birds float on the water. The fascinating sadness of the place seems accentuated by the sight of these fleets of somnolent birds, in the middle of the day, and it's as if the void becomes intertwined with the deep sadness, which from time to time finds its voice in the shrieking of a gull. A magnificent landscape, boosted by his enthusiastic state of mind that comes from feeling he's in a foreign land.

Timidly moved, Riba recalls a poem by Wallace Stevens, "The Irish Cliffs of Moher":

> *They go to the cliffs of Moher rising out of the mist,*
> *Above the real,*

Rising out of present time and place, above
The wet, green grass.

This is not landscape, full of the somnambulations
Of poetry

And the sea. This is my father or, maybe,
It is as he was,

A likeness, one of the race of fathers: earth
And sea and air.

There's Dublin, slightly hazy in the middle of the bay. A girl goes by with a portable radio playing "This Boy," by The Beatles. And the song gives him a sudden feeling of nostalgia for the time when he too was close to the "race of fathers." He's not young anymore and doesn't know if he can bear such beauty. He looks at the sea again. He takes a few steps toward the rocks and immediately feels that he ought to stand still, because if he keeps on walking he'll probably end up staggering along, blinded by tears. It's a secret emotion, hard to communicate. Because how can he tell the truth and let his friends know he's fallen in love with the Irish Sea?

This is my country now, he thinks.

He's so absorbed in all of this that Ricardo has to shake him awake, blowing the smoke from his Pall Mall into Riba's face.

"What are we up to?" his friend asks.

Riba looks at Ricardo, his flowery, Polynesian-patterned shirt. He finds him ridiculous. He imagines him dressed this way in the Austers' house.

Before, when he drank, Riba didn't distinguish between strong and weak emotions, or between friends and enemies. But his recent lucidity has slowly given him back his capacity for boredom, and also for excitement. And the Irish Sea—over which he now imagines a great mass of gray clouds with silver edges floating—seems to him the most superb incarnation of beauty, the highest expression of that which disappeared from his life for so long and which now—it's never too late—he has found all at once, as if he were in the middle of a great storm, feeling like a man who senses his life is going downhill, yet is faced with the unmistakable beauty of a gray sea edged with silver, and which he'll never forget as long as his memory serves him.

He recalls some words of Leopardi's that have been with him for years. The poet said that the view of the sky is perhaps less enjoyable than that of the land and the fields, because it's less varied, and also far from us, not a part of us, belonging less to what is ours.... And nonetheless, if the view of the Irish Sea has moved Riba, it's precisely because he doesn't feel it's his, it doesn't belong to his world at all, it's strange to him; it's so different from his universe that it's touched him inside leaving him deeply moved, a prisoner of a foreign sea.

Themes: All banal. Excessive hunger, for instance, which has taken hold of the group and made them desperately start looking for a place to have lunch.

Riba thinks about the theme of his own hunger—a special hunger, separate from the rest of the group's—and remembers when he used to read manuscripts at the publishing house and noticed that in many of them, almost as if it were a set rule, certain trivial themes appeared on the surface of the story as if they also had the right to a certain rank. And he also remembers that, the further he got into these stories, the more noticeable it was that one important theme gradually shifted to another, preventing a stable center from existing for any length of time. And not just this, but on the surface of the stories only the shadows of certain elements remained, that is, precisely the least significant themes: the hysterical need to find a restaurant, for instance, which is the theme right at this moment, when he feels he's almost having a nervous breakdown from hunger, and even more so because he's so exhausted after having walked so far.

At a moment when the Irish Sea has come to be the center of Riba's life, the circumstance has arisen—it can be modestly explained—that for the narration (supposing someone wanted to describe what is happening right now—now when actually, in these very moments, nothing is happening) the theme would be confused with the action, and the action and theme would turn into one single thing; this, moreover, could not be very easily summed up and wouldn't be enough for any grand reflection, unless one would like to go on about humankind's proverbial hunger since the beginning of time.

Action and theme: The need to find, as soon as possible, a restaurant.

As they look for a place to eat by the sea, Riba wonders whether his friends might not have conspired to prevent his setting foot on the streets of Dublin. For whatever reason, ever since he's arrived, they've done nothing but skirt around the city. He can't complain, because there's no question that these walks are what have led to his encounter with the unforgettable, freezing, sad beauty of this coastline. But this doesn't stop it from seeming strange to him that he still hasn't set foot in Dublin.

"We'll go to the city after this," says Nietzky as if reading his thoughts.

Nietzky has started to scare him a little. It's odd how our perceptions of others change so easily from one day to the next. Today it seems to him that Nietzky has a sinister side. He talks and acts differently from the person Riba imagined might be related to his *angelo custode*. At times he's rude; it's curious to observe how he never used to seem this way. But perhaps Nietzky doesn't deserve to be seen in such a bad light. Maybe Riba's disappointment comes from realizing something, which he obviously couldn't see long before: Nietzky is nothing like a guardian angel, he's simply a selfish young man, with certain demonic features. It would have all gone better if he hadn't idolized him. Young Nietzky isn't related to his *duende*, nor can he in any way be the complementary father Riba imagined he might find in him. Nietzky has absolutely nothing fatherly about him. To think he could have had two father figures was a grave error on Riba's part. At the very least, the trip will have served to make him realize this, to understand that his friend from New York isn't a protective father or an angel of any kind, is actually slightly conceited. For example, he's conceited when he talks about what they're going to do tomorrow, he's unbearably arrogant, wearily imparting to them his vast knowledge of Bloom and Joyce, and treating them as if they are poor ignoramuses on the general topic of Bloomsday. And he's pathetically conceited when he sings, in perfect English, the traditional Irish song "The Lass of Aughrim," heard at the end of John Huston's *The Dead*. He sings it very well, but soullessly, and ruins a very moving tune.

"Who decides when we go to Dublin?" asks Riba rebelliously.

"Well, whoever takes charge, and at the moment, as far as I can see, that's not you," says Nietzky, who suddenly starts speaking cruelly to Riba, as if he's read loud and clear his recent malevolent thoughts.

In the Globe restaurant in Howth where they have lunch, they're served by an unbearable Spanish waiter from Zamora, wearing a spotless blue jacket. He speaks such perfect English that at first none of them realizes he's not from Howth or that he's not even Irish. When they find out, Riba decides to get revenge in his own way.

"What's wrong with Zamora to make you leave it so quickly?" he asks, a variation of the curious question about Toro and Benavente *he* was asked the other day in the bank manager's office in Barcelona.

The waiter denies having fled Zamora. His colloquial way of speaking is admirable, because everything he says sounds emphatically true. It's clear his entire being is suffused with life, with authentic life, although the one problem he has—what stops Riba from envying him in the slightest—is that this very uninhibited language doesn't stop him from being a waiter, but rather totally the opposite. Maybe he's a waiter because since he was a child, he's been fluent in this way of speaking so genuine and so Spanish, and now, any sort of change is impossible. In other words, he lives as a prisoner of his Spanishness, completely possessed by his Spanish-waiter's language, by his terribly traditional and complex-free speech, which seems only normal, the only eternally authentic way of speaking for a hundred thousand miles.

They ask the waiter about last Thursday's European elections and he tries to pass himself off as the world's best informed person and in the end becomes literally unbearable. As he talks, he slowly loses all his credibility. Indeed, he lost it the very moment he started talking. He's like the protagonist of a story in which a man in an elegant, meticulous blue jacket keeps his garment the whole time, but whose pockets gradually become more and more threadbare.

He talks and talks about Thursday's elections, but they're barely listening. Here in Dublin today, Sunday, the corpse of the ill-fated "yes" vote to the Lisbon Treaty is still warm; the Irish rejected this treaty last Thursday, and there are posters and other paraphernalia from last week's intense and confused electoral battle still lying around.

"Ireland's like that," says Nietzky somewhat disdainfully.

What? Riba feels he ought to kill him. And the thing is, he's already thinking like the biggest fanatic of all those in love with the Irish Sea.

"And what are you here for?" asks the Spanish waiter.

"A funeral," says Riba.

They all, apart from Nietzky, think he's being witty and laugh at his joke. The waiter leaves their table in confusion, and Riba notices he has a horrid pencil behind his ear.

The pencil of Latin literature, thinks Riba.

Time: Five in the afternoon, immediately after coming out of the Globe restaurant, Howth.

Action: They get back into the Chrysler and take a long detour, driving around the ring road and heading for the other end of the bay. After bypassing the entrance to Dublin again, they go to Finnegans pub, in the middle of Dalkey: a quiet town with narrow streets, where, mainly on Vico Road, the second chapter of *Ulysses* takes place, and where, as we know, thanks to the great Flann O'Brien, seemingly accidental encounters take place, and where the shops pretend to be closed, but are open.

Ricardo, his voluminous raincoat in hand—it's obvious he didn't need to bring it—thinks the town is very genteel. Javier says he's been there many times and it's the most enchanting place in the world. Young Nietzky doesn't believe Javier or share Ricardo's view.

"Believe me," Javier says, "in a pub here in town, after he was dead, Joyce worked as a bartender. He confessed to the customers who recognized him that *Ulysses* was a pain in the ass and a joke in poor taste."

Ricardo searches in vain for an open shop among those pretending to be shut, somewhere he can buy batteries for his camera.

They carry out an inspection of the pub with the Joycean name that's been chosen—they agreed to this days ago by email—as the setting for the founding act of the Order of Finnegans. It was chosen by Nietzky, who claims to come to this pub every year.

Would it surprise or collapse you to know that the Mollycule Theory is at work in the parish of Dalkey? [Flann O'Brien, *The Dalkey Archive*].

Swap "Mollycule Theory" for "Order of Finnegans" and everything fits much better. The pub is packed, probably because they're showing one of the European Championship games on the television, but also because in Ireland pubs are almost always full. Javier and Ricardo order beer, Nietzky a whiskey with ice.

A tender and ridiculous cup of tea with milk is the teetotaller Riba's embarrassed order. Since the cruel jokes about his sad drink keep coming, he tries to dispel them by asking his friends if they knew there was a character in Borges's story "Death and the Compass" called Black Finnegan who owned a pub called Liverpool House.

"So we're also in a Borgesian pub," says Javier.

"And the Order could be a bit Borgesian as well, it's not going to be all Joyce," suggests Ricardo.

"We could just include the Borges line as a motto on the Order's coat of arms. I think that might be enough,"says Riba.

"Do we have a coat of arms?" asks Nietzky.

Riba proposes a legend that could be inserted into the coat of arms: "Black Finnegan by name, an old Irish criminal, who was crushed, annihilated almost, by respectability ..."

Atmosphere in Finnegans: Much clinking of pint glasses and rowdiness. A blonde woman who's had a lot of work done and a man with a dense gray beard, his loose jaw trembling as he speaks. A foreign soccer team scores a goal, which provokes an almost endless cry of jubilation among the clientele. It turns out the Polish national team has loads of Irish supporters. Thick smoke, although in theory no one is smoking. It's as if this smoke came from a deeply rooted past that hasn't budged an inch from the pub. Meshuggah, as Joyce would say, off his chump. A long silence at the table of the future Knights of the Order.

"I haven't come up with anything for the funeral for the Gutenberg age," Nietzky suddenly bursts out.

Javier and Ricardo think he's carrying on with the joke Riba made earlier. But as he then gives a lengthy explanation, they gradually discover his words are totally serious. It will involve holding a requiem tomorrow for one of the pinnacles of the golden age of printing, *Ulysses*, and for the age itself. A requiem, above all, for the end of an era. He hadn't said anything about it up until now because he'd forgotten.

"You forgot?" asks Javier, incredulously.

Action: Riba says the requiem might seem like a silly idea, but it's absolutely not. Because if one thinks about it calmly, it has a religious meaning, it's a prayer for the end of an era. They, the members of the Order of Finnegans, will be the poets of this funeral prayer. It would be good to hold this funeral. After all, if they don't do it, it won't be long before others do.

Time: Thirty minutes later.

Action: They've been talking and arguing endlessly. Nietzky has drunk four whiskeys in a row. Javier, in the meantime, has become a fan of the Polish national team and maintains, in his characteristically categorical tone, that they're the best team in the world. Ricardo's got an exaggeratedly indignant scowl permanently stuck on his face. What's he grumbling about? The requiem, mainly.

"But what's so bad about organizing a funeral for the Gutenberg era, a requiem that's a grand metaphor for the end of the print age, and also for the almost forgotten closure of my publishing house?" says Riba with such subdued sarcasm no one even notices.

"You haven't made us come to Dublin so you can turn yourself into a metaphor, have you?" says Ricardo.

"And what's so bad about our Riba wanting to be an allegory, a witness to the times, a notary to a change of eras?" Nietzky intervenes, drunk as a skunk.

"But have we come here so that our dear friend can become a witness to the times? That's the last thing I expected," says Ricardo.

"Well, that and so I can feel alive," protests Riba with surprisingly genuine bitterness, "and have a trip to tell my parents about when I go and see them on Wednesdays, and feel I'm opening up to other people and not being such a *hikikomori*. Have pity on me. That's all I ask."

They look at him as if they've just heard an alien speak.

"Pity?" asks Javier, almost laughing.

"All I want is for the funeral to be a work of art," says Riba.

"A work of art? Ah, this is new!" Nietzky intervenes.

"And also for you all to understand that retiring is tough, that I've got too much time on my hands and sometimes I think I've got nothing left to do, and that's why I'd like you all to be more sympathetic and understand that I'm trying to organize things to escape the boredom."

His voice sounds so broken that they're all frozen for a moment.

"Don't you see?" Riba carries on, "There's nothing left for me to do, except ..."

He looks down. Everyone stares at him, as if asking him to make an effort, as if begging him, please, to complete the sentence and say something that will save them from feeling so embarrassed and awkward. They want this episode to be over soon.

He lowers his head even more, it's as if he wants it to sink into the ground.

"Except ..."

"Except what, Riba? Except what? For God's sake, explain. What's left for you to do?"

He'd like to say, but he won't: to find his spirit, the *first person* that existed in him and vanished so early on.

But no, he won't say it.

For the sake of his health, he's been going to bed early for over two years. And as he himself says, if he ever breaks this routine and goes to a dinner party—the last time was that evening at the Austers' house—everything gets very complicated. For this reason, at ten o'clock, having eaten nothing but a squalid little sandwich, his friends drop him off at the entrance to Morgans hotel. He's going to bed without having seen Dublin. It's no big deal, but he thinks he could have been there by now; his friends could have been kind enough to go into the city at some point. But anyway, he'll wait till tomorrow. They'll see Dublin tonight, because they've arranged to meet Walter to give him his car back, and then they're going to check out some bars and maybe some clubs. They tell Riba they expect to see him fresh-faced in the morning, at breakfast time. If he can't sleep—they remark jokingly—Irish TV is always very enjoyable. And don't drink the minibar dry, Ricardo advises him with unnecessary cruelty.

A last-minute question. Riba wants to know who Walter is. It seems somehow to be an unsolved mystery. They have a car and Walter is the one who loaned it to them. But why do they have this car and who is Walter?

Sometimes his friends don't act like friends but like writers or former authors, and then they're like everyone else: bastards. No one is prepared to give him an explanation about this Walter. It's as if ever since an hour ago, when they learned he wasn't going out with them, his friends, his ex-authors, stopped counting him among the living.

His head bowed, he goes into the hotel, a little annoyed with them. As he walks past the John Cox Wilde, which is now buzzing, he acts as if he hasn't even seen the pub. He's faced with a risk, because fate has surely planned to get him drunk there tonight. And so he doesn't even look at it. But finally he gives in and glances over at the place, his curiosity gets the better of him. He goes in and resists, as much as he can, the constant waves of a nagging desire to have a drink, despite thinking that just one wouldn't do any harm and might help him sleep better tonight. But he resists, because he knows it wouldn't be just one drink and his will would easily cave in. This is why it's better not even to start, not to try one drop. No alcohol at all.

He acts almost like a hero of "the anti-alcohol resistance." He clenches his fists and thinks that he'll turn around and go up to his room. It amuses him to think that if someone saw him in here, they'd think he'd started drinking again. In the end, he leaves the bar.

On his way to the elevator, he passes a young man wearing a black suit who seems to recognize him. For a minute, the guy hesitates and seems about to stop and talk to him. Riba also hesitates. But he doesn't know him at all and it would be ludicrous to stop and talk to this stranger. In the end, the man coughs, looks away and quickens his pace.

In the elevator, the piped music is so depressing that for a minute he has the impression that the music itself, no matter how modern, is only bringing back memories of ruins: he tries to remember details of loved ones, houses, faces, but all that appears are ruins and more ruins. His life is in decline, he has to acknowledge it, but so is the world, and this gives him some consolation. He must try to make a connection, somehow, with enthusiasm. And in any case not cease in his exploration of the *foreign*. Dublin is a great first port of call in his struggle against the familiar, against the interbreeding of Catalan concepts and landscapes too often repeated and now too cramped for him. His native land, fatal land. He feels he's truly fleeing from it at last. He should make up his mind once and for all and start this long journey toward enthusiasm, even if it were just to honor his grandfather Jacobo, such a supporter of euphoria....

A ghostly brush against his shoulder. A coldness on the nape of his neck. But there's no one else in the elevator. He looks at himself in the mirror and shrugs his shoulders, as if he's trying to have fun all by himself now. What's this icy draught? The elevator doors open; he steps out into the long, empty corridor, slowly walks down it. In the time it would take for the briefest flash of light in the world, he walks past his Uncle David, his mother's brother, dead for more than twenty years. He's not about to panic, but it's the first time he's seen the ghost of a relative outside his usual surroundings. In any case, the apparition was so fleeting that if he really saw it then he might have to start admitting that an instant like this is sort of a glimpse or connection point between the past and the present. Hadn't he heard of interconnected points in space and time whose topology we might never understand, but between which the so-called living and the so-called dead can travel and thus encounter each other?

Time: Half past one in the morning.
   Day: Bloomsday.
   Style: Somnambulistic.
   Place: Dublin, Morgans hotel. Room 527.
   Action: Riba wakes abruptly from a deep sleep, as someone tries to enter his room using their swipe card. Still half asleep, he remembers the red suitcase someone left in the room this morning. He gets up fearing the intruder's swipe card will end up working. When he can't get in, the person on the other side nervously knocks three times on the door. Some unintelligible words are heard. The voice of a young man. It's a little scary. The old panic of someone coming into your house or your hotel room in the middle of the night.
   "Who's there?" asks Riba, half sleepy, half scared.
   "New York," the voice of the young man replies.

Did he really say New York? Riba didn't hear very well, but that's what he thought he heard. New York. He goes back to bed, disconcerted and with a certain amount of comic awareness, as if retreating inside the room could protect him from something. He tries to think he's dreamed it all. But he's awake, and though he's still quite sleepy and clumsy thanks to the one and a half Orfidal he took a while ago, he's aware that all this couldn't be more real. The thing he's feared so much would happen to him one day is taking place. Someone is trying to get into his room in the middle of the night.

Two more knocks on the door.

"The suitcase is in reception," he says to whoever is out there. And he almost shouts out of fear when he says this, as if he was scared that the person trying to get into his room wanted only to kill him.

A long silence follows. Riba is motionless, barely breathing.

Some footsteps in the corridor, and then on the stairs. The man goes away.

Day breaks very early in Dublin, something he hadn't expected at all. At seven minutes past five, the very first light of day can be seen in the room, and he half opens his eyes. On the television, which he left on, he sees the mute image of a bridlepath lined with bare bushes. There's no one on the path, until suddenly a funeral procession appears, led by a very majestic horse. Riba realizes he's watching a Dracula film. Another shock for today, he thinks drowsily. All at once he remembers the disturbing events of last night. After the intruder appeared, he fell back asleep quite easily, and luckily, the man didn't reappear. It must have been the owner of the red suitcase. And it's more than likely that he didn't say he was called New York, but some other thing that sounded like it and that Riba didn't hear properly. No one's called New York.

Perhaps he should have opened the door and made sure. He checks the time again. It's only ten after five in the morning, a dreadful time to begin any kind of activity. To start with, it's too early to go down for breakfast. Will his friends have returned yet from their night on the town? It would be awful to go out into the corridor and find them all there, drunk, barely able to recognize him. Or the other way around, to find them overly happy to see him, and what's more, to run into the enigmatic Walter and for him to embrace Riba enthusiastically. It's too early for that sort of thing. He'll even have to wait to call his parents in Barcelona and wishing them a happy anniversary. Because today—he's just remembered—is their sixty-first wedding anniversary.

Even so, he tries to liven up and recalls a Ralph Waldo Emerson quote: "Write it on your heart that every day is the best day in the year." Today must be, he thinks. After all, he's been waiting for it for weeks. Then, he remembers his grandfather Jacobo: "Nothing important was ever achieved without enthusiasm!" What a great phrase, he thinks once again. It's clear he's trying to liven up any way he can. He wants to feel euphoric on this Bloomsday. But he'll have to wait. He's used to that. He'd like to feel that enthusiasm his grandfather always tried to instill in him, but at this time in the morning—this morning of the best day of the year—it's all turning out to be a little bit difficult. It seems as if even thinking is turning out to be complicated. He's so sleepy he only manages to think he's not managing to think much yet. Unexpectedly, he remembers: a day when, as he was coming out of the cinema he asked a young usherette—who vaguely reminded him of Catherine Deneuve—what she thought the film was about. And as she replied, telling him it was a story of undying love, he felt himself briefly falling in love with her. He has always liked women who look like Catherine Deneuve, and would go so far as to say that his whole life has been deeply marked by this.

It's clear his mind is already starting to wake up. The proof is that he's now gripped by a certain amount of enthusiasm. But he realizes that his euphoria must coexist with the awkward memory of the incident last night, which now he sees almost as a dream, or the start of a good story, although he won't tell his friends about it later as if it were a story, or as if he were a writer. It's possible the stranger was someone who thought he was still staying in room 527. Maybe it was a young man who stayed in this room with his lover. Perhaps that morning he had left the room very early and the woman, fed up with him and not knowing when he'd be back, decided to break things off, paid for the room and left his suitcase up there, so that, when he returned, the fool would realize he'd been abandoned to his fate.

What would have happened if Riba had opened the door a few hours ago? This guy was hoping to find his lover there. Maybe the stranger would have got the biggest shock himself. And what's clear is that, if Riba had opened the door to him, a story would have been set in motion. A writer would no doubt have found the beginning of a good story there, thinks Riba.... His head nods gently. It seems he's woken up too early and is going to fall back asleep. But he immediately recovers from this false return to slumber.

Shortly afterward, precisely when he's most awake, he falls into a stupor of words and questions with very little meaning. He thinks, for example, about the color of Ireland and asks himself if one day this predominant color, green, will go away. What does this question mean? Isn't it an idiotic question? He looks over at the TV and watches how, after scanning the horizon to look for the sun, Dracula hurls a curse at the sky. From the movement of his lips Riba thinks he's understood what he said, but it doesn't seem very likely. He thinks the vampire said:

"Restless as a child's bottom."

How strange, he thinks. Would the young man who came to look for his red suitcase and said he was called New York have spoken like that? His mind becomes somewhat confused again. And how strange it all is, he thinks. He pulls the sheets over his head, as if he were starting to feel scared again. If he could choose his future, he'd go on sleeping forever. If anyone knocked at the door now, he'd think it was the genius he's been looking for all his life.

He remembers a day when, with excessive care, Celia read the label on a bottle of mineral water at home, turning it around slowly, without stopping. And now he does something similar in his room. He picks up a bottle of crystal-clear Irish spring water and repeats those gestures of Celia's.

Loneliness. Celia over there in Barcelona. His friends, probably sleeping off their hangover. His parents on the day of their sixty-first wedding anniversary, but it's so early in the day he can't even call them.

Alone, dreadfully alone. Although, all things considered, with each moment that passes, the feeling of loneliness grows less. Because this strange background murmur doesn't cease, the sensation of noticing the almost palpable presence of someone at his side, stalking him. Damn it, he thinks, I'm going to end up getting used to this company. He tries to incorporate some humor into the moment, but doesn't really know how. He thinks that, if it's anyone, this ghost can only be the creator of his days, or the spirit—the lost genius—of his childhood. Or someone who's using him as a guinea pig for his experiments. Or Uncle David himself, although he doesn't think so. Or the masterly author he always looked for and never found. Or no one. In any of these cases, it must be someone who, as Joyce would say, has faded into impalpability through death, through absence, through a change of manners. Whoever it is, admitting the unmissable disparity—this someone or no one—must be like that famous reality, toward which one can get closer and closer, but never close enough; because reality knows how to slip away behind an infinite series, of footsteps, levels of perception, false soundings. And in the long run, reality turns out to be inextinguishable, unreachable. One can find out more and more about it, but not everything. Even so, it's advisable to try to find out a little more, because in certain investigations surprises do occasionally occur.

Breakfast is served in a room adjacent to the lobby, an ultra-modern black and white space, a tiresome, painfully hip locale. He's never seen such a dark, lowly-lit place for having breakfast: it looks like Dublin at night, but very late at night and before it was built, when this place too was one of the darkest on earth. Because, for starters, you can't see a thing. And when he eventually gets used to the darkness, he starts to make out a series of brusque businessmen, each eating breakfast alone, their expressions stern and unsmiling, their briefcases on the floor. All he can see around him are sullen businessmen dressed in stiff suits. Those are "the Morgans," he thinks. They don't interact with each other, although one would hope that a certain enthusiasm for the things of this world would be visible on their faces. The Morgans seem to live in a migrainey, morbid, unsociable sort of enthusiasm. In order to be on a par with them, Riba asks for coffee in the same reserved, standoffish tone they use. A few of them throw him glances of complete indifference and seem to frown.

He amuses himself by imagining that one of the Morgans is eating cooked kidneys for breakfast, as Bloom does at the start of *Ulysses*. It comforts him to think that, when breakfast is over, it'll be a more appropriate time to call his parents. One of the Morgans is staring at him so hard it makes him uncomfortable. It makes him think of a similarly sullen man he met in the Roverini on Madison Avenue, on his second trip to New York. Like that one, this man seems strangely familiar; it's as if he knew him from a long time ago and knew everything about him, and yet as if at the same time the man, who looks quite Italian, were really a genuine and total stranger; more than that, it's as if he were the person he knew least of all the millions of strangers in the world.

Maybe he's spying on him. Or it could be that Walter man. Or a friend Nietzky recruited last night, who'll come up to him any minute to introduce himself and say something like how he was the first to buy all the books Riba published at his publishing house. So you are the famous *first person*, Riba would say then if this guy came over to say something like that. But the supposed Italian doesn't come over, he sits motionless, simply staring at him, until he gets bored and chooses instead to bury himself in his copy of the *Irish Times*, which they hand out on your way into the dining room. Riba wonders what would happen now if he went over to the man and told him that he sometimes thinks he recognizes the lost spirit of his childhood in strangers. The other man would either think he was a madman or was trying to chat him up. He'd never understand the spiritual nuances, this manoeuvre where he was only trying to connect as closely as possible to that little boy on a long-ago Barcelona patio, wanting to reconcile himself with his childhood spirit, with the *first person* he knew so fleetingly and who separated from him so early on. But the surly Morgans aren't in the mood for any kind of subtleties.

Another one, the one sitting at an adjacent table very involved in some papers covered in figures and mathematical equations, looks at Riba now with absurd suspicion, as if he thought he wanted to copy his notes. This is all Riba needs, for someone to think he's nostalgic for the world of business or needs to copy other people's formulas for success.

He looks at the supposed Italian and confirms that the man's stare of a few seconds ago has given up the ghost. This allows Riba to observe him better. He really reminds Riba of the young Morgan he saw a few months ago in New York's Roverini. But he soon sees it's not the same guy, not at all. This one, if possible, looks even more sullen.

What a shame he can't tell his parents he's thinking of them so fondly now on the day of their wedding anniversary, and that he's doing so sitting opposite one Irish grump, and next to another, who's almost childlike in his fear that someone's going to copy his work. But Riba knows that, when he talks to his parents, he'll only wish them a happy anniversary and will say nothing to them about these Morgans. He's got enough problems with them since his visit last Wednesday ended so badly.

In order not to sink into self-reproach he concentrates again on the world of the sullen strangers. He thinks of all the ones he's ever met in his life. The first that comes to mind is a burial insurance salesman, a friend of his grandfather's who used to visit them every summer to renew their endless policies. He was extraordinarily sullen, as if he believed he had to be like that in order to be closely linked to his profession. And the worst thing: you could never tell what he was thinking.

"As a man thinketh, so is he," he remembers his grandfather used to say. But was it his grandfather who said this? Did his grandfather, the least sullen man Riba has ever known, say so many things? He feels he's worse than Spider, perhaps because he's slept so little. And when he looks back over at that young, stern-faced, staring Morgan he sees that not only is the stranger no longer there, but that he's vanished and not even the slightest trace of his presence remains. It's as if he were never there.

He tries to remember that he has to go through the day completely enthused, but it's hard to convince himself this will be possible. Where did that Morgan go? He found him deeply upsetting, but he hadn't given him permission to disappear like that. He feels even more annoyed than when he was a child and his spirit abandoned him. And absurdly vindictive toward this Morgan who has left.

That young man—he thinks—so full of life, and at the same time insubstantial as a ghost. Recently, lots of people have been in the habit of disappearing a few seconds after having appeared.

And he remembers a little girl he used to play with in the summer holidays, in Tossa de Mar. Time flies like an arrow, the child used to say, and fruit flies fly too.

Back in his room, waiting for the revelers to wake up, he takes refuge in the book he's brought with him and starts to read a biography of Beckett, by James Knowlson. He published it but didn't read it at the time, and decided the trip to Dublin would provide an ideal opportunity to do so. The time has come to read this book he published five years ago and which, by the way, lost him so much money. He knows he could do other things. For instance, go to the executive lounge on the first floor and check his emails. But he wants to stick to his decision to undergo travel therapy and to distance himself from the internet and computers. He's come to Dublin with this book on Beckett because he always thought one day an opportune moment to read it would arrive, but also because, shortly before leaving Barcelona, it struck him that Beckett was a great friend of Joyce's—he's heard it said he was his secretary too, but this isn't true—and was born in Foxrock, County Dublin, on April 13, 1906, twenty-six months after the day on which *Ulysses* takes place. Precisely twenty-six months have passed since Riba suffered his physical collapse. Twenty-six months was also exactly how long his parents' engagement lasted.

Now he reads the section where Knowlson comments on how the young Beckett fled Ireland and above all escaped from May, his mother, but didn't have a much better time in London. He was depressed and jobless the whole time he was there. He applied without success for the post of assistant curator at the National Gallery. He suffered all sorts of physical discomforts in the form of cysts and eczema. He soon saw that he'd be forced to return to his Dublin home. The worst thing was that he went back, and his mother, convinced he was behaving strangely and had psychological problems, tortured him by making him return to London and paying for two years of intensive psychotherapy for him there, which led him to end up detesting forever the old capital of the empire and the empire itself. He was never a good Irishman, but he acted like it when it came to despising England. He traveled around Germany afterward, where he learned—Knowlson says—to be silent in another language, absorbed in front of Flemish paintings.

Even so, he did return to Dublin and to life with his mother. Uncomfortable in the house where he was born, in Cooldrinagh, in the village of Foxrock. Long walks at dusk to Three Rock and Two Rock, always returning home via Glencullen, generally accompanied by his mother's two Kerry Blue terriers. Days of fog and lethargy, of indecision. Long hikes around the beautiful coast of the county: lighthouses, wind, harbors. Long strolls around one of the most beautiful areas on earth. And one single conviction during those days of much indecision: now he would hate London forever. And a question preyed on the no-longer-so-young Beckett: what if I went to France and fled from the beauty of the lighthouses and the last piers of the ports at the end of the world of my noble, beloved, sweet, revolting native land?

Two days later, Beckett says goodbye to Dublin once and for all and sets off for Paris, which soon becomes his life's destiny. He experiences something there he forever calls a *revelation* and that he once summed up thus: "Molloy and the others came to me the day I realized my stupidity. Only then did I start to write what I felt." When the biographer Knowlson asked him to be less cryptic about the matter, Beckett didn't mind explaining it further:

> *I realized that Joyce had gone as far as one could in the direction of knowing more, [being] in control of one's material. He was always adding to it; you only have to look at his proofs to see that. I realized that my own way was impoverishment, in lack of knowledge and in taking away, in subtracting rather than adding.*

With this *revelation* of Beckett's, the Gutenberg age and of literature in general had started to seem like a living organism that, having reached the peak of its vitality in Joyce, was now, with his direct and essential heir, Beckett, experiencing the irruption of a more extreme sense of the game than ever, but also the beginning of a steep decline in physical form, ageing, the descent to the opposite pier to that of Joyce's splendor, a freefall toward the port's murky waters and its poverty, where in recent times, and for many years now, an old whore walks in an absurd worn-out raincoat at the end of a jetty buffeted by the wind and the rain.

Reading makes him sleepy again, perhaps because he woke up too early. But he doesn't attribute this sudden low to that, but rather to the fact that he's started reading on the other bed, the one he didn't sleep in last night. He remembers Amy Hempel, whose character says in one of her stories that she'd discovered a trick to get to sleep: "I sleep in my husband's bed. That way, the empty bed I look at is my own."

He looks at his empty bed and puts himself in the shoes of whoever might be observing him from the place he is now. The rumpled sheets on the adjacent bed would induce first boredom and then an instant loss of consciousness in this person. He imagines he gets right under the skin of the man and he ends up falling asleep, and a recurring nightmare of a cage gets to him too, except this time God is outside the cage. He's a scruffy guy who's always mechanically smoothing down his hair. He imagines that, under the gaze of the messy-haired man, he says to the absentee, the one who slept last night in the now empty bed:

"It was never a problem, but it's starting to be one now, and it unsettles me. I try to communicate with myself, but it's impossible to do so. There's no greater distance than the space between two minds. As much as if you suspect I'm that *first person* who existed in you and vanished so early on, or if you think I'm the author of your days, or the spirit of your childhood, or simply the shadow cast by your publisher's sorrow; the most distressing thing of all would be for you to think that I am happy. If only you knew."

•

No one was further from suicide than Beckett. When he visited the grave of Heinrich von Kleist he felt a deep unease and scant admiration for this Romantic artist's final suicidal gesture. Beckett, who loved the world of words and loved gambling, led a life where he wrote ever shorter, more minimal novels, works that were more and more stripped down and sparse. Always worstward. "Name, no, nothing is nameable, tell, no, nothing can be told, what then, I don't know, I shouldn't have begun." A stubborn walk toward silence. "So leastward on. So long as dim still. Dim undimmed. Or dimmed to dimmer still. To dimmost dim. Leastmost in dimmost dim."

He changed his language to impoverish his expression. And in the end his texts appeared more and more purged. The lucid delirium of poverty. Going through life forever hindered, precarious, inert, deformed, unsettled, numb, terrified, unwlecomed, naked, sickly, shaky, defenceless, exiled, inconsolable, playful. Beckett, skinny and smoking in his room in Tiers-Temps, a nursing home in Paris. His pockets full of cake for the pigeons. Retired, like any other elderly person with no family, to an old people's home. Thinking of the Irish Sea. Waiting for the final darkness. "Much better, in the end, if sorrow disappears and silence returns. In the end, it's how you've always been. Alone."

So far from New York.

"I'd like to be born," he hears someone say in the next room.

He interrupts his reading of the biography. It might be true that he'd heard this if it weren't for the fact there's no one in the adjacent room. Not a single sound has been heard there since he arrived. He hasn't heard anyone go into the room. And anyway, the sentence was uttered in Spanish. It's his imagination. It's not exactly serious. He'll continue to talk to it, to his imagination. He invents any name and says it before challenging it to come in.

"If you're out there, knock three times."

Enter ghost. Perhaps who's come in is this first person he's obsessed with, this first good man who became hidden thanks to his catalog.

It's well known that ghosts come from our memories, they almost never arrive from distant lands, or outside us. They are our tenants.

"What about the red suitcase?"

"I never travel," the ghost says. "I'm forever trying to be born. And to learn English, which it's about time I did."

Time: Eleven o'clock in the morning.

Date: Bloomsday.

Place: Meeting House Square, a square that developed from the place where a century ago a large part of the Quaker community of Dublin was concentrated.

Characters: Riba, Nietzky, Ricardo, Javier, Amalia Iglesias, Julia Piera, Walter, and Bev Dew.

Style: Theatrical and festive.

Action: The traditional public reading of *Ulysses* on the stage of the theater built in one corner of the square. A seated audience occupies all the chairs in Meeting House Square. More of the audience is on the terrace outside a café. Occasional passersby and people stand and talk, some of them very animatedly. A well-expressed pleasure at the costumes of the readers.

Riba finds himself with Julia Piera, a Spanish poet who's lived in Dublin for two years and is also a friend of Javier and Ricardo and who immediately offers to add them to the list of people who will take their turn to read a section from the book on the little stage. They're already at the end of chapter five, so the most likely thing is that, thanks to a curious coincidence, they'll get to read bits from chapter six. Nietzky and Ricardo put their names on the list and are given readings at around half past twelve.

With anxious curiosity, Riba observes all the people dressed up as Leopold Bloom, Molly Bloom, Stephen Dedalus. He's attaining small degrees of unsuspected happiness. Everything, absolutely everything, seems new to him, and life does too. He thinks the feeling must be similar to that of having traveled to another world. There's an air of wonderful unreality. Of being somewhere else.

He records everything in a commonplace book he's bought in a bookshop of the nearby photography gallery and that he's decided to inaugurate with a list of the things that catch his eye this morning.

A word-for-word account of what he has written down up to now:

A man dressed as the "inner landscape of a skull."

A wonderful fat girl who thinks she's Molly Bloom.

The Israeli writer David Grossman, who's put himself down on the list to read a fragment of *Ulysses*.

Bev Dew, the young daughter of the South African ambassador, in a wide-brimmed flowery hat and an ankle-length dress. Very beautiful. Fragrant face. Apple-faced. Accompanied by her laconic and strange brother Walter, a friend of Nietzky's from school and shadowy owner of the Chrysler.

The poet Amalia Iglesias, who waves to Javier, who was her neighbor years ago in Madrid.

A Portuguese man dressed up as David Hockney!

"Full devotion to funerals!" Nietzky says. He's probably been drinking again.

An anonymous, bony figure. To employ a Beckettian description: haughty forehead nose ears white holes mouth white threadlike finished invisible stitching.

Julia Piera again. Sensuality, beauty, vivaciousness.

A few more than obvious ghosts, even one wearing a white sheet. Me, comically reflected in a shop window again.

A sort of Finnish ogre with a straw hat and silver-handled cane.

A man in a raincoat bearing a quite astonishing resemblance to Beckett as a young man.

A Jesuit called Cobble, friend of Nietzky's, who suddenly stops dead and starts talking in a suspiciously low voice to Amalia Iglesias.

The reading is running conspicuously late, as if from their Irish vantage point they wanted to poke fun at British punctuality. They're so behind that Nietzky doesn't take the floor until 1:10 p.m. He reads in a ridiculous, very correct and lilting English. His friend Walter's sister, however, seems almost moved listening to him. Riba feels unexpectedly jealous, and then this reaction worries him. Extreme beauty, youth. He likes Bev, he can't deny his arousal, his sudden sexual desire. Above all he likes her voice. In the middle of this sort of euphoria he's experiencing, in the middle of unexpected levels of happiness, he thinks that maybe Bev reminds him of one of those girls with beautiful, glittering voices from the novels of Scott Fitzgerald: that timbre in which the jingle of coins can be heard, the beautiful cascade of gold in every fairy tale. Yes, he likes Bev, among other things because in some way her glamour brings her closer to New York. Or maybe he just likes her, and that's it.

Meanwhile, up on the stage, the reading of Joyce's novel continues. Simon Dedalus, Martin Cunningham, and John Power are already sitting in the hearse and chapter six is trotting along at the same pace as the horses toward Prospect Cemetery.

> —*What way is he taking us? Mr Power asked through both windows.*
> —*Irishtown, Martin Cunningham said. Ringsend. Brunswick street.*
> *Mr Dedalus nodded, looking out.*
> —*That's a fine old custom, he said. I am glad to see it has not died out.*
> *All watched awhile through their windows caps and hats lifted by passers. Respect. The carriage swerved from the tramtrack to the smoother road past Watery Lane.*

"It's really a requiem for my profession and above all for me, as I'm all washed up," Riba says to Javier as he glances anxiously at Bev, as if wanting to point out to his friend that he's saying all this because she reminds him that he's old now, after all he's nearly sixty and seducing her would not be the easy task it might have once been for him.

They're standing on one side of the square, by the first row of seats of the ever-increasing audience.

"You don't have to convince me of anything anymore," Javier says. "And even less when we're on the sixth chapter already and I'm feeling imbued with your idea for the requiem. I've even thought about writing a story about someone who holds funerals all over the world, funerals in the form of works of art. What do you think? It's someone trying to learn to say goodbye to everything. Saying goodbye to Joyce and the age of print is not enough for him, and he starts to turn into a collector of funerals."

Reba responds, "He could have this slogan printed on his hat: 'Full devotion to funerals!' It's what Nietzky said just now."

Javier can't hear these last few words properly because an unnecessarily loud voice booms out from the stage.

"How awful! I don't think the visit to the terrible Hades needs so much shouting," Javier comments.

The sun comes out and obviously no one was expecting it, although everyone has immediately noticed it with great cheer. Riba goes back to his commonplace book and writes that, due to the sun's recent appearance, people at the tables outside the café are now sitting open-mouthed, "as if they were already home and it was evening and they were watching television."

The sun's come out, but up there the reading continues on an ever gloomier stage: "A raindrop spat on his hat. He drew back and saw an instant of shower spray dots over the gray flags."

Bev and Walter Dew come over, slightly enigmatically, across these same gray flagstones. It looks as if the South African ambassador's son is about to say something, but in the end he lives up to his incurable curtness—Nietzky has already warned them that his friend is president of the elitist Dublin Laconic Society, and doesn't tend to open his mouth much.

Bev smiles and asks, in her near-perfect Spanish, how they're going to manage today without the Chrysler to get around on this wonderful Bloomsday. Not even she and her brother have the car today, because their father's using it. There can be no doubt that hidden in the laconic man's sister's voice there's real charm. It's a sensual voice, with light, life, heat, he even hears sweat. A radiant, sparkling voice, although this sparkling contrasts at times with the girl's opaque intelligence.

"Trains and taxis," Javier replies, "it's not a problem. We came here in a taxi today. Otherwise we'll walk, it's fine."

Riba doesn't even move, he's rooted to the spot looking at Bev, hoping that maybe she'll say something else.

"Isn't that right?" Javier asks him. "Well, look at this, our beloved editor has joined the laconic circle."

"Oh, yes," Riba reacts. "There are taxis everywhere. All you've got to do is raise your arm when you're out on the road, in front of the hotel, for example, and one soon stops."

When he's finished saying this, he feels, he's almost certain, that he's said too much. And he remembers there was a time when he felt genuine panic at turning into a chatterbox.

Some distance away from Riba stands Ricardo, slightly cautious, a Pall Mall in hand as ever, talking to Nietzky.

"Listen up. To me the worst thing is that Riba's been imagining me all this time as some sort of Romantic artist type. It's madness. I can't understand why he's incapable of seeing me as a normal person, a family man, an office worker, a busy husband who goes to the supermarket on the weekends and takes the garbage out every night. I mean, I'm nothing more, nothing less than that."

"I didn't know you were so normal," says Nietzky.

On the stage, the relentless reading of the novel continues:

White horses with white frontlet plumes came round the Rotunda corner, galloping. A tiny coffin flashed by. In a hurry to bury. A mourning coach. Unmarried. Black for the married. Piebald for bachelors. Dun for a nun.
  — Sad, Martin Cunningham said. A child.

State of the sky: Very bright, getting more and more sunny.

Action: In his corner, Riba thinks about the child he was. A strange moment. He imagines the coffin he would have had if he'd died young. And he also imagines the shadow of his spirit—the guardian angel lost at such a young age—accompanying the coffin in silence. Then the voice of his childhood playmate. Time flies like an arrow and fruit flies fly too.

Not far off, Ricardo and Nietzky continue their now lengthy conversation.

"What can the Rotunda corner be?" Ricardo asks.

"The Rotunda corner? The corner of Death. At least that's what it seems like, doesn't it?"

"But also like Gothic Rotunda, that font invented in I don't know which century. But it's true, it would be normal for the Rotunda to be Death. About being normal. Didn't you know I was?"

Short silence.

"What? Normal? Well, no." Another brief silence. "I associate you with art and as far as I know, art is never normal. It's labyrinthine, fantastically deceitful and complex, my friend. Look at Walter, for instance."

"Is Walter an artist?"

"In his own way he is. He's not normal, even when he's taking out the garbage."

In another corner of the square, Bev has just noticed Riba's notebook.

"What are you writing in there?" she asks.

Riba reckons that maybe, if she's addressed him so familiarly, it's because she doesn't see him as that old or decrepit. He cheers up suddenly, actually he cheers up a lot, enormously so. It was worth taking the Irish leap for something like this alone. The girl's question has given him an opportunity to shine, and given that he's already taken the much desired English leap, he understands that now he can even reconcile himself with his French past—he's already quite keen to do so—and become an echo of the Parisian Perec, his eternal idol, and a superb expert in questioning the everyday, the commonplace.

"Oh, nothing," he replies. "I'm taking notes on what seems not to be important, what isn't spectacular, what happens every day, what comes back every day. The trivial, the everyday, the obvious, the common, the ordinary, background noise, the usual, what happens when nothing is happening …"

"What did you say? Don't you think Bloomsday is spectacular? But that's awful, baby, that's awful you don't think it's spectacular!"

Did she say "baby"? It's not the most important thing, but her tone of voice didn't sound nearly as wonderful as before, this is true. And although everything can be improved on, the bad first impression he's doubtless managed to have of the girl is beyond repair. He thought ingenuously that the South African ambassador's daughter's intelligence was equal to her beauty and all he's achieved is to come across like a fool, as someone incapable of valuing the spectacular qualities of Bloomsday. Good heavens, this is hopeless now. And it won't do any good to think this "baby" of hers was vulgar and unnecessary as well, nor will it do any good to think the girl looks like or is a total idiot. Even if she is or looks that way, he was the one not to rise to the occasion and everything is beyond hope now. And so is his age, and what's worse: his blatant decrepitude. It's better to take a few steps and move away, to help the famous fruit fly to fly.

When, after walking in a slow zigzag across the square, Amalia gets to where Nietzky and Ricardo are, they finally discover, thanks to her, that the Rotunda isn't Death, or a typeface, nor can it be associated in any way—everything would fit too neatly if it could—with the death of the age of print. No. It's simply the old maternity hospital of Dublin, the first one in Europe.

Birth and Death. And Amalia's laughter.

At the same time, Bev has returned to her attack on Riba. She looks at him, laughs. What can she want now? Will she go on about how spectacular the day is? She's very beautiful. Despite his recent letdown, he'd give anything to hear her voice again. He's bewitched, he admits it, but she makes him feel like he's in the States. Will she call him "baby" again?

"My favorite writer is Ragú Candor," Bev says in her attractive voice, just as sensual as before although now she has a French accent. "And yours?"

Riba, much taken aback, understands that whatever happens he's now faced with a second chance and starts to think carefully about his answer. In the end, he chooses not to make mistakes and opts for this Candor as well, a man he's never heard of. What a coincidence, Riba says, he's my favorite too. Bev looks at him in surprise and asks him to repeat that. Ragú is my favorite, Riba says, I like his stylistic restraint and the way he deals with silence. I thought you were more intelligent, Bev says. Ragú Candor is for silly girls like me and now you seem silly too.

She's won the game. And what's more, Riba was wrong again and the worst of it is that—the idea of getting along with Bev now ruled out forever—he feels he's aged ten years. He's incapable now of seducing young girls. He's made a fool of himself, he's finished. Without drink he lacks the humor that at least made him more daring and funny. His face darkens, and gradually acquires a slow, mournful look.

Up there, on the stage—as if it were a parallel story—the reading of the novel goes on and the funeral cortège continues slowly on its way at the height of a sunny morning: "Dunphy's corner. Mourning coaches drawn up drowning their grief. A pause by the wayside. Tiptop position for a pub. Expect we'll pull up here on the way back to drink his health. Pass round the consolation. Elixir of life."

The Rotunda was always a good excuse to take to drink.

Time: A quarter to four.

Date: Bloomsday.

Place: Martello tower, in the village of Sandycove, a circular tower on the outskirts of the city of Dublin, the place where *Ulysses* begins: "Stately, plump Buck Mulligan came from the stairhead.... Solemnly he came forward and mounted the round gunrest."

Characters: Riba, Nietzky, Javier, and Ricardo.

Action: They have climbed up the narrow spiral staircase to the round gunrest, and are now contemplating the Irish Sea from up there. The day is still calm and the sky is a surprisingly uniform white. The tide is high, and the surface of the sea, taut and burnished like rippling silk, looks higher than the land. Riba is hypnotized for a few moments. Strange sea of an intense blue, dangerous like love. He imagines that the sea, in reality, is only a pale gold gleam that extends out to the impossible horizon.

As time is getting on, because they've arranged to meet the Dew siblings and Amalia and Julia Piera at the gates of Glasnevin Cemetery, Nietzky decides to found the Order of Knights right here, high up in the tower. What's more, he considers the setting a nobler one. They went to Finnegan's pub yesterday and when they pass it again going to Dalkey to get the train home, they'll have too little time to stop and found the Order there.

They're alone on the gunrest, but Riba has the feeling that the wind is carrying broken words and that, what's more, there's a ghost hidden on the spiral staircase. Javier, who hates *Ulysses*, is pretending he's Buck Mulligan and shaving his chin. Nietzky reads the rules he drew up yesterday: "The Order of Finnegans has as its sole purpose the veneration of James Joyce's novel *Ulysses*. The members of this society are obliged to honor the work and to honor Bloomsday every year, and when possible, go to the Martello tower in Sandycove and to feel there that they are part of a now ancient race that began like the sea, without name or horizon, and which today is in danger of dying out...."

In quite a hurry and after the symbolic inauguration of the Knights, it's decided that every year one new member can be admitted, "only if and when three-quarters of the Knights of the Order agree to it." And then, with no time left to lose, they go to catch the train. They walk for half an hour along the road to Dalkey and from there, without stopping at Finnegans, take the train back to Dublin singing a song about Milly, the fifteen-year-old daughter of the Blooms who left Dublin to study photography and who only appears obliquely in *Ulysses*:

> O, Milly Bloom, you are my darling.
> You are my looking glass from night till morning.
> I'd rather have you without a farthing
> Than Katey Keogh with her ass and garden.

Time: After five o'clock.

Character: Riba.

Theme: Riba's old age.

Action: Takes place entirely in Riba's imagination, on the train returning to Dublin from Dalkey. With his friends singing "O, Milly Bloom" in the background, he imagines that this ghost haunting him and taking notes of everything happening on the train, and whose breathing he can practically hear, is a young novice in the world of letters; someone who's spent weeks getting more and more involved in an adventure that's driving him mad and which, moreover, he doesn't know whether or not will end up leaving him buried under the books of his future oeuvre: an oeuvre that sooner or later will prevent him—a parallel story to that of Riba as a publisher, who these days sees his true personality obscured thanks to his catalog—from knowing who he is, or who he might have been.

He imagines that the young novice has chosen him as a character, a guinea pig for his experiments, as the character of a novel about the real life, without any exaggeration—of a poor old retired publisher who's somewhat desperate. He imagines that young man observing him closely, studying him as if he were a guinea pig. For the novice it's a question of finding out if devoting himself to good literature for forty years has been worth the trouble, and he tells the story of the daily life, without too many surprises, of the character he's observing. At the same time as considering whether such literary passion is worth the effort; he tells how the retired publisher is still looking for the new, the revitalizing, the *foreign*. He comes as close to the character as he can—sometimes in the most physical sense—and narrates the problems the man has with his wife's Buddhism, while commenting on his movements—having a funeral in Dublin, for example—to fill an empty space.

He imagines that in the novel, the novice has set out to subvert a certain kind of conventional approach, but isn't trying to transform literature into something mysterious, rather attempting to make it possible for the literary publisher to be seen as a hero of our time, as an individual who bears witness to the disappearance of publishers of distinction and reflecting on the difficult situation of a society headed toward stupidity and the end of the world.

He imagines that suddenly this novice comes so close to him that Riba ends up sitting on top of him and blocking his view, suffocating him so the poor young man can only see a huge blurry blot, which is actually the *written* publisher's dark-colored jacket.

Taking advantage of this opportune blot that momentarily paralyzes the novice's narrative powers, Riba manages in every sense to put himself in the other man's place, and to take over his way of seeing things. He then discovers, not without surprise, that he shares absolutely everything with him. To start with, an identical tendency to narrate, and interpret—with the distortions peculiar to a highly literary reader—those everyday events that touch his life.

Then the train goes into a tunnel and he is finally left with no imagination. Zero imagination. Total darkness. A bit of clarity comes when they emerge from the tunnel and he sees the light of dusk again. He thinks he's missed everything already. And then suddenly, he feels a ghostly touch on his back. For a few moments he sits motionless in his seat, and little by little starts to understand that the novice is still there, lying in wait.

Time: Fifteen minutes later.

Style: As theatrical as in the Meeting House Square and maybe more gloomy than festive, although things could change at any moment.

Place: The Catholic cemetery of Glasnevin. A million people are buried here. Founded by Daniel O'Connell, it is eerie at this time in the evening. There are many patriotic monuments, decorated with national symbols or personalized with sports paraphernalia and old toys. Curious towers on the walls, which were used to look out for grave robbers who worked for surgeons at the end of the nineteenth century.

Characters: Riba, Javier, Nietzky, Ricardo, Amalia Iglesias, Julia Piera, Bev, and Walter Dew.

Action: Outside the gates to the place, Riba becomes emotional when he sees the iron railings. They're the same ones Joyce names in chapter six. Are they really railings or a line from *Ulysses*? Faced with this dilemma, Riba is lost for a long time, and after a powerful mental journey, his gaze ends up returning to the cemetery gates. "The high railings of Prospect rippled past their gaze. Dark poplars, rare white forms. Forms more frequent, white shapes thronged amid the trees, white forms and fragments streaming by mutely, sustaining vain gestures on the air."

"The same poplars," Amalia whispers. They cross the threshold of the main gates and the eight of them walk through the terrifying cemetery, which looks like it's come straight out of the Dracula film

Riba saw this morning. All that's missing is some artificial fog and for Paddy Dignam's corpse to rise up from the grave. Riba continues to remember: "Funerals all over the world everywhere every minute. Shovelling them under by the cartload doublequick. Thousands every hour. Too many in the world."

Ravages of death, ravages of the Rotunda.

An unexpected, inspired tirade from Ricardo when they're already a few yards inside the cemetery. He says he's had a sudden revelation and understood everything all at once. He now sees how pertinent the funeral for the Gutenberg age is, for we mustn't lose sight of how much Joyce loved wordplay.

"And I don't know if you've realized that Bloomsday," he says, "sounds like Doomsday. And the long day *Ulysses* takes place on is nothing less than that."

In the end, Ricardo says, Joyce's book is a sort of universal synthesis, a summary of time; a book designed to make a few anecdotal gestures signal an epic, an odyssey in the most literal sense of the word. That's why whoever had the idea for a requiem had the greatest idea of all.

They walk slowly down the main path in Glasnevin and come to a beautiful lilac tree, which Ricardo photographs after explaining to them all, with unnecessary solemnity, that he's almost certain it appears in *Ulysses* toward the end of the cemetery scene. Nietzky thinks the tree is the same color as the lilacs at the Rotunda, which he takes to represent Death, and talks—without the others really understanding him—about the beauty of the Rotunda's lilacs, as if there had to be a logical and purely commonsensical relationship between the lilacs and Dublin's maternity hospital. Riba comes to the conclusion that young Nietzky is talking for the sake of talking and has had a lot to drink again, besides.

Oblivious to his status as a fallen angel, Nietzky reflects aloud on the disparity between the length of men's lives and that of lilacs and other trees. Julia Piera yawns, and then her gaze wanders to a mother and daughter in mourning, standing by a grave, the girl's face streaked with dirt and tears. The mother with a long face, pale and bloodless. Mother and daughter, a hideous pair as if plucked from a drama from another century, as if they'd stepped out of a period film about life in the Rotunda.

And Ricardo, totally oblivious to this, makes questionable macabre jokes. Minutes later, in the middle of an argument in overly raised voices about the gloomy beauty of the place and the by now hackneyed lilac tree, Bev asks for everyone's attention so they can observe how the cawing of the crows blends with their argumentative visitors' shouts.

There are crows, but no one's heard them cawing. A brief silence. A pause. The wind. "You will see my ghost after death." Ricardo finds this phrase, lifted from *Ulysses*, carved onto a gravestone beside one of the smaller paths, in the Murray family crypt. Another photo opportunity, obviously. "How wonderful the Murrays are," someone says. More group portraits. Now everyone squeezes around the tomb of the Joycean family. A cemetery worker wields Ricardo's camera as if he were a great photographic artist and gives them all orders to pose with more style. When the session is over, someone realizes they've been walking around for quite some time now and still haven't gone into the chapel at the end of the cemetery, the place where the brief and sad funeral for Dignam the drunk was held. This seems like the ideal place for the funereal words for the Gutenberg age, and actually for everything, for the world in general.

Javier asks how they're going to make sure the requiem is a work of art. They all look thoughtful. Then the laconic Walter speaks up. He offers to recite the prayer. It will be a short piece, he says, very artistic, thanks precisely to its brevity and depth. Everyone looks at Walter, they all stare incredulously at him and carry on walking along the path that leads to the chapel. A laconic man's words can always have an artistic side, Riba thinks. "It's a prayer for writers," Walter says, with an unnecessarily doleful air. And he tells them it was composed by Samuel Johnson, on the day he signed a contract to write the first complete dictionary of the English language.

Then repeats what he's just said, in English, despite it not being at all necessary. Walter has a great involuntary sense of humor. At the same time, it's surprising that even before intoning the funeral prayer, he's said so much already, even a few unnecessary words. What a waste, Riba thinks. Another long pause. Everyone's gaze drifts to a bench, the last one on the left shortly before going into the chapel. Two men who look like tramps have just sat down there, two guys who are remarkably pale. "Two stiffs who've come out to get some fresh air," Ricardo says, as if his flowery Polynesian shirt made him feel more alive than anyone else. Laughter.

A gentle evening breeze moves the lilac tree. Actually, Johnson was praying for himself, Walter clarifies. And he says it so naturally it's as if Johnson were simply one of them. No one in the group has heard of this prayer before. In any case they all think it's a good idea to use a prayer of Johnson's to intone a funeral hymn. After all, Walter says, Dr. Johnson is the only person in the world to have dedicated a genuinely brilliant essay to the theme of epitaphs. He himself specialized in them for a while, writing them in verse and giving them to the best tombs in London. So Dr. Johnson seems like the ideal person for this epitaph for the Gutenberg age, Walter says.

Everyone is delighted that Dr. Johnson's writers' prayer is the one that will be used as an epitaph for the print age. Everyone that is except Riba, who at the last minute discovers that, as hard as he tries, he can't identify at all with writers, against whom he actually bears a certain grudge, because when it comes down to it, they're the involuntary cause of this sorrow that at times reappears in the middle of his recurring nightmare about the cage and God. Deep down, Riba fears that this writers' prayer is pursuing him and making him regret what he stopped doing, his brain forever pierced by his publisher's sorrow, by that intimate hydra gnawing away at him.

The wind moves the lilac tree again.

And what's more, Riba thinks, they're taking this ceremony too seriously. They don't realize that the apocalyptic is now, but it was already there back in the mists of time and will still be there when we have gone. A very informal man or feeling is what's apocalyptic, and doesn't deserve so much respect. The important thing is not that the print age is foundering. The serious thing is that I am foundering.

"For himself," Walter is still saying, "Johnson was praying for himself."

Then Nietzky says that there are prayers for sailors, for kings, for distinguished men, but that he didn't know there could be a prayer for writers.

"And what about publishers?" Javier asks.

Riba remembers a dream in which he saw Shakespeare studying *Hamlet* to play the part of the ghost.

"Johnson was praying for himself," Walter insists.

They go into the little chapel, and Riba recalls the obese gray rat that in Joyce's book toddles about by a crypt close to Paddy Dignam's. He remembers his friend Antonia Derén, whose anthology on the various appearances of rats in the most illustrious contemporary novels he published a few years ago.

"One of those chaps would make short work of a fellow. Pick the bones clean no matter who it was. Ordinary meat for them. A corpse is meat gone bad," Bloom thinks at the funeral.

Walter waits for a great silence to fall and then, when he sees the suitable conditions for his prayer have arrived, he utters it in a solemn, quivering voice: "O God, who hast hitherto supported me, enable me to proceed in this labor, and in the whole task of my present state; that when I shall render up at the last day an account of the talent committed to me, I may receive pardon by the grace of God. Amen."

No one, except Riba, can understand what is going on when Walter then suddenly starts weeping inconsolably. In theory, he's not a writer and so this problem linked to literary talent shouldn't affect him. The thing is, even if he were, it wouldn't really be very logical for him to start weeping like this. After all, no writer has ever shed a single tear about this. But Riba knows that's precisely where the clue to solving this enigma lies. Writers don't cry for themselves or for other writers. Only someone like Walter who sees everything from the outside and who has a special intelligence and sensitivity, understands how much one should cry whenever one sees a writer.

Riba is poking fun at the funeral, but he wants to rise to the occasion and be as sincere and authentic as Walter. And out of the options he's considering on various pieces of paper in his pocket, he plans to read, as a funeral prayer, the text of a letter from Flaubert that reveals how uncontrollably seduced the writer felt by the figure of St. Polycarp, martyr and bishop of Smyrna, to whom this expression is attributed: "My God! What century—or what world—have you made me born into?"

In order to better read this letter, first he tries to get as emotional as Walter. Right here, he thinks, is where Dignam's coffin once was, which I imagined so many times when I was reading *Ulysses*. Here was this coffin in this chapel, and it doesn't look like things have changed much since Joyce's time. Everything looks exactly conserved in time, identical to the book. The bier, the entrance to the chancel, are all identical. The chancel is the same, there's no doubt. There were four tall yellow candles at the corners, and the mourners knelt here and there, in these praying desks. Bloom stood behind, near the font, and when all had knelt, he carefully dropped his unfolded newspaper from his pocket and knelt his right knee upon it. Right here. This is where he fitted his black hat gently on his left knee, and holding its brim, bent over piously, more than a century ago now. But everything's the same. Isn't it moving?

Then he takes a step forward and walks to the middle of the altar and from there prepares to recite his dirge in the form of Flaubert's letter to his lady friend Louise Colet. But at that moment a street vendor enters and approaches the group, with his little cart of biscuits and fruit. Somewhat thrown by his appearance, Nietzky intervenes with nervous energy, and without anyone having let him through or given him permission, starts to read, aloud and very fast, the section from *Ulysses* where a priest blesses Dignam's soul. He reads somewhat hastily and awkwardly and adds many words of his own, ending like this: "All the year round that priest prayed the same thing over them all and shook water on top of them all. On Dignam now. And on top of an age that today dies with him. Never, ever, nothing. Never more, Gutenberg. Bon voyage, into the void."

Pause. The wind.

And then in a sing-song, priestly voice:

"*In paradisum.*"

They all repeat the litany tersely, annoyed, perhaps because they feel something more than skeptical, and they have the impression that Nietzky couldn't have been more false and mocking in his farewell sentiment for an era. "Some of us," Walter says, "were not born for superficiality." Once again, his involuntary humor. Stifled laughter. What can he have meant to say? Maybe it's too simple. Nietzky was awful. And superficial, of course.

Riba finally gets ready now to recite his funeral prayer when a young couple comes in unexpectedly. Dubliners, probably. The man is tall and has a beard, the woman has long blonde hair carefully combed back. The woman crosses herself, the two speak in low tones, one might say they're asking what sort of gathering is being held here in the chapel. Riba goes closer to hear what they're saying and discovers that they're French and are talking about the price of some furniture. Brief bewilderment. The sound of a cart transporting stones can be heard. Now everyone looks at Riba, undoubtedly so that he'll bring to a close the ceremony he would have finished by now if not for the street vendor, the French couple, and Nietzky with his nervous energy. Ricardo too wants to join in with the prayer, and faced with such indecision, he gets there before Riba: "I don't think any more words are necessary. Gutenberg interred, we've entered other ages. They will have to be buried too. We'll have to burn phases as we go, perform more funerals. Until Judgement Day arrives. And then conduct a funeral for that day too. Then lose oneself in the immensity of the universe, listen to the endless movement of the stars. And organize obsequies for the stars. And after that I don't know."

The French couple is whispering louder now. Are they still talking about furniture? Riba decides to give the letter from Flaubert to Julia Piera, who takes the floor to read, with a few variations of her own, this sort of dirge of an essay: "All this makes me sick. Nowadays, literature looks like a great urinal factory. This is what people smell of, more than anything! I'm always tempted to exclaim, like St. Polycarp did, 'Oh my God! What century—or what world—have you made me born into!' and to flee, covering my ears, as this holy man did whenever he found himself faced with an unseemly proposition. Anyway. The time will come when the whole world will have turned into a businessman and an imbecile (by then, thank God, I will be dead). Our nephews and nieces will have a worse time. Future generations will be tremendously stupid and rude."

Riba, as an ex-businessman, preferred Julia to read this letter. He wouldn't have been able to stand his friends' giggles when it came to talking about businessmen. The crunch of gravel is heard. An obese gray rat, Riba thinks. The distant cry of a seagull is also heard. The biscuit vendor seems to have gone for good. Riba waits for silence, and then taking two steps forward, more stately than plump Buck Mulligan at the start of *Ulysses*, he reads his personal requiem for the grand old whore of literature and recites "Dublinesque":

> *Down stucco sidestreets,*
> *Where light is pewter*
> *And afternoon mist*
> *Brings lights on in shops*
> *Above race-guides and rosaries,*
> *A funeral passes.*

> *The hearse is ahead,*
> *But after there follows*
> *A troop of streetwalkers*
> *In wide flowered hats,*
> *Leg-of-mutton sleeves,*
> *And ankle-length dresses.*

> *There is an air of great friendliness,*
> *As if they were honouring*
> *One they were fond of;*

187

Some caper a few steps,
Skirts held skilfully
(Someone claps time),

And of great sadness also.
As they wend away
A voice is heard singing
Of Kitty, or Katy,
As if the name meant once
All love, all beauty.

Minutes after the funeral oration for the honest old whore of literature, before leaving Glasnevin, they stand looking at a sign on the cemetery wall near the exit that prohibits cars from going over twenty miles an hour as they're leaving. There's laughter at the sign, maybe in an attempt to diffuse some of the tension that's built up in the last few minutes. The French couple talk to the street vendor. Beyond them, the two cadaverous-looking tramps are still sitting on their bench. Far away, the screech of a seagull seems to imitate a crow. Or is it a crow?

"Let's get out of here," Javier says emphatically. Everyone seems to agree. They go back to Milly Bloom's song, which they all sing happily now, as if they'd just escaped from an awful nightmare. Yes, that's enough of this place.

They speed up and look as if they've just arrived from a trip to the country. The railings of *Ulysses* are slowly left behind. And that fragment:

"The gates glimmered in front: still open. Back to the world again. Enough of this place."

At the very gates of the cemetery is the ancient pub, Kavanagh's, also known as the Gravediggers. This pub isn't named in Joyce's chapter, but nevertheless it was here in 1904, next to the gates. It's a squalid place, as far as they can see, which must have a hair-raising atmosphere late at night, something no one here doubts in the slightest, as already, right now in the evening light, at first glance and from outside, you can see that the very structure of the bar itself is reverberating and shuddering, as if about to explode.

Action: After all the ups and downs of the day, everyone goes into the Gravediggers set on sinking down to the bottom somehow. They go in very thirstily.

The Rotunda always was a good excuse to take to drink.

The customers of the Gravediggers have literally turned the pub into pandemonium. At this time of day, the Gravediggers is the capital of Hell, the city of Satan and his acolytes, the city built by fallen angels. It's at the opposite extreme from the Pantheon in Paris, for example. That sobriety, that elegance. Riba has started thinking of Paris again, of all things French. He interprets it as a passing nostalgia for the time of his admiration of Paris. That pantheon, those serene spaces where one can try to reunite all the gods.

The poet Milton made it possible for one to imagine the capital of Hell, Pandemonium, as a very small place. The demons had to make themselves tiny to get into it. Here, in this bar in Dublin, all the customers seem to have reduced their size to be able to be with the rest of the monsters in such a reduced space. The preferred noise of the agitated clientele is a string of staccato chatter, like a hyena's laugh or the shrieks of a baboon, getting slower at the same time as it acquires a shriller pitch.

They're all proper atheists, the barman says, amusingly and absurdly, in a Spanish he assures them he learned in Barcelona. No one really understands what he's talking about. The racket gets more deafening every night, the barman explains without explaining anything. No one knows what the relationship between the noise and atheism can be exactly, but it doesn't seem like the best moment to explain. The deafening party continues. Riba, who now really can hear the cawing Bev said she heard before, imagines that the customers and other gravediggers are like crows who flap down onto the pub's roof every evening at dusk, and then penetrate the most unlikely places in the tiny, hellish bar and growl, threatening each other and singing obscene songs about Milly Bloom and other invented ladies of Dublin, all dead now. And meanwhile the bar reverberates and shudders and the atmosphere is alcoholic to the most delirious extremes.

The Gravediggers presents the most serious temptation to drink Riba has encountered since he came out of his health crisis. Who knows, maybe the secret name of the pub is the Coxwold. Riba is terrified at the mere possibility of falling off the wagon again and doesn't lose sight of the threat the infernal place poses. Perhaps it's here that the prophetic, moving, and terrifying vision of his dream might come true, this vision to be found inside the same dream that's led him to Dublin and to this cavern of crows vibrating with the terrible air of the end of a party as in the cantina El Farolito from that novel by Lowry he's always admired so much.

Everyone here looks as if they've come from the cemetery, he's thinking, and at that moment his cell phone rings. A call from Barcelona. It's Celia phoning to tell him that she's had a call from Calle Aribau and that his parents are indignant because he still hasn't wished them a happy sixty-first wedding anniversary. Oh no, Riba thinks. He'd completely forgotten. Maybe Dublin has liberated him too much from his parents' gentle tyranny.

"Where are you now?" Celia wants to know.

"In the Gravediggers. A pub on the outskirts."

Perhaps he shouldn't have said this. Being in a pub, and also the name of this one, could get him into trouble.

"No, Celia, I haven't had a drop to drink. Don't cry."

"I'm not crying. What makes you think I'm crying?"

There's too much noise in the pub. He goes outside so he can talk. The racket subsumes the entire area around the pub and the high railings. He has a long conversation with Celia and makes another mistake, because when he describes the bar he tells her it looks like that place after death, a world called hell. "I don't like your vision of the other world," she says in a dangerously Buddhist tone. He immediately tries to change the subject, but Celia wants to know if he's sure he hasn't had a drink. And he has to take a few minutes to calm her down. When he finally manages to soothe her, he hangs up and stands lost in the noisy atmosphere around the door to the Gravediggers. He stands there thinking about the Coxwold premonition. He dreamt that scene of inconsolable weeping with Celia at the entrance to the bar with such intensity that, even though it's only the memory of a dream, it's still one of the most impressive memories of his life. He came here to Dublin to encounter the sea, but also to encounter this unlived memory, this moment which, just as happened in his New York dream, has hidden within it something some people call *the moment of true sensation*. Because that weeping seemed to contain, in its most absolute fullness, the core of his existence, the secret universe of all his great love for Celia and infinite joy at being alive and also the tragedy of having been, two years ago, on the point of losing it all.

Perhaps Celia should be here now, and a couple of good drinks should have left the two of them crying emotionally, collapsed in an embrace on the floor, at the entrance to this hellish pub: fallen, but together forever in their love and in their essential weeping, and with Buddha's permission, going through an intense experience of great epiphany, a moment right in the center of the world.

The noise inside the Gravediggers is so loud that now he's talking to Walter using only signs. No one can understand him, not even Walter, an expert in sign language. But Riba on the other hand knows very well what he's saying. He's telling Walter that all life is a demolition job, but the blows that carry out the *dramatic* part of this task— the sudden hard blows that come, or seem to come, from outside— the ones that a person remembers and that make him blame things, and those that, in moments of weakness, a person tells his friends about, don't reveal their effects immediately. The blows come from inside, those blows that furtively encroached upon your interior self from the moment you decided to become a publisher and look for writers, and especially for a genius. These blows are related to a dull, muted pain a person doesn't really notice until it's too late to do anything, until you realize once and for all that in a certain sense you'll never again be who you were and that the blows were well-aimed.

•

He doesn't touch a drop, but perhaps because he's returned, after twenty-six months, to a completely alcohol-infused environment, he remembers that his greatest error, linked to his love of drink, was his inexcusable need to show others the most abject side of his being, and the fact that he always he used to make an effort to speak the truth about what he was thinking, whether or not this hurt whoever might be listening. Taking for granted that his charming side was always visible, he took pains to reveal his abject side. And he did this driven by a need, on the one hand, to escape all social protocols (which made him feel ill) and on the other, because of a desire to align himself with the purest and most original surrealist movement, that which held that any idea that passed through one's head should be immediately put out there and doing so constituted a moral obligation, because this way the most intimate side of everyone's personality was put on display. Naturally this, shall we say, aggressive compulsion brought him numerous problems, lost him contracts and friendships and destroyed his public image. Now, since he stopped drinking and went over to the other side and reveals only, in a positively overwhelming way, the most attractive side of his being, he has the feeling he's lost the suicidal but brilliant "open country" of his previous experiences. He's remained in a state of stifling serenity and politeness and cleanliness that sickens him. It's as if now he were merely an elegant impostor who pilfered the genuine, moving images from the minds of others. Of course he couldn't feel less inclined to have a few drinks and return uselessly to being abject. He'd much rather feel that, for some time now, sobriety has been helping him to recover his tragic conscience, as well as to look for his center, his algebra and his key, as Borges would say, and his mirror.

An hour later, imagination and memory transport Riba to the end of the sixties and the edge of a forest on the Costa Brava battered by gale-force winds. He finds himself on this confused forest edge, the sky grown dark and a wind rising, blowing dust over the surface of the scorched earth, creating, at first swirls, and then freak cobwebs that gradually formed a persistent and obsessive geometric poem in his mind. He remembers that back then he was still very young and hadn't yet published even one book or knew what he was going to do with his life. He would have been very surprised to learn that, forty years later, he'd want to be in that situation once more, that is, to be again in front of the forest battered by gale-force winds without yet having done anything with his life.

The hurricane in this memory having blown over, Riba goes back to the Dublin night, which now, compared to this memory, seems a mild one. He's in the doorway to the pub, he came out to get some fresh air.

This is my country now, he thinks again.

As he opens the door to the place, he hears "Walk on the Wild Side," the song that always evokes New York for him. His friends are coming out of the pub and it looks as if they're bringing the party into the street. Suddenly they all realize the temperature has dropped and they need to find taxis and go back into the town center. A fog obscures the railings of the cemetery, where visitors are still leaving.

Riba's gaze darts among those present and stops at a group not from the pub but from the graveyard. Near these people, as if he'd come from nowhere, is a tall, lanky, solitary man. He's not with anyone. Where the hell did he come from? It's the same guy he saw this morning in Meeting House Square. He looks like a young Samuel Beckett. Round tortoiseshell glasses. A lean, bony face. Eagle-eyed, the eyes of a bird that flies high, that sees everything, even at night. He's wearing a scruffy beige raincoat and is looking at Riba intensely, as if he can sense his spirit soaring, and also as if he doesn't want to transmit a certain dark unhappiness emanating from his birdlike face.

He doesn't look happy, but Riba prefers to think that the young man has just felt for the first time the emotion that any mortal with literary pretensions experiences when he discovers that the practice of his art makes him sense the fluttering of brilliance. Could it be that this young man's art consists of the intimate humility of learning to observe in order to then try to narrate and decipher? If this is true, there would be no more mystery. But Riba doubts this is the case and so, fearfully, he asks Ricardo if he has any idea who the lanky-looking fellow in the mackintosh might be. Amalia hails a taxi. Walter scans the foggy horizon in search of a second vehicle. Bev and Nietzky argue politely about who's going to get into the car Amalia has stopped. Finally Nietzky loses the battle and stands watching the first taxi leave with the resignation of a man watching a gravedigger help attach the ropes to a coffin to lower it into the grave. Walter, who is the one who seems to have best understood Nietzky's deathly expression, carries on looking for a second taxi.

Riba's gaze follows the stranger in the raincoat and after a short while he sees him walk slowly into the fog and soon afterwardvanish, disappear into it. He doesn't see him again. What could have become of the guy swallowed up by the mist? Dracula disappeared like this too. What's more, Dracula had the ability to turn himself into fog. Is Riba the only one who saw him? He asks Ricardo again if he noticed the young man in a raincoat who was also there this morning in Meeting House Square. "What selfinvolved enigma did Bloom risen, going, gathering multicoloured multiform multitudinous garments, voluntarily apprehending, not comprehend?" Such ease, incidentally, to disappear, like Dracula in the mist. In this same graveyard, in another time, Bloom saw his creator.

If I have an author, it's possible he has a face like that, he thinks.

"Well, what do you know," Ricardo says. "Always someone turns up you never dreamt of."

JULY

The moon shone, having no alternative, on the nothing new. It's raining. It's midnight. He feels that the more time he spends in this rocking chair, the more it will take on the shape of his body. An enormous hangover. He has a terrible fear that his kidneys will explode and he'll die here, right now. Cold sweat. He fears that first thing tomorrow morning Celia will leave him. Fear of fear. Even colder sweat. Twelve o'clock on the dot on the clock of anguish.

Time: Midnight.

Place: A fifth-floor apartment in a building in north Dublin.

Atmosphere: Dissatisfaction. He hates himself for yesterday's mistake, but also for having been so clumsy and not having been able to find a writer truly able to dream in spite of the world; to structure the world *in a different way*. A great writer: at once anarchist and architect. It wouldn't have mattered if he were dead. A real genius, just one would have been enough. Someone able to undermine and reconstruct the banal landscape of reality. Someone, dead or alive ... An even colder sweat.

Physical state: Glacial. A massive headache. A feeling of "what for?"

Details: A suitcase and a carry-on bag in the hall—not on the landing, because the neighbors aren't trustworthy here. They indicate that Celia, who's asleep now, is very angry about yesterday and also about today; she'd wanted to give him one last chance this afternoon when she'd returned from her long Buddhist meeting, but he had been so comatose and stupid that she must have decided at that moment to leave tomorrow.

Action: Mental, unmitigating. Out of an obvious professional obsession—reading too many manuscripts, and to top it all, not a single masterpiece—he reads the events of his life more and more literarily. Riba is now in his rocking chair, and after having slept off his hangover all day long and having drunk two Bloody Marys a while ago to try to get over it, he's attempting to reconstruct the terrifying events of the night before. He is doing so in a panic that he might remember too well what happened and die as soon as he does. His remorse at having started drinking again makes him wonder if it mightn't be better to give the slip to the disagreeable and emotional memory of last night's events and take refuge in a book that he has close at hand, an old copy of Vladimir Nabokov's lectures on literature to his students at Cornell. He hopes that by reading these wise lectures, he'll end up feeling sleepy again, which he doesn't now because he's slept all day. He doesn't want to fall under the dangerous hypnosis of the computer, sit in front of it and risk Celia waking up and finding him in *hikikomori* mode again, which is the last thing, rightly or wrongly, she'll be able to stand now.

After twenty-six months of abstinence, he'd completely forgotten how bad a hangover feels. How horrendous. Now the headache seems to be letting up a bit. But an uncontrollable buzzing and remorse are drilling into him. The buzzing—probably very closely related to his old *writer's malady*—is disconcerting, because it brings back, absurdly and obsessively, the memory of the list of wedding gifts from when he married Celia, so many years ago now: that miserable and discouraging assortment of lamps, vases, and crockery. It's all very strange. If he doesn't do something, the rocking chair will take on the shape of his body.

More details: The rocking chair is unvarnished teak, guaranteed against cracks, rot, and nocturnal creaking. The sky he glimpses through the curtains is strangely orange, with violet tints. The rain starts to get heavier and now lashes the windowpanes. Since he arrived at this house, he's been obsessed by the reproduction of "Stairway," a small Edward Hopper painting the owner of the apartment has hung next to the window. It's a painting in which the viewer looks down a staircase to a door open onto a dark, impenetrable mass of trees and mountains. He feels he has been denied what the geometry of the house offers. The open door is not a candid passage to the outside, but an invitation paradoxically extended to stay where he is.

"Go," says the house.

"Where to?" says the landscape outside.

This feeling, once again, is unhinging him, disorienting him, making him very nervous. He decides to ask for some discreet help from Nabokov's book, which is beside him. And then, for a moment or two, he stares at the hazy moon again and at everything he can see out there. The hangover, the abundant rain, "Stairway," and that atrocious sky have him bound to a terrifying anguish. But also directly to a feeling that this is a game. For a moment, "anguish" and "game" intertwine perfectly, as they have so many times in his life. His feet are cold and that could be related as much to the hangover as to the game and the anguish and the stairway that seems to descend inside his own mind.

"Go," says the house.

He covers his dramatic feet with a checked blanket, quite a ridiculous blanket, and pretends to write a sentence mentally, to write it in his head—he has that unusual and luxurious feeling of writing in his head—five times in a row:

It's midnight and the rain lashes the windowpanes.

It's midnight and the rain ...

Then, he starts other games.

The next one is even simpler. It consists of going through all the authors he's published and studying why not even one of them ever presented his readers with a true, authentic masterpiece. Also to examine why none of them, in spite of occasionally showing signs of almost supernatural talent, was an anarchist and at the same time an architect.

Here he pauses and remembers that in one of the letters received from Gauger, who writes to him, every once in a while, from the Chateau Hotel in Tongariro, his secretary attributed the absence of genius in all the writers they published to the profound despondency prevalent in our times, to the absence of God, and definitively—he said—to the death of the author, "announced back in the day by Deleuze and Barthes."

Marginal note: The ongoing correspondence from that hotel in Tongariro is particularly worrying for Riba, who can't understand why his former secretary keeps writing to him, unless it's simply to keep up appearances, and even more, hold at bay suspicions that he embezzled a substantial amount of money from the publishing company.

Other details: From this game of going through all the authors and studying why not even one ever submitted a true masterpiece is derived another even more perverse game, which consists of asking himself the painful question of whether the brilliant author for whom he'd searched so long and hard wasn't actually himself, and if he hadn't become a publisher in order to have to look exclusively for that great talent in others, and thus to be able to forget the dramatic case of his own personality; he's actually hopeless at being brilliant as well as hopeless at writing. It's very possible that he turned to editing in order to avoid this baggage and be able to dump his disappointment on others, not exclusively on himself.

He immediately feels he has to contradict himself and remembers that he also took up publishing because he's always been an impassioned reader. He discovered literature by reading Marcel Schwob, Raymond Queneau, Stendhal, and Gustave Flaubert. He became a publisher after a long time; and then there's the time he now considers *black* in which he betrayed his first literary loves, reading only novels with protagonists who earned more than a hundred thousand dollars a year.

A commentary: It's well known that when a person sees a glint of gold in books, he's taking a qualitative leap in his editorial vocation. And some of that could apply to Riba, except that, beforehand, he was a reader of good novels, and also a committed reader; he didn't just go into the business to make a lot of money, that is, for what is vulgarly referred to in Spanish with the verb *forrarse*. Ah, *forrarse*! What a strange expression. Was there any equivalent in English? To make a mint? To line one's pockets? In fact, he soon realized he was heading for ruin and still didn't want to give it up, and the miracle was that he lasted in his profession for thirty years.

He always had good relationships with foreign publishers, whom he usually saw at the Frankfurt Book Fair and with whom he exchanged information and books. With editors in his own country, however, he never had a great rapport. They always seemed fatuous to him, less knowledgeable about literature than they pretended to be: bigger celebrities and more egocentric than their authors whom they branded as egomaniacs to delirious extremes. Curiously, his friends in Spain have usually been writers, and the vast majority younger than him.

Even though he never stumbled upon a truly great genius, he had a deep respect for the vast majority of his authors, especially those who understood literature as a force directly linked to the subconscious. Riba has always believed that one loves most books that produce the sensation, when opened for the first time, that they've always been there: places never visited appear in them, things never seen or heard before, but the sense of having a personal memory of those places or things is so strong that somehow you end up thinking you've been there.

Today he takes it for granted that Dublin and the Irish Sea have been in his mental landscape forever, forming part of his past. If one day, now that he's retired, he goes to live in New York, he'd like to begin a new life, he'd like to feel like a son or a grandson of an Irishman who emigrated to that city. He'd like to be called Brendan, for example, and for the memory of his work as a publisher to be easily forgotten in his native land, forgotten with the malice and treachery so typical of his tight-fisted and indolent compatriots.

Could he, if he so desired, go back to that night when he danced that foxtrot until dawn, go back to his wedding day, go back to being the brilliant and heartless publisher who, at the height of his success—

it didn't last long—made caustic declarations and pointed out the ideal way forward for literature? Or is he going to be left forever staring, like an idiot, at the electric light and wondering whether to have a third Bloody Mary and thus liberate himself from the rocking chair? Is he going to remain forever unable even to get up and walk normally through the house? The buzzing comes again. Obsessively, he goes back to the discouraging and truly obsessive trousseau, the wedding gift list: lamps, vases, old-fashioned crockery. An author's trousseau, he thinks.

The rain is getting heavier and heavier and is now too persistent to be a summer shower. Since yesterday the downpour has been interrupting the usual fine weather at this time of year in Ireland. For weeks it hasn't rained in Dublin. He's into the second week of a twenty-day holiday with Celia in an apartment in the north of the city, the area on the other side of the Royal Canal, not very far from Glasnevin Cemetery, where he's wanted to return for days now, perhaps to see if he might again glimpse that ghost who vanished before his very eyes on that afternoon of June 16 in front of The Gravediggers pub; that ghost, a relative of Dracula's, with the great ability to turn himself into fog.

During their first days on the island, he and Celia stayed on Strand Street in the coastal town of Skerries, a pleasant place with a great variety of sea and coast and a long, curved harbor full of shops and pubs. But Celia felt too disconnected from her Buddhist contact in Dublin—she'd been having long meetings every afternoon since they arrived with a religious society or club—and they moved to the pretty town of Bray, near Dalkey, where they also felt uncomfortable; they finally ended up in this apartment in a building near the Royal Canal.

The thing keeping Riba entertained now is trying to avoid remembering in too much detail what happened yesterday. He fears remembering yesterday's horrors. So he looks again at the book of Nabokov's lectures as if this might be his only hope, finally deciding to fully enter the Nabokovian commentary on one of the chapters, chosen at random (the first chapter of Part Two), of Joyce's ever-difficult *Ulysses*:

Part Two, Chapter I
Style: *Joyce logical and lucid.*
Time: *Eight in the morning, synchronized with Stephen's morning.*
Place: *7 Eccles Street, where the Blooms live, in the northwest part of town.*
Characters: *Bloom, his wife; incidental characters, the pork-butcher Dlugacz, from Hungary like Bloom, and the maid servant of the Woods family next-door, 8 Eccles St …*
Action: *Bloom in the basement kitchen prepares breakfast for his wife, talks charmingly to the cat …*

Riba ends up closing the book of lectures, because the theme of *Ulysses* now sounds antiquated to him, as if the funeral on June 16 in Dublin had been so effective as to draw to a close an entire era, and now he is living only at ground level, or at rocking-chair level, as if he were a Beckettian vagabond; as if he were now resigned to the inevitable, preferring to remain at the mercy of the memory of last night's tragic alcoholic relapse.

Fortunately, this rain today is not the terrible London flood, it's not the same apocalyptic storm as when he was there with his parents, fifteen days ago, that savage rain. He'll never go back to that city. Deep down the trip was a concession to his elderly parents, an attempt to assuage his guilt for not having been in Barcelona for their sixty-first wedding anniversary. And also a way of saving himself, even if just once, the hateful task of having to tell them about his visit to a foreign city.

"So you've been to London."

He just couldn't be bothered, when he got back, to have to answer his mother's question and tell them things about that city, so he decided to take both of them, his father and mother, to London.

It was complicated—he thinks now, almost motionless in his rocking chair—that trip to London, because his parents hadn't moved from Calle Aribau for years. But if anything, the excursion confirmed that they have a free-flowing communication with the great beyond wherever they are. In London, gatherings occasionally formed around his parents: agglomerations they pretended not to notice, perhaps because since time immemorial they'd always known how to bear the weight of so many ancestors naturally.

Perhaps he's become very Irish. The thing is he didn't feel comfortable in London. He didn't like many things, but he has to admit that he did love the double-decker buses and the three elegant and solitary green-and-white-striped deck chairs he photographed in Hyde Park. He was sorry his friend Dominique wasn't there because he would have liked to see the Tate installation with her; but she'd had to leave quite suddenly for Brazil, where she lives most of the time. He didn't like many things about London, even though other things amused him. The strangest was when he saw his parents in the middle of the very street that Hammershøi depicted in "The British Museum." Riba hadn't been able to find this street on his previous trip, but he suddenly discovered that it did exist and it was called Montague Street and was in such plain view that Celia had found it as soon as they approached the British Museum. She was carrying the photocopy of the painting that Riba had brought to London for that very reason: a very wrinkled photocopy Riba kept in his pants pocket. Right there, in Montague Street, was where the greatest ghostly turmoil gathered around his parents, who seemed to know everybody and to have been living in that neighborhood their whole lives.

Riba thought that, if he had been a poet or a novelist, he would have exploited the great narrative goldmine he had at his disposal in his parents' animated ghostly gatherings: gatherings not restricted, as he'd always thought, to the closed space of the apartment on Calle Aribau, but taking place—as was now perfectly obvious—anywhere in the world, in broad daylight, in any bustling city street in any suburb of the universe, including London.

He didn't like that city, but he walked around with interest, for a long time, through the surly and labyrinthine East End, the center of Spider's gray life. And he was fascinated by the huge and somewhat ancient railway stations, especially Waterloo. He went into ecstasies for a few moments, in Bloomsbury, in front of the building of the enigmatic Swedenborg Society, and recalled the extraordinary revelation that occurred to the Swedish philosopher one day as he stood on the second-floor balcony of that house: if he wasn't mistaken, the revelation was that, when a man dies, he doesn't realize he's died, since everything around him stays the same, for he is at home, his friends visit him, he walks the streets of his city; he doesn't think he's died, until he begins to notice that in the other world everything is as it is in this one, except it's slightly more spacious.

They were good moments he spent there in front of the Swedenborg Society, but in general he didn't like London; although that didn't stop him doing things all over the city. Patiently, Celia and his parents accompanied him around Chelsea as he whimsically tracked down the two houses where Beckett had lived as a young man in the 1930s. One was situated at 48 Paultons Square, a beautiful spot just off the King's Road. And the other at 34 Gertrude Street, where the writer rented a room from the Frost family and went out every day to the sessions of psychoanalysis his mother paid for from Dublin and which little by little created in him a mood favorable to hating that city, although not writers like Samuel Johnson, about whom he wanted to write a play. "You can't imagine how much I hate London," Beckett wrote to his friend Thomas McGreevy, a key person in his life because he was the one who put him in touch with James Joyce. For the young Beckett, that letter, in which he explained in detail how very much he hated London, was nothing more than the preamble to his decision, the next day, to pack his bag and return to Dublin, where the martyrdom of his difficult relationship with his mother awaited him.

There was a great photograph to commemorate 34 Gertrude Street. A big, suddenly youthful smile from Riba looking at the camera Celia was pointing at him. Glorious moment. He felt happy and almost proud of having been able to find the two lodgings of the young Beckett so easily.

"And without knowing a word of English!" he repeated happily, forgetting the none too minor detail that Celia, who spoke the language with ease, had figured it all out.

That photo of 34 Gertrude Street was one of the key mementos of the trip and also one of its few memorable events. Because, for the rest of the time, London put him in a very bad mood. Almost nothing he saw in that city seemed to amuse him. He discovered that he was still fascinated, and would be for a long time—much more than anywhere else—by New York and this wild sea of Ireland that he now had so close to home and on which the rain beat down tonight with relentless cruelty.

Now, as his hangover slowly, very slowly recedes, he reaffirms his old idea that anyone who has visited New York and this rough Irish Sea must look down on London with superiority and stupor. He ends up seeing it as Brendan Behan did that day when, comparing it with many other much better places, he described it as a wide flat pie of redbrick suburbs, with a currant in the middle for the West End.

He's turned into one of those Irishmen who amuse themselves with their constant and ingenious cutting remarks about the English. He guesses that he'll soon forget London, but never Dominique's brilliant installation, which he visited with his parents and Celia in the Tate Modern. It was an experience at the edge of reason, because his parents were so literal and seeing, with natural astonishment, the end of the world, they were left impressed and mute for a long time.

It was raining especially hard and cruelly outside the installation, while inside loudspeakers reproduced the sound of the rain artificially. And when they were about to leave that place of refuge for "survivors of the catastrophe," they rested for a while on the metal bunkbeds that accommodated, day and night, refugees from the flood of 2058, a year when undoubtedly all the people Riba loved, without exception, would be dead.

By that year, all his loved ones would be sleeping forever, they'd be sleeping in the infinite space of the unknown, that great space that could finally be represented by the rain lashing the windowpanes of the highest windows of the universe. No doubt, in 2058 all his loved ones would be like those high windows Phillip Larkin talked about: *the sun-comprehending glass, / And beyond it, the deep blue air, that shows / Nothing, and is nowhere, and is endless.*

High fantasy is a place where it's always raining, he took the opportunity to remember there in London, in the middle of that general atmosphere of great catastrophe and universal flood. All over the place, in Dominique's installation, were human replicas of Spider, numerous displays of walking ghosts and other men sleeping. His mother ordered a lime flower tea in the bar overlooking the river on the Tate's top floor, while his father looked permanently surprised.

"Do you realize what we've seen? We're right at the end of the world!" he kept repeating, sounding cheerful and contrite at the same time, while contemplating the great view of London under the spectacular and destructive rain.

Then with a great sense of involuntary humor, his mother—once she'd recovered with whatever tea they'd served her instead of lime flower—said to her husband with a sudden worried grimace:

"Stop laughing, Sam, and take notice, once and for all, of what's going on. For the past few weeks it's been raining constantly. It can't be true that it rains so much, in Barcelona, in London. I think it's in the Great Beyond that it's raining all the time."

And then, as if she'd reached the most important or maybe most obvious conclusion of her life, added:

"I suspect we're all dead."

A few days ago he finished reading James Knowlson's biography of Beckett. As soon as he got to the end he decided to reread *Murphy*, a book he'd delved into enthusiastically and with irrepressible astonishment when he was very young, as if he'd found the philosopher's stone. The book made so great an impression on him that he has never since been able to look at a rocking chair without thinking of poor, old unhinged Murphy. What fascinated him most about the book was the central story in which nothing seemed to happen, but in reality lots of things were going on, because in fact that story was full of brutal micro-events; in the same way, although we don't always notice, many things happen in our own apparently listless daily lives; lives that seem flat, but which suddenly appear to us loaded with tiny matters and also serious little discomforts.

Riba plays at rocking the chair in such a way that the moon rocks with it. It's a gesture of profound hopelessness. As if seeking to ingratiate himself with the moon, since he's not going to be forgiven by Celia now. The gesture is futile in any case, because the moon doesn't bat an eyelid. Then he begins thinking about writers of first novels, so-called novices, and he meditates on how seldom ambitious young novelists choose the material closest to hand as subjects for their first books; it's as though the most talented ones feel pushed to gain experience in the most arduous manner.

Only this would explain, Riba thinks, why the novice, that ghost he suspects is lying in wait for him, would notice someone like him, who isn't close at hand. Just a desire to make life difficult for himself. Because, how can a poor novice narrate from outside what he barely knows?

Riba has read enough in his lifetime to know that when we try to comprehend the mental life of another man we soon realize just how incomprehensible, changeable, and hazy the beings we share the world with are. It's as if solitude were an absolute and insurmountable condition of existence.

How arduous for a novice to talk about his tiny great events, or serious slight discomforts: all those matters that really only Riba himself would be able to explain and even qualify in great depth because, as is logical, only he truly knows them fully: the fact is only he knows them.

Only he—no one else—knows that on the one hand, it's true, there are those serious slight discomforts, with their monotonous sound, similar to rain, occupying the bitterest side of his days. And on the other, the tiny great events: his private promenade, for example, along the length of the bridge linking the almost excessive world of Joyce with Beckett's more laconic one, and which, in the end, is the main trajectory—as brilliant as it is depressing—of the great literature of recent decades: the one that goes from the richness of one Irishman to the deliberate poverty of the other; from Gutenberg to Google; from the existence of the sacred (Joyce) to the somber era of the disappearance of God (Beckett).

Depending on how you look at it, Riba thinks, his own daily life over the past few weeks is starting to reflect that story of splendor and decadence and sudden collapse and descent to the pier, opposite that of the splendor of a now unsurpassable literary period. It's as if his biography of the past few weeks were running parallel to the story of literature: one that saw the great years of the existence of God, and then his murder and death. It's as if literature had discovered, with Beckett, that after the divine Joyce's vantage point the only path left was a criminal one, that is, the death of the sacred, being left to live at ground level or in a rocking chair.

It's as if—just like in that Coldplay song—after having ruled the world and experienced great heights, all literature could do was sweep the streets it used to own.

How difficult and how complicated it is for the poor novice, he thinks. He doesn't envy young authors at all, having to take on this whole muddle. It's midnight and the rain continues to lash the windowpanes, and the moon carries on in its own way. His hangover is fading, but not that much. The worst thing is there are still blank spots in his memory of last night. And Celia, who might be able to help him, is sleeping, and has probably decided to leave him tomorrow.

There's only one thing that he's completely sure happened yesterday: part of the premonition of the Dublin dream came true when he, tragically, started drinking again; Celia ended up embracing him in the early hours of the morning, on the way out of McPherson's, the pub on the corner. They both fell and rolled on the ground, in the rain, moved and terrified at the same time at the misfortune that had unexpectedly befallen them. But what especially surprised him is that he recognized that same powerful emotion he'd felt in the hospital when he had that prophetic dream.

As soon as he remembers the final scene of yesterday's tragedy, he tries to get the rocking chair to remain stiller than anything around it, even for a moment. It's as if he wanted to stop time and go back to try to make amends and even attempt to prevent last night from happening. As he tries to stop everything, a deep silence gradually settles, and it even seems the light has grown dimmer and is now more like a color closely resembling lead. It's strange, because up to now he could hear the neighbors. The world is still for a fraction of a second. The shining glint of some scenes from the pub last night. Fright. Dismay. The more he remembers, the more the feeling of anguish grows and also the discovery of something impossible: he can't go back without falling prey to attrition, the idea of which has always horrified him. What does all this mean? This impossibility, this silence, this attrition, this pain, this stillness—which, in any case, have yet to come entirely into being—do they mean something? Outside, the night sky is still strangely orange. Riba could not feel any lower. How rich Joyce's prose was. Only the rocking chair lets him be higher than the floor. He suddenly remembers Beckett's *Endgame*: "Mean something? You and I, mean something! Ah that's a good one!"

So maybe what happened with Dr. Bruc in Barcelona before traveling to Dublin for the second time might not mean anything either? After informing him of the results of his tests, the doctor suggested he volunteer for a clinical trial investigating "paricalcitol's role in preventing cardiovascular fatalities" in patients with chronic renal failure like him.

"You might say," Riba interrupted her, "that you're actually asking me if I'd like to be your guinea pig."

She smiled, and instead of answering directly, she explained that paricalcitol was a metabolically active form of Vitamin D used in the prevention and treatment of secondary hyperparathyroidism, which was associated with chronic renal failure. It would mean collaborating in a study—led by a laboratory in Massachusetts—of the types of changes in gene expression when certain patients were treated with paricalcitol.

Riba insisted on asking again why she thought of him as a guinea pig and explained, as if confiding a secret to a friend, that for weeks he'd been feeling watched, though he didn't know by whom. It was, he told her, as if he'd actually become somebody's guinea pig, and that's why her medical proposal had suddenly set all his alarm bells ringing even louder. He couldn't explain it, but it seemed as if, overnight, people had started thinking of all sorts of experiments to do on him.

"You don't think people see you as a mouse?" the doctor said.

"A mouse?"

The doctor realized how sensitive he was, but still placed an information sheet in front of him and the contract—*Advised Consent for Associated Pharmacological-Genetic Research (DNA & RNA)*—so he could study it at home or on his trip to Dublin, in case he decided when he came back that he did want to volunteer to help with the advancement of science.

Now at midnight, in this house in Dublin, he looks again at the papers his doctor friend gave him in Barcelona. He re-reads them so carefully and anxiously that the "Information Sheet" ends up sending him into a tremendous metaphysical panic, perhaps because he connects it with that undeniable fact, which he sometimes forgets, but which is the heart of everything: his kidneys are failing, and although at the moment the situation is stable, cardiovascular problems could appear in days to come. In short: death is visible on the horizon, that horizon that begins and ends in his rocking chair.

But perhaps, Riba tells himself now, the biggest problem of all isn't so much being at death's door, or being dead without knowing it—as his mother sensed in London when she saw the rain wasn't going to stop—but the disturbing sensation of not having really been born yet.

"To be born, that's my idea now," Beckett's character Malone confessed. And further on: "I am being given, if I may venture the expression, birth into death."

The idea, now that he thinks of it, was also in Artaud: that sensation of a body *possessed* that struggles to rescue itself with difficulty.

But what if it was yesterday, just as he was on his way out of McPherson's, that he was born into death? In the prophetic dream

he had in the hospital when he was seriously ill, the feeling of being born into death was clear and seemed to be right at its heart
when he and Celia—who in turn seemed to be at the center of the
world—embraced beneath the rain, on their way out of a mysterious pub.

And yesterday, in real life, he again felt something similar. Within
the disgrace, there was an enigmatic emotion in that embrace scene.
An emotion that arose from birth into death or from feeling alive
for the first time in his life. Because it was a great moment despite
its brutality and tragedy. One moment, at last, at the center of the
world. As if the cities of Dublin and New York were united by a
single current, and this was none other than the very current of
life, circulating through an imaginary passage; there were various
stations or stops on this "journey" that had all been decorated with
replicas of the same statue that were even an homage to a gesture,
to a sort of secret leap, to an almost clandestine but existing movement, perfectly real and true; and that was the English leap.

He worries that the noise he's making in the kitchen will wake up
Celia, but he hears some chairs being dragged across the floor upstairs—where they always finish dinner very late. He realizes the
neighbors will wake her before he does. He decides not to have a
coffee and then begins a mute and autistic protest against the noisy
upstairs neighbors and pisses in the sink with a marvellous sensation of eternity.

Someone buzzes the intercom.

Late as it is, the sharp, shrill sound surprises him. He goes out
into the hall and timidly picks up the intercom phone, asking who
it is. Long pause. And all of a sudden, someone says:

"Malachy Moore *est mort.*"

He stands petrified. Moore and *mort* sound similar, although they
belong to two different languages. He ponders this trivial detail to
keep from being completely overwhelmed by fear.

Now he remembers. It's terrible and weighs on his soul. He spent
a long time yesterday in McPherson's talking about Malachy Moore.

"Who's there?" he asks over the intercom.

No one answers.

He looks down from the balcony, and just like last night, there's nobody in the street. Yesterday's great muddle began in exactly the same way. Someone rang the bell at the same time. He looked out and there was nobody there. History repeats itself.

Whoever has just said that Malachy Moore is dead might be the same person who yesterday, in Spanish and with a Catalan accent, called and explained that they were conducting an evening survey and wanted to ask him just one single question, and without giving him time to respond, said:

"We just want to know if you know why Marcel Duchamp came back from the sea."

But no, it doesn't seem to be the same person as yesterday. Perhaps it is just a coincidence that the two calls came twenty-four hours apart. This person tonight has spoken in French without the slightest trace of a Catalan accent, and it could just as easily be Verdier as Fournier, one of the brand-new friends he made last night in the bar. As for last night's call on the intercom, it had to have been perpetrated by an expert in *The Exception of My Parents*, his friend Ricardo's autobiographical novel. Because that question about Duchamp appears hidden within the pages of that book.

Whoever called yesterday can't be the same person as today, a moment ago. The man on the intercom last night was someone who read *The Exception of My Parents* and could only be that Catalan friend of Walter's they'd met two days earlier and to whom they'd given their address. Yesterday's caller couldn't have been anyone else, unless it were—something unlikely, surely—Walter himself with a Catalan accent. The strange thing was that whoever buzzed last night didn't come back later—if only to laugh at his cleverness—to reveal himself. Riba still doesn't know why this friend of Walter's, who went to the trouble of making that midnight joke, then vanished from the scene. And he understands even less why whoever just rang also now vanished. They do resemble each other in that respect.

He goes back to the intercom and demands again that whoever's down there identify himself.

Silence. Just like last night at midnight. Nothing but quiet, quiet under the infernal leaden light of the front hall that harbors two sad chairs and a bare lightbulb hanging from the ceiling, along with that suitcase and carry-on bag with which Celia threatens to leave tomorrow.

At midnight yesterday, when he didn't see anybody, he thought Walter's friend must have taken refuge in McPherson's. Absolutely everything arose from that misunderstanding. McPherson's is a pub run by a man from Marseille and a number of his regulars are French. He and Celia had sat out on the patio of this establishment a couple of times, always in the daytime. Yesterday he ended up there, believing that he'd find Walter's friend and would be able to ask him why he'd played that late-night joke.

Although he doesn't want to remember too precisely—he's afraid it'll upset him—he's gradually getting back his memory of what happened, and all at once he remembers how, at this very time, after the question about Duchamp and after having seen there was nobody down in the street, he was seized by a huge sense of anxiety and decided to go and see how Celia was doing and thus feel in some way supported by her company. He'd left her sleeping and didn't know if the intercom would have woken her, or whether her face would still be wreathed in the beatific expression she'd been wearing recently. He needed her to help him get over his bewilderment caused by the call about the sea and Marcel Duchamp. So he went into the bedroom and got quite a surprise. He remembers quite clearly now, it was a distressing moment. The incredibly harsh expression on Celia's sleeping face shocked him, so rigid and paralyzed and more like a lifeless soul than anything else. He was left literally terrified. She was sleeping, or she was dead. She looked dead, or maybe she was petrified. Although everything indicated that she badly needed to be reborn, he preferred to think that Celia was near a divine spirit, some god of hers. After all, he thought, religion is useless, but sleep is very religious, it will always be more religious than any religion, perhaps because when one is sleeping one is closer to God....

He had stayed there in the bedroom for a while, still hearing the echo of the question about Marcel Duchamp and wondering if the time hadn't arrived to overcome his fear and to head down—it was an old, private metaphor of his—the metaphysical avenue of the dead. It has always seemed, thought Riba, that, on that general avenue, one single deceased person isn't anything or anybody. Everything's relative and so it's easier to see that there's more than one crooked cross, more than one headstone surrounded by barren thorns in this world so big and so wide, where the rain falls ever slowly upon the universe of the dead....

Oh! He realized that, aside from a certain desire to be absurdly poetic, he wasn't controlling what was going through his mind very well, and stopped. The world big and wide, the universe of the dead ... As if a logical consequence of how complicated everything was, and also another more than likely consequence of last month's funeral in Dublin and his world ending in London and the enigmatic words coming through the intercom, Riba ended up thinking of the scene in John Huston's *The Dead* where the husband watches his wife on the stairway of a Dublin house, still, stiff but unexpectedly lovely and rejuvenated—lovely and youthful on account of the story she'd just remembered—paralyzed at the top of the stairs by the voice singing that sad Irish ballad, "The Lass of Aughrim," which always reminded her—giving her a sudden beauty—of a young man who died in the cold and rain of love for her.

And he couldn't help it. Last night, Riba associated that scene in *The Dead* with that young man from Cork who, two years before he'd met her, fell in love with Celia and then, after a number of diabolical misunderstandings, left Spain and returned to his own country, where soon afterward he killed himself by jumping off the furthest pier in the port of his home town.

Cork. Four letters to a fatal name. He always associated that city with a vase in their home in Barcelona. The vase always struck him as a nuisance, but he'd never gone so far as getting rid of it due to

Celia's strong opposition. Sometimes, when he was depressed, he found that he got much more depressed if he looked at old photographs, the cutlery, the paintings inherited from Celia's grandmother. And that vase. By God, that vase.

Riba had never been able to tolerate the sinister story of that suicidal young man. When occasionally it occurred to him to remind Celia of that poor boy from Cork, she always reacted by breaking into a smile, as if the memory made her feel young again and profoundly happy.

Yesterday, watching her sleep so rigidly but so beautifully, and unsure whether she was alive or petrified, he couldn't resist a depraved temptation, a vengeful urge, and imagined her in those days of her youth, closer to a prostitute on the jetty at the end of the world than to the serene Buddhist she was today. He imagined her that way and then said mentally to his sleeping wife, with that strange softness of imagined but unspoken words:

Celia, my love, you cannot suspect how slowly the snow is falling through the universe and upon all the living and the dead and upon that young imbecile from Cork.

That's what he said mentally, though she remained immersed in her indecipherable dreams, faintly illuminated by the light from the hall: her hair all messy, her mouth half open, breathing deeply. The rain lashed wildly against the windows. In the bathroom, one of the taps hadn't been turned off properly and was dripping, and Riba went to turn it off. The light grew a little dimmer and then began to tremble, as if the world were ending. Although the door to the apartment was closed, it seemed like all that remained was to wait for Duchamp to come back from the sea, come back to get rid of that blasted vase.

It would be best to get used to the idea that Malachy Moore has died. He'd rather think that than speculate on the idea that the Frenchmen he'd met yesterday, Verdier and Fournier, might have played a trick on him to get him to come to the pub again tonight. He doesn't really know why, but he thinks the voice that told him Malachy Moore was dead had meant it.

But as soon as he's given him up for dead, he notices that something, in a vague and indistinct tone of protest, has gently begun to deflate in the atmosphere. It's as if the space through which his shadow normally wanders were emptying itself, and as if with this absence, the previously chilly nape of his neck and his back had begun to heat up. In some part of this room, something is giving way at quite a pace. At such a pace that it already seems to be entirely gone. Someone has left. Maybe that's why now, for the first time in a long time, it seems there is no longer somebody there lying in wait. Not a single shadow, no trace of the specter of his author, or of the novice who uses him as a guinea pig, no God, no spirit of New York, no sign of the genius he always sought. He feels panic in the midst of this sudden stillness, so extraordinarily flat. And he remembers the flat instant that followed the moment Nietzsche announced that God had died, and then the whole world started living at ground level, miserably.

He could swear he's entered an ambiguous realm of the deceased, a region that dazzles him in such a way that he can't look straight at it, as with the sun, which no one can look at for very long. Although at heart, like the sun, this region is no more than a benign force, a source of life. One can be born into it, because one can be born into death. He will try. After all, yesterday that rebirth was possible. He will try to get his faded retired publisher's life back on track and improve it. But something has completely given way in the room. Someone has left. Or been erased. Someone, perhaps indispensable, is no longer here. Someone is laughing on his own somewhere else. And the rain lashes more and more wildly against the windowpanes and also through the empty and deep-blue air, and what is nowhere and is never-ending.

Since he has a tendency to interpret the events of his world each day with distortions typical of the reader he has been for so long, he now remembers the days of his youth when it was common to argue about the *death of the author* and he read everything relating to this thorny issue, which worried him more from one day to the next. Because if there was one thing he wanted to be in life it was a publisher and he was already taking the first steps to becoming one. And it seemed like very bad luck that just as he was preparing to find authors and publish them, the figure of the author should be questioned so strongly that people were even saying that, if it hadn't already, it was going to disappear. They could have waited a little longer, young Riba lamented every day back then. Some friends tried to encourage him, telling him not to worry, because it was only a dubious trend of the French and American deconstructionists.

"Is it true the author has died?" he asked Juan Marsé, who he occasionally bumped into in his neighborhood. That morning Marsé was accompanied by a tall, dark-haired girl with an unforgettable apple-shaped face, and the poet Jaime Gil de Biedma.

Marsé threw young Riba a frightful look, which he still hasn't forgotten.

"How funny, that's like asking if it's true we have to die," he heard the girl say.

He remembers that he really fancied that woman—facially so similar to Bev Dew, now that he thinks of it—and he also remembers that he even fell suddenly in love with her, the very same as what happened not long ago with Bev. He was especially enamored of her face. Her fresh, fragrant apple face. And also because hanging over her furrowed brow, an impalpable shadow on her face, was an expression that struck him as a direct invitation to love.

"The author is the ghost of the editor," said Gil de Biedma, half smiling.

And Marsé and the tall girl with the apple face laughed a lot, probably at a private joke he couldn't share.

Certain scenes from last night come back to him in violent flashes. He remembers when, having already had quite a bit to drink, he was talking to those two Frenchmen at the bar in McPherson's and at a certain point, after they'd talked of the beauty of the Irish Sea and about the Spanish victory in the European Championship and asked Riba something about the decor of Irish houses, the conversation slid, though he can't remember why, toward Samuel Beckett.

"I know someone who's lined his house with Beckett," said Verdier.

A house lined with Beckett. He'd never heard of such a thing. In its day—in the days when the publishing house received so many manuscripts—it would have been a good title for one of those novels certain weak and indecisive authors used to submit with titles even feebler and more faltering than they were.

The two Frenchmen, Verdier and Fournier, knew so much about Beckett's appalling squandered years in Dublin that, between one shot of gin and another, at some point he started calling them Mercier and Camier, the names of two Beckett characters.

Verdier, a great Guinness drinker, was explaining precisely why the key to Beckett's personality lay in his Dublin years. Sitting in his rocking chair, Riba could not now recall many of the things Verdier told him, but he did remember perfectly hearing about the extremely dangerous game the writer used to play from an early age, when he'd climb to the top of one of the pine trees surrounding the house where he was born and jump down, grabbing a branch just before he crashed to the ground.

Riba remembers perfectly Verdier telling him this, probably because it impressed him more than the other things and perhaps also because it reminded him of what he tended to do with the rocking chair when he rocked it as far back as possible and then dropped back so he could feel himself almost falling, closely linked to the calamitous pretension of the world that he now associated with the death of the author and of everything.

Fournier was also very talkative, and at a certain moment, emphasized again and again that Beckett has always been an example of a writer who risks everything, has no roots, and shouldn't have any: no family, no brothers or sisters. He comes from the void, said Fournier. Several times he said that he came from the void. The ravages of alcohol. Riba suddenly remembers the exact moment when he asked Verdier and Fournier if they'd ever seen an individual in Dublin who resembled the young Beckett.

He remembers telling them that, since he'd seen that guy twice over the course of Bloomsday in two different places; it was very likely that they might have bumped into that young Beckett lookalike on more than one occasion.

Verdier and Fournier, almost in unison, told him they knew someone like that. In Dublin this Beckett double was relatively famous, said Fournier. The young double was a great walker, studying at Trinity College, but he was seen all over the city, in the most unexpected places. Many people knew him, yes. He stood out precisely because of his resemblance to the young Beckett; they didn't think there was anything mysterious about it and believed he was the young Beckett himself, simple as that. Although many in Dublin knew him as Godot. But that wasn't his name, of course. His name was Malachy Moore.

"But it's Beckett himself, I'm telling you," concluded Verdier.

Still somewhat scared, he is gradually completing the forced reconstruction of what might have happened yesterday. As the hangover subsides, new fragments of his night out begin to appear and now, crystal-clear, the terrifying memory arrives of the instant when last night at home, after the question about Duchamp over the intercom, he decided to make some enquiries outside, far from his labyrinthine room and that crushing solitude. And he remembers the mad moment when, after leaving a note for Celia, he decided to make a move and called the elevator and a few seconds later stepped out into the street. The rain hit him in the face and he suddenly felt like he was back in the harsh solitude of the night and the elements. He was walking very slowly so his flimsy umbrella wouldn't take off, and take him off with it, when all of a sudden he saw the great danger that was just around the corner, beside the only unlit streetlamp.

He feared it, but maybe he didn't imagine it could be such an obvious danger, right out of an Irish film, complete with rain and even a bit of fog. He felt, for a moment, that if he managed fully to recover the daring bravery of his youth, he would regain some of the spirit of those times when he wasn't afraid of anything. He plucked up courage as he analyzed the situation. No matter how much he wanted to, it wasn't advisable for him to turn back now, because he'd already been seen. Faced with such a fate, all he could do was hope to emerge unscathed. Obviously, terribly, those two potential villains were there, those two scary guys on the corner acting as if they were there because it was the best place they could be on a rainy night like this. One was skinny and blond, dressed in a really outdated punk style, with a big, very crooked nose. The other was fat and black with a big paunch and messy dreadlocks hanging down over his shoulders.

The blond with the crooked nose was especially frightening. Neither of the two looked at him although there was nobody else in the street. Riba didn't know what to do. He thought the best thing would be to just keep walking as if nothing was wrong, speed up a little as he passed them until he reached the entrance to the pub, which was only fifty meters beyond the danger: walk right past them without even looking their way, as if they didn't make him at all suspicious or it hadn't occurred to him that they might have been the ones who'd left the message on the intercom, or anything like that.

Although, thinking it through, it was more than obvious that those two guys were not the kind of people to mention Marcel Duchamp on an intercom. The closer he got to the corner, the more Riba felt panic growing inside him, but he kept walking, it was clear he had no choice. He turned up the collar of his raincoat and walked on. And the biggest problem arose from his own mind when, as he got closer to the two undesirables, he began to feel more insecure and old than ever. He was shattered, he noticed his heart was beating very rapidly and he felt a very powerful fear spread throughout his body. He had to admit he was really old, quite grossly old. Never had the words to the poem "Dublinesque" suited him so well as in that moment, because, as if by magic, his brief nocturnal stroll to the pub was turning him into the old whore in the mackintosh at the end of the world, that is, into the unexpected reincarnation of the last spark of wretched literature and at the same time into a washed-up old man freezing to death walking down stucco sidestreets, where the light is pewter and down which he was walking himself, the last literary publisher in history, turned into his very own funeral.

Actually, thinking about it now, even that sordid Dublin street was marvelous if he compared it to the dull reality of Spain and its terrible landscape. As he advanced toward the two probable thugs, he felt nostalgic for the times when the night held no secrets for him and he sailed through the most difficult situations practically unnoticed. And all of a sudden, as if humor could save him from everything, he began to hear, as an unexpected echo, Milly Bloom's song, and it was as if the ghost of poor Milly was trying to come to his aid. Then he started remembering other situations when, as now, he'd consigned the danger to the background by thinking of things other than those that should really be worrying him. For example, as a boy, he'd been on the verge of drowning, because the sea at Tossa de Mar had carried him out beyond safety, and not knowing how to swim, he'd clung onto an air mattress; but instead of thinking he was going to die, he'd started conjuring up a scene from *El Jabato*, his favorite comic, in which the hero goes through a similar situation and at the last minute is rescued by Noodle the skinny poet, another character in the comic strip.

And when he came up to the likely thugs, he was so distracted and concentrating so hard on recalling the skinny poet Noodle—whose name struck him at that moment as an allusion to the fragility of human life—that he passed the two guys without even noticing he'd left them quite easily behind. They didn't seem to see him either, or maybe they just saw a specter pass, or a dead man, and didn't want to bother him. The fact is that he suddenly realized he hadn't even noticed them as he walked right past, and now, he had to get used to the idea that he had completely left them behind. Looking back might be fatal, so he kept going, now thinking of his youth and the great many dull nights he'd wasted holding a glass of whiskey, leaning forward to listen to other people's nonsense. He had so much free time back then that he squandered completely, stupidly away to nothing.

Seconds later, like a ghost lost in the night, he reached the door of McPherson's. There weren't too many people inside. No sign of Walter's Catalan friend. He realized immediately it had been a mistake to look for him there. But now it was too late. The few customers in the bar were watching him, waiting to see if he'd come in or not, so he took two more steps and walked inside. He immediately felt that he'd sunk down into the deepest recess of a buried memory. Whatever the case, the best thing he could do was to carry on as if nothing was wrong. "Once you're in, you're in it up to your chin," as Céline used to say.

At the bar he could see only a middle-aged man at one end of it, scratching his crotch with a meditative air, and beside him a very skinny guy with a classic boozer's look, cloth cap, and hobnailed boots, staring furiously at the spark of golden light at the bottom of his glass of whiskey. There were also a few amorous couples on the velvet benches, red and black benches that smelled of railway carriages. He didn't yet know that the two guys at the bar were French and that he'd end up christening them Mercier and Camier.

He remembered he walked into McPherson's feigning self-confidence and that, even before wondering what he'd have to drink, he leaned on the bar and decided that he'd concentrate and try to get his brain to start the process of conceiving himself the same way Murphy did his own self. He then imagined his brain as a big empty sphere, hermetically sealed against the exterior universe, which, as Beckett would say, was not an impoverishment, since it didn't exclude anything not contained within it, because nothing ever existed or ever would exist in the exterior universe that wasn't already present as virtuality or as actuality—as virtuality elevating itself to actuality, or actuality falling into virtuality—in the interior universe of his mind.

After this considerable and futile mental effort, he felt almost devastated. He thought of the reproduction of "Stairway," the small Hopper painting in the apartment that had been obsessing him since the first day. The painting itself had told him not to go out. It was a painting that invited one not to go outside. Even so, he had decided to open the door and brave the rain and the street. Hopper, having painted a door open to the outside, invited him, quite clearly if paradoxically, to stay indoors, not to budge an inch. But now it was too late. He had defied the painting and left.

"You, sir, are the essence of vulgarity," he remembered a rejected author had once told him in his own office. Why had this phrase remained so deeply ingrained in his mind and why did it reappear at the trickiest moments, when he needed more self-confidence than usual?

He timidly asked for a gin with water. Marcel, the bartender from Marseille, said something to him in French to show him he remembered him from when he'd been there with Celia on the patio. Then he served him the gin. Riba drank it down in one gulp. Two years' thirst, he thought. And from then on he didn't think anything clearly anymore. The alcohol went straight to his head. One goes away suddenly, he thought. And in a flash returns. With the intention of changing. Head hung. Head in hands. The head, headquarters of everything. Motionless in the full moon the last publisher.

It's difficult to know—for Riba himself—what exactly it was he'd just thought. Eventually, you have to pay for two years of abstinence. Anyway, he understood more or less the way things were going. Motionless, in the full moon, the last publisher. Wasn't he the last publisher? He had been spending his nights in the rocking chair facing the moon, with the Gutenberg galaxy buried, and believing that all the stars were deceased souls, old relatives, acquaintances, charlatans. But no, this wasn't the right interpretation. It was just the ruthless effects of alcohol. A drinker's thoughts. Head hung. Head in hands.

"Another gin," said Riba.

Was he the last publisher? That would be ideal, but no. In the paper every day he saw photos of all those new, young independent publishers. Most of them looked to him like insufferable, uneducated beings. He never thought he'd be replaced by such idiots and it was hard for him to accept, a long and painful process. Four idiots had dreamed of replacing him and had finally achieved it. And he himself had ended up making way for them, had helped them prosper by speaking well of them. It served him right for having been such a bastard, for being far too gracious and generous with the falsely discreet young lions of publishing.

One of those new publishers, for example, spent all his time proclaiming that we're living in a transitional period toward a new culture and, wishing to prosper without effort, made claims for quite obtuse prose writers he claimed had found a goldmine in the "new language of the digital revolution," so useful for covering up their lack of imagination and talent. Another one tried to publish foreign authors with the same taste and style as poor Riba and in fact succeeded only in imitating what he'd already done much more competently. Another wanted to copy the most spectacular heads of the Spanish publishing world; he dreamt of being a media star and his authors were mere pawns of his glory. In any case, none of the three seemed shrewd enough to endure the thirty years he'd endured. He'd heard they were planning some sort of homage to him in September and that the digital revolutionary, the imitator, and the aspiring superstar were at the head of it. But Riba thought only of fleeing from them. Behind that move were hidden motives, very little genuine admiration.

He gulped down a second gin, which was followed by others. After a short time, he felt like he was Spider, or rather, an arrow in a cobwebbed cellar of steel-gray light. There were so few people in the place that there was no point in looking for Walter's Catalan friend among the clientele. In any case, no one there could be suspected of having called him on the intercom. And it began to seem obvious that someone had managed to get him mixed up in a little mystery, which he might be able to clear up the next day, or maybe he never would. It was, in any case, futile to look for the solution to the enigma between the four walls of that place. And he had made a huge mistake by going out at night. His gaze fell again on the two men in Irish caps he'd seen on his way in and who were sitting quite close to him at the bar. He thought he heard them speaking French and timidly approached them. Just then, one of them said:

"*Souvent, j'ai supposé que tout …*"

He stopped as he saw Riba approach and the phrase hung half-finished in the air. He supposed that everything what? That phrase turned into another mystery, probably forever now.

When minutes later, Riba nobly tackled his fifth gin, he was totally absorbed in a long chat with the Frenchmen. For a while he talked about cocktails he'd drunk in days gone by in bars all around the world and of sapphire swimming pools and white-jacketed waiters who served cold gin at certain clubs in Key West. Until in the mirror over the bar he began to see multi-colored rows of bottles of alcoholic beverages, as if he were on a carousel. And suddenly, with the first whiskey—he'd decided to abandon the gin in a flash—he asked the two Frenchmen a question about the decor of Irish houses, and without really knowing how, ended up causing Samuel Beckett to appear in the conversation.

"I know someone who has his house lined with Beckett," said Verdier.

"Lined?" said Riba, surprised.

Although he asked him to explain this, Verdier refused to do so point blank.

A little while after the third whiskey, Riba interrupted Verdier somewhat nervously, just when Verdier was at the most critical stage of his predictions for Saturday's races. Verdier looked stunned, as if he could barely understand why he'd been interrupted in such a way. Taking advantage of the confusion, Riba asked—and it seemed like he was asking the entire neighborhood—if they'd ever seen a guy in Dublin who looked a lot like the writer Beckett when he was young.

That was when, almost in unison, Verdier and Fournier told him that they knew someone just like that. In Dublin that double of

Beckett's was relatively famous, said Fournier. And the conversation entered a more animated phase, and at one point, Verdier even had a lovely memory of Forty Foot, a Beckettian location found in Sandycove, right in front of the Martello tower, which in fact appears in *Ulysses*. It's the spot with steps carved into the breakwater from which, since time immemorial, Dubliners enjoy diving in all the seasons of the year. That's where Beckett's father taught his sons, Sam and Frank, to swim, by throwing them in, with tough cruelty. Both stayed afloat and became fiercely fond of swimming. In fact, whenever he returned to Ireland, Beckett always went to Forty Foot, although the place he swam in more frequently, his favorite spot among all those of his native land, was a marvellous inlet under the hill of Howth.

"A truly Beckettian place. Windy, radical, drastic, deserted," said Verdier.

"Abode of gulls and coarse sailors, an end of the world scenario," added Fournier.

When they were at their most animated, Celia entered the pub like a gale-force wind, shouting at Riba with a thunderous rage that seemed endless. For a while, Celia seemed like a bottomless pit of insults and wailing.

"This is the end," she said when she managed to calm down a little, "you've committed the mistake of your life. The mistake of your life, you stupid man."

While Verdier and Fournier instinctively withdrew to the part of the pub farthest away from the bar, Riba suddenly discovered it was again possible for him to experience an intense moment at the center of the world: a moment that, in spite of having already been foreseen in the prophetic dream, arrived now with the same volcanic force and energy he had already felt in the apocalyptic vision that, at the time, served as a warning that one day in Dublin he might find himself on the edge of a strange happiness.

It wasn't exactly the ideal scenario; Celia wouldn't stop shouting and the situation was embarrassing. But he guessed, allowing himself to be guided by the model of the dream he'd had two years before in the hospital, that Celia would soon become more affectionate. And what he guessed turned out to be true. When she tired of shouting, she hugged him. And they went on to experience a moment at the center of the world. There was a reason that moving embrace was in the premonitory Dublin dream. They hugged each other so hard that, as they left the pub, they staggered and lost their balance, and just as the dream had predicted, they fell to the ground, where they remained in each other's arms, as if they were a single body. It was an embrace at the center of the world. A horrible hug, but also spectacular, emotional, serious, sad, and ridiculous. It was an essential embrace, right out of—never truer—a dream. The two of them sat there afterward on the curb on the south side of that north Dublin street. Tears for a disconsolate situation.

"My God! Why have you started drinking again?" said Celia.

A strange moment, as if there were a hidden sign bearing some message in their pathetic crying and the surprising fact that Celia's question was identical to the one in the dream.

Then, a partly logical reaction, he sat waiting for Celia to continue acting with great fidelity to the scene in the prophetic dream and to say:

"Tomorrow we could go to Cork."

But Celia didn't go so far as to say that. In contrast, the word "Cork," the great absentee, strolled onto the stage, but as if completely suspended in the air, as if it were floating there in order to reappear perhaps later on, in an even more terrifying situation. In the shape of that vase at home in Barcelona, for example.

Riba seemed to understand fully at that moment that the fundamental essence of that strange dream he'd had in the hospital two years ago was simply regaining the awareness and the joy of being alive.

Celia did not say they could go to Cork the next day, but that didn't make the moment any less strange, unique, any less a moment at the center of the world. Because he suddenly felt that he was linked to his wife beyond everything, beyond life, and beyond death. And that feeling was so serious in its most profound truth, it was so intense and so intimate, that he could only relate it to a possible second birth.

She, however, didn't really share these feelings, was merely indignant about his ill-fated fall off the wagon. Even so, in the scene of the mortal embrace there was also emotion on Celia's part and he saw that she too—although not to the same extent as he did—she appreciated the unexpected intensity of this unique moment at the center of the world.

"When the dead cry it's a sign that they're beginning to get better and to recover the awareness of being alive," he said.

"When the dead cry it's because they've drunk themselves to death on whiskey," answered Celia, perhaps more realistically.

He took a while to respond.

"What a shame," he said, "that we die, and get old, and everything good goes galloping away from us."

"That we get old and die," she corrected him.

And so the spell of the moment was gradually broken.

But the moment had occurred. It was, in fact, an instant at the center of the world. Although there was nothing at all central about the moment that followed, the one in which she gave him a terrible look and their lives returned to an ordinary state. Now she wouldn't stop looking at him, with hatred once again. But mostly with contempt.

And what did he do? Was he able to look at her with contempt? Was he able to tell her she was a simpleton because she'd become a Buddhist? No, he couldn't, and didn't dare. He was still under the effects, the echoes of the great emotion he'd experienced. He heard the deep murmur of the Irish Sea and some words that told him it would always be better to be held in contempt by everyone than to be held on high. Because if one settled into the worst position, the lowest, and most forgotten by fortune, one could always still hope and not live in fear. Now he understood why he'd had to situate himself at ground level to manage to have some sense of survival. It didn't matter that he'd grown old and been ruined and was at the end of everything because, after all, this drama had been useful in helping him understand why—within the so well-known incompetence of man in general and the no less famous incompetence of his time on this earth—there still existed a few privileged moments that one must be able to capture. And that had been one of them. And what's more, he'd already experienced it in a dream of almost incomparable emotion, two years ago in the hospital. That was one of those precious moments he'd surely been fighting for, unknowingly, over the past few months.

Hugging Celia, he imagined right then and there, for a few moments, and very much in spite of their uncomfortable position on the ground, that just like other times he was wandering the streets of the world alone, and all at once found himself at the end of a pier swept by a storm, and there everything fell back into place: years of doubt, searching, questions, and failures suddenly made sense, and the vision of what was best for him asserted itself like a great fact; it was clear he didn't have to do anything, except go back to his rocking chair, and begin there a discreet existence, worstward ho.

"The lamentable change is from the best." He remembered, then and there, Edgar, the Earl of Gloucester's son in *King Lear*, saying, that it always happens to us when we're settled into the best. "The worst returns to laughter. Welcome, then, thou insubstantial air that I embrace! The wretch that thou hast blown unto the worst owes nothing to thy blasts."

Now he is in the worst way, but something's not working because the worst is not returning him to laughter. He's paid a high price for his nocturnal epiphany on the final pier and nevertheless nothing is as he expected it to be. Without realizing, he has settled into the worst of the worst, a lower stratum than anticipated. His hangover is not abating. And the small Hopper painting will not look any different for love nor money.

With horror he's beginning to see the first consequences of his mistake. To begin with, he's clearly sensing that both God and the genius he always sought have died. To put it another way, without having given his consent, he sees himself now settled in a deplorable pigsty within a repugnant world.

They are all gone, as Henry Vaughan said. "They are all gone into the world of light," is how the first line of that seventeenth-century English poem actually reads. But from the pigsty he's holed up in now, worstward ho, that illuminated kingdom is not exactly visible. And this is undoubtedly one of the great disadvantages of the hovel the apartment has finally turned into. So Henry Vaughan's line is reduced to a foul and miserable: "They are all gone." End of story.

The nostalgia for the lost or never found genius returns. There was a time, while devoting himself to searching one out, that he took it for granted that one obvious sign of the presence of that genius in a piece of writing, or in an action written in life, would be the ability to choose themes far removed from one's own circumstances. Until not long ago, Riba had always imagined that genius busying himself with his daily life as a retired publisher, a life that would be precisely quite far removed from the life of that novice. Until not a moment ago, he had the impression that for a novel to have genius, it was essential that throughout, a superior spirit, more intuitive and more intimately aware than the characters themselves, should be placing the whole of the story under the gaze of future readers; this, without participating in its passions, motivated only by the agreeable excitement produced by the energetic approval of one's spirit to expose what one has been so attentively contemplating.

Whether or not it's a coincidence, the fact is, since he's given up Malachy Moore for dead, he doesn't sense that the person who's been lying in wait for him so fervently is still there, the one who has been observing him with maniacal, perhaps professional interest. Nostalgia for the genius. Or for the absentee. Nostalgia even for the novice. The truth is that, more or less as Henry Vaughan was saying, they are all gone. They have all vanished, and perhaps for a long time, maybe forever. He remembers the youngsters who made fun of Cavalcanti because he never wanted to go on a bender with them. "You refuse to be of our company. But when you've proved there is no God, then what will you do?"

The rain falls, as if trying to flood the entire earth at last, including this house in north Dublin, this almost tragic house with a rocking chair and a big window and a painting of a stairway, in front of the Irish Sea, this house so well appointed for going worstward ho, and if I may be allowed to say so—forgive the interruption, I do need to distance myself somewhat, but if I don't say it I'll burst out laughing—so completely lined with Beckett.

What will he do now that he's discovered that neither God nor the brilliant author exist and that, furthermore, no one looks at him anymore, and on top of that, there is nothing but misery in his ground-level Beckettian world. As he listens to the rain falling, he again senses, realizing that not only has something given way in the room, but also someone has now literally gone. There is no longer a shadow, not a trace of the specter of his author, or of the novice, or of God, or of the New York *duende*, or of the genius he always sought. It's only intuition, but it seems clear that, ever since he's felt settled into the worst of the worst, he's been heading toward something even lower. No one's lying in wait for him any longer, no one's watching him, there isn't even anyone hidden or invisible behind the deep blue interminable air. No one's out there. He imagines slipping a smooth watch into his trouser pocket and starting down the stairs of a remote presbytery. But soon he wonders why he is making such an effort to imagine so much if no one, absolutely no one, sees him. Desolation, solitude, misery at the ground level. Settled into the worst of the worst, the world now only resembles a tiny mound of shit in the most rotten, least pure, least fragrant space. Nostalgia for perfumed faces, for apple faces. Things have gotten so bad; perhaps it would be best if Malachy Moore hadn't died and continued to be a presence—a shadow if you will—that at heart, even if only a shadow, at least he was a presence with some sort of encouraging force.

He knows Malachy Moore was a great walker and that many called him Godot. That he'd been seen all over Dublin, in the most unexpected places. That he had Dracula's great ability of turning himself into fog. He doesn't know much else, but doesn't think he's so hard to imagine: Malachy Moore grew in an irregular way, especially his bone structure. Everyone was immediately struck by his eyes. Although he was short-sighted, his eyes were sharp and expressive, and gleamed with the profound light of intelligence behind the round lenses of his glasses. His hands were cold and lifeless and he never gave a firm handshake. When he roamed the streets, his legs resembled a stiff pair of compasses. He was an absolutely brilliant author, even though he'd never even written anything. He was the author Riba would have liked to discover. He seemed taller than he actually was. And if one caught a glimpse of him up close—before, following his most notorious custom, he disappeared into the fog—one would see straight away that he was not such a tall person, although his stature was above average. The impression of height came from his thin build, his mackintosh all buttoned up, and his tight trousers. Something in his appearance, with the fundamental contribution of his head, reminded one of some highland eagle—watchful, restless—soaring over valleys. A bird to keep an eye on.

Although he's stuck in his rocking chair, he keeps hearing the gradual and almost irresistible call of his computer and after a while, knowing that Google sometimes works just like a police file, he gives in to temptation and goes and sits in front of the screen, like a perfect *hikikomori*, trying to discover in the entries on Malachy Moore, the young man in the mackintosh he saw in Glasnevin who made him think he might be looking at his author.

He looks at the entries, but only finds information on baseball or soccer players of that name, none of whom could ever be the genius in the raincoat he thought he saw a few weeks ago. He clicks on *Images* to see if by chance anyone pops up resembling a young Beckett, but there's nothing of the sort, although there is a photo of three gentlemen, the caption of which has nothing at all to do with anyone called Malachy Moore: *Sean McBride, Minister of External Affairs Irish Republic, Bernard Deeny, and Malachy McGrady at the 1950 Aeridheacht.*

In order to carry on doing something before his two sleeping pills kick in, he checks the word Malachy, without the Moore, and there he finds information about an honorable Irishman, St. Malachy, a character completely unknown to him, but whom he has the impression he's heard spoken of a thousand times. He reads about this St. Malachy of Armagh of Ireland, who was born Maelmhaedhoc O'Morgair in the year 1094 and was a Catholic archbishop, who is remembered ten centuries later for the two prophecies supposedly revealed to him at the end of a pilgrimage to Rome.

St. Malachy's prophecies take Riba to Benedictus, the mysterious current Pope. And looking up the latest news on him, he discovers that Benedictus alias Ratzinger is a pope who spends most of his time in his room, reading and writing and preparing encyclicals. He travels much less than his energetic predecessor. As they used to say John Paul's apartment looked like a Polish tabernacle, because there were always people coming in and out, they say the papal apartment of Benedictus/Ratzinger resembles a vault, that it's reminiscent of the room in which the poet Hölderlin shut himself up for forty years. Why that room specifically? He tries to find out, unsuccessfully, to whom it would have occurred to link Ratzinger with the sublime Hölderlin. And he ends up thinking of Hölderlin's room in Tübingen, that room lent to him by the carpenter Zimmer and in which the poet lived for forty years. He thinks of *The Invention of Solitude* by Paul Auster, where it's said that Hölderlin's madness was faked and that the poet retired from the world in response to the ridiculous political attitude that racked Germany after the French Revolution. According to this, Hölderlin's most deranged texts had been written in a secret, revolutionary code, and furthermore, with the private joy of a confined man.

"Confining oneself to a room…" he remembers Paul Auster wrote.

He thinks how someone who could observe him from outside would see him. Someone like Malachy Moore, for example, who has now died. No one was ever able to prove that the dead can't see us.… A great clap of thunder … Again, he feels entirely awake. A shame, now that he was starting to enter into a restorative dream, a dream that would take place entirely on Hopper's stairway.

Mixed with fear, his yawns are imaginative curves taken by a slow, imaginary racing car that sometimes speeds up suddenly. On one of these curves, at the wheel of this strange car, he's just discovered that his personality has things in common with that of Simon of the Desert, that anchorite who spent his life on top of a pillar in a Buñuel film. Simon stood in penance on top of the eight-meter-high pillar, while he has been doing the same, for a while now, with a more modern touch: sitting in front of a computer and with the feeling that the more time he spends in front of the screen, the more the computer, in a very Kafkaesque way, is imprinting itself on his body.

He suddenly realizes—no one is safe from the racing car's whims—that a crippled dwarf and his goats are surrounding him. The devil appears to him dressed as a woman and tries to tempt him. Suddenly the feminine demon, as if in an imitation of what happened to Simon of the Desert, takes him on a trip—swifter than swift—to a cabaret in New York, and he's glad to have arrived in that city so quickly, and what's more, to have been unexpectedly liberated from the Gutenberg galaxy and the digital galaxy, both at once. It's as if he'd approached the world beyond them, which can be nothing but the final cataclysm. After all, as John Cheever said: "We are never in our own times, we're always somewhere else."

In the cabaret, the voice of Frank Sinatra rings out at a thousand revolutions per minute, a song with lyrics that, depending on how you look at it, are terrible: "The best is yet to come."

Everyone in the cabaret has insomnia. Outside, it's pouring. Although New York is the most spectacular place he's ever seen in his life, he'd rather be in Dublin. New York resembles a holiday more than anything and Dublin is more like a working day. He remembers those lines of Gil de Biedma's that marked his youth: "*After all, we don't know | if things are not better this way, | limited on purpose.... Maybe, | maybe working days are right.*"

"Go on, drink. It's the end of the world."

Black dancers attempt impossible dances.

New York's very grand, but maybe, maybe it's true that working days are right. And Dublin. Maybe Dublin is right too.

He's always admired writers who each day begin a voyage into the unknown and yet who are sitting in a room the whole time. He goes back to thinking about rooms for recluses. He thinks of the philosopher Pascal, for starters, maybe because he was the first one Auster quoted in that chapter of *The Invention of Solitude* about rooms—square, rectangular, or circular—in which some took refuge. Pascal was the one who came up with that memorable idea that all our misfortunes stem from the fact that we are unable to stay quietly in our own room. What happened to Riba yesterday in McPherson's is living proof of this, a clear demonstration that a rocking chair is preferable to the elements and the rain.

Auster mentioned many other rooms. The one in Amherst, for example, in which Emily Dickinson wrote her entire oeuvre. Van Gogh's in Arles. Robinson Crusoe's desert island. Vermeer's rooms with natural light ...

Actually where Auster says Vermeer, he could just as well have said Hammershøi, that Danish painter of the obsessive portraits of deserted rooms. Or Xavier de Maistre, that man who traveled *around his room*. Or Virginia Woolf, with her demand for a room of her own. Or the *hikikomoris* in Japan who shut themselves up in their rooms in their parents' houses for prolonged periods of time. Or Murphy, that character who didn't move from the rocking chair in his room in London ... The sleeping pills seem to be taking effect again, and as he dozes, he feels he is getting into the skin of Malachy Moore when he knew how to slip away into the fog, and he is soon seeing all sorts of things in the deepest darkness.... But has Malachy Moore died? Google doesn't know anything. It's futile to search any further in Google.... He wants to believe it was a joke played on him by Verdier and Fournier, who took a shine to him last night. He can imagine the scene. Verdier saying: "Let's go tell the whiskey king that his Malachy Moore was murdered at midnight...." He imagines things like that, until finally he falls asleep. He dreams that Google knows nothing.

He never thought he'd attend another funeral at Glasnevin Cemetery, and much less so soon. An altar boy, carrying a brass bucket of something no one can guess, is coming out of a door. The priest, in a white tunic, has come out behind him adjusting his stole with one hand and balancing a little book in the other against his toad's belly. They both stop next to Malachy Moore's coffin.

If I believed I was being pursued by an author, thinks Riba, it's now entirely possible that he's right there, four meters away from me, on that catafalque. And a moment later he wonders if he'd be able to admit to anyone that he is thinking such a thing. Would they take him for a lunatic? Surely it would be useless to explain that he's not crazy, and that all that happens is that sometimes he senses or picks up too much, he detects realities no one else perceives. But it would probably be useless to explain all this, much less to say that his wife has left him and that's why he's so deranged. It's the penultimate Tuesday in July and it's only just stopped raining a couple of hours ago. It's strange. So many days—months, even—with so much rain. Now even the disappearance of the clouds seems odd, such calm weather.

Yesterday, just as he feared, Celia left him. It didn't matter that he was already awake when she woke up, because he failed to prevent her leaving. He tried everything and it was impossible to stop her.

"You can't go, Celia."

"I'm not staying."

"Where will you go?"

"My people are waiting for me."

"I'm sorry for being such an idiot. And anyway, who are your people?"

"You still reek of alcohol. But that's not the only problem."

"What is the problem?"

"You don't love me."

"I do love you, Celia."

"No. You hate me. You don't see the horrible things you do or how you look at me. And that's not the only problem either. You're a disgusting drunk. You never leave that rocking chair. You live in a pigsty. You always throw your dirty clothes on the floor and I have to pick them up after you. Who do you think I am?"

A long list of complaints followed in which, among other things, Celia accused him of endless stupid behavior and of encouraging cobwebs to grow in his brain and of not having accepted getting old and taking the loss of his publishing house and the power it used to give him so badly. And finally she again accused him of having fallen off the wagon just because he didn't know what to do with his life anymore.

"You live without a god and your life lacks meaning. You've turned into a poor little man," she sentenced finally.

At that moment, Riba couldn't help but remember the previous day when, as soon as he gave Malachy Moore up for dead, something had given way swiftly in his room and he had settled into the worst of the worst. Now he was still in this place, the lowest of all. He was only saved by inhabiting the same paradox that united so many poor men like him: that sensation of being trapped in a place that only makes sense if it were actually possible to leave.

From Celia's point of view, the whole conflict didn't originate from her at all, nor was it caused indirectly by her change of religion, because she saw this change as completely normal, not at all problematic. The conflict had to come from somewhere else, surely from the meaningless life he was leading and also as the most direct consequence of this: his lamentable tendency recently toward extreme melancholy. Of course the life they'd lived before wasn't exactly ideal either, despite the fact that, helped immeasurably by alcohol, he'd been more sociable. She, in any case, had long felt by then that literature had nothing to say to her; it didn't change her vision of the world or make her see things in a different way. Instead, all that hot air depressed her profoundly without any author who was close to God or to anything. Andrew Breen, Houellebecq,

Arto Paasilinna, Derek Hobbs, Martin Amis. She felt distant from all those names, which for her had simply increased a list—Riba's catalog—a list now lost in time: former guests who once came to dine at her house; people who believed in nothing and who drank till dawn and who it was very difficult to get rid of.

A taxi was waiting downstairs for Celia, and almost from the moment she reached the landing and put her suitcase and bag in the elevator, Riba began to think how he could get her back. He spent all day calling her cell phone, but there was never any answer. And his anguish at her absence was increasing, and by a long way, exceeding any other anguish he'd had for any other absence. Yesterday, when Celia left with a loud Buddhist slam of the door—even now the slam still strikes Riba as Buddhist—he stood in the house trembling with fear, fearing everything, including the unwanted emotions that might get to him through the enigmatic intercom. And he regretted never having once taken note of the address of the place in Dublin where she attended her Buddhist meetings. Without Celia, he was filled with such an absolute fear of the world that he spent longer than ever sitting motionless in the rocking chair, staring at the reproduction of the small Hopper painting.

"Leave," the house said to him.

And he stayed in the rocking chair, half terrified, half obligingly, and even pretending that the painting of the stairway really had trapped him.

But as evening fell, as if he'd suddenly remembered that when it gets dark we all need someone, he got his strength back and began to move around the house, almost frenetically, until this unexpected restlessness ended up taking him all the way outside, where he trusted a stroke of luck would lead him to Celia, perhaps still walking round and round Dublin dragging her suitcase, in search of some society for the protection of Buddhists.

But it was he who started walking in circles, confused and lost in the city, bewildered, desperate. A nagging idea kept coming back to him of converting to Judaism—his mother's former religion, after all—so Celia would see he'd taken a spiritual turn in his life.

But most likely it was all futile. Celia had probably actually left the island by now.

He walked sadly along gay Grafton Street, stopping in front of all the shops with their awnings out. He took grievous delight in the muslin prints and silks, the young people from all over the world, the jingling of harnesses, the still echoing hoofthuds from bygone days lowringing in the baking causeway. He passed, dallying in front of the display windows of Brown Thomas, the venerable shop with its cascades of ribbons and flimsy China silks. He saw the grand house where Oscar Wilde spent his childhood, and then walked to the house where Bram Stoker, the creator of Dracula, lived for so many years. For a while, he could be seen walking along, ghostlike, as if he were one of those fellows that turned up so often in some of the most celebrated novels he published: those poor desperate romantics, always alone and without any direction or God, sleepwalking down lost highways.

On O'Connell Bridge he remembered that no one ever crosses it without seeing a white horse. He crossed it and didn't see anything. There was a white pigeon perched on O'Connell's head. But obviously a pigeon was not what he was looking for. "I feel ridiculous like this, without a white horse," he thought. And he retraced his steps. On Grafton Street, with patriotic fervor, he heard a street band playing "Green Fields of France," the ballad about the soldier Willie McBride. His Irish patriotism suddenly blended with an abrupt nostalgia for France, and the combination was stimulating. After that he spent a long time in the bar of the Shelbourne Hotel, and thought of phoning Walter from there, or Julia Piera, his Dublin contacts, but he didn't have the nerve. After all, he wasn't that close to them, and besides, he didn't think they could help him on the subject of Celia's departure. He could also call the two Irish writers he'd published years ago and who'd drunk his entire wine cellar dry, Andrew Breen and Derek Hobbs, but he remembered in time that he wouldn't be able to communicate with them. That day at his house, it had been Gauger who'd looked after the two restless Irishmen.

At 27 St. Stephen's Green, a few yards from the street where Dracula's creator had lived, he gave in to alcohol again. In the great bar of the Shelbourne Hotel, he unexpectedly *dracularized* himself with four shots of whiskey. Through the window overlooking the street he followed, bloodymindedly, the progress of a miserable godforsaken cat, with no owner … no author, no novice, no wife. For a while, the alley cat was him. He was a cat deep in spiritual and physical discomfort. He had a little straw hat tied on his head, making it quite clear he'd had an owner until very recently. As he walked he shook his paws, which were very wet. Riba followed his progress feeling like he wanted to bite his neck. Bite himself? Once again, alcohol had left its mark on him. He decided to leave, to go back to hiding out in his rocking chair because he couldn't risk running into Celia in one of these two places and her seeing him in that state again.

He phoned his parents in Barcelona.

"So you've been to Dublin," his mother said.

"I'm still there, Mama!"

"And what are your plans now?"

That damned question about his plans again. The question had already taken him very far once before, to where he is now. Dublin.

"I'm going to Cork because there's a revelation waiting for me there," he told her. "I'm hoping to talk to Celia's former lover."

"Isn't he dead?"

"You know perfectly well, Mama, that a little detail like that means absolutely nothing."

After these words, he had to hang up immediately, before everything got even more complicated.

He was about to ask for the bill in the increasingly lively bar of the Shelbourne when, flipping distractedly through the pages of the *Irish Times* that someone had just left on the next table, he came across the tiny and sinister death notice for Malachy Moore. He froze. So it was true, he thought, almost disheartened. The funeral was the next day, at noon, in Glasnevin. He was so shocked, it was as if he'd known the dead man his whole life. And as had happened weeks earlier in Barcelona, what again struck him as a great setback was that, the whole story of his life having been so tranquil for the last two years, this fictional side that he hadn't counted on and had no desire for should have grown so alarmingly. For if there was anything he'd particularly valued lately, it was the agreeably steady pace of his normal life, that daily world so calm and boring into which he thought he'd settled perfectly forever: his moderate life of long waits in Lyon or his long wait to go to Dublin, and then a long wait in Barcelona to return to Dublin, without it ever crossing his mind that there he'd end up at the funeral of a great stranger.

He's still astonished by the fact that it's not raining today. He arrives late at the cemetery, when they've already closed the coffin and it's impossible to see the dead man's face. In any case, the most likely thing is that today they're burying the person who a month ago, in the same place, he confused with his author.

In the front row are the parents and two girls who must be the sisters of the deceased. The two young women bear hardly any resemblance to Beckett, perhaps none at all. As for the parents, they seem more likely to be related to Joyce than to Beckett. However, most of the people there are young, which leads him to think that this person who died was in the prime of life. He has no reason to think differently; the funeral is very likely for that fellow glimpsed a month ago beside the gates of this cemetery: that glassy young man so prone to disappearing that finally he really did vanish.

He never thought he'd attend another funeral in Glasnevin, and much less that it would be for the young man in the round glasses, presumably his author. When the time comes for the speeches, he doesn't understand anything they say, but he can see that the first and second of the young people to speak in Gaelic are overcome by emotion. And to think that he'd thought of his author as a lone wolf, and when he says his author he's also saying that genius author he'd looked for so hard for his whole life and never found—maybe he has found him, but in this case he's been found after he was already dead. And to think that he'd imagined his author as a man with no friends, forever approaching a pier at the end of the world.

He doesn't understand any of the funeral speeches, but he thinks this is the real, the final funeral of the great whore of literature, the same one who caused this unparalleled pain, the publisher's sorrow that he's never been able to escape since. And he remembers that:

> As they wend away
> A voice is heard singing
> Of Kitty, or Katy,
> As if the name meant once
> All love, all beauty.

He doesn't understand anything they say. Due to his complete fragility, even in the way he stands, the first of the two young men to speak reminds him of Vilém Vok when he reflected aloud on his chimeric attempt to mature toward childhood. The second seems more sure of himself, but ends up bursting into tears and provoking a general outbreak of grief among those present. There is the emotional collapse of the parents. Someone faints, probably a relative. A small, great Irish drama. The death of Malachy Moore ends up seeming like a much more serious event than the end of the Gutenberg era and the end of the world. The loss of the author. The great Western problem. Or not. Or simply the loss of a young man with round glasses and a mackintosh. A great misfortune in any case, for the inner life and also for all those who still desire to use the word subjectively, to strain and stretch it toward thousands of connections of light still to be established in the great darkness of the world.

Action: The sorrow of the publisher.

On his way out of the funeral, seeing that the parents and two sisters are receiving the condolences of relatives and friends, he joins the line. When his turn comes, he shakes one of the sister's hands, then the other's, nods to the father and then turns to the mother and says in formal Spanish and with a conviction in his words that surprises himself:

"He was a hero. I never met him, but I wanted him to get better. I was following his condition for days, hoping for his recovery."

Then he makes way for the person behind him. It's as if he were saying that Malachy Moore had spent the last days of his life in a military hospital, mortally wounded from combating against the forces of evil. Or as if he had somehow wanted to tell them the author had been murdered by all of them together in one more stupid incident of our times. He thinks he hears the melody of "Green Fields of France" in the distance and is silently moved. The English leap, he thinks, has taken me further than I expected, because my feelings have changed. This seems like my land now. The draughty streets, end-on to hills. The faint archaic smell of the Irish docklands. The sea, awaiting me.

In some place, at the edge of one of his thoughts, he discovers a darkness that chills him to the bone. When he's getting ready to leave, he suddenly sees the young Beckett, standing right behind his two distressed sisters. They exchange glances and the surprise seems to register on both sides. The young man is wearing the same mackintosh as the other night, although more threadbare. The young man has the look of a fatigued philosopher and the unmistakable air of living a hindered, precarious, inert, uncertain, numb, terrified, unwelcoming, inconsolable life.

Maybe Dublin is right. And perhaps it is also true that there are interconnected points in space and time, focal points among which we so-called living and so-called dead can travel, and in this way, meet.

When he looks back in the direction of the young man, he's disappeared, and this time it's not the fog that has swallowed him up. The thing is he's no longer there.

Impossible not to go back to thinking there is a wrinkled piece of fabric that sometimes allows the living to see the dead and the dead to see the living, the survivors. Impossible too not to see Riba now walking along, overrun by ghosts, suffocated by his catalog, and weighed down by signs of the past. In New York the day is surely mild and sunny, fragrant and sharp like an apple. Here everything is darker.

He walks ahead weighed down by signs from the past, but he has taken the reappearance of the author as an incredibly optimistic sign. He feels like he's experiencing another moment at the center of the world. And he thinks of "The Importance of Elsewhere," that Larkin poem. And letting himself be swept up in the celebration of the moment, by the excitement of finally *being elsewhere*, he speaks like John Ford, in the first person plural.

"We are us, we are here," he says softly.

He doesn't know he is speaking unwittingly to his destiny marked by solitude. Because the fog has begun to take up a position around him, and the truth is it's been a while now since the last shadow on earth was interested in stalking him.

But he's still enthusiastic about the reappearance of the author.

"Well, what do you know. Always someone turns up you never dreamt of."

New Directions Paperbooks—a partial listing

César Aira
An Episode in the Life of a Landscape Painter
Ghosts
The Literary Conference
Will Alexander, The Sri Lankan Loxodrome
Paul Auster, The Red Notebook
Gennady Aygi, Child-and-Rose
Honoré de Balzac, Colonel Chabert
Djuna Barnes, Nightwood
Charles Baudelaire, The Flowers of Evil*
Bei Dao, The Rose of Time: New & Selected Poems*
Nina Berberova, The Ladies From St. Petersburg
Roberto Bolaño, By Night in Chile
Distant Star
Last Evenings on Earth
Nazi Literature in the Americas
The Skating Rink
Jorge Luis Borges, Labyrinths
Seven Nights
Coral Bracho, Firefly Under the Tongue*
Kamau Brathwaite, Ancestors
William Bronk, Selected Poems
Sir Thomas Browne, Urn Burial
Basil Bunting, Complete Poems
Anne Carson, Glass, Irony & God
Horacio Castellanos Moya, Senselessness
Tyrant Memory
Louis-Ferdinand Céline
Death on the Installment Plan
Journey to the End of the Night
René Char, Selected Poems
Inger Christensen, alphabet
Jean Cocteau, The Holy Terrors
Peter Cole, Things on Which I've Stumbled
Maurice Collis, Cortes & Montezuma
Julio Cortázar, Cronopios & Famas
Albert Cossery, A Splendid Conspiracy
Robert Creeley, If I Were Writing This
Life and Death
Guy Davenport, 7 Greeks
Osamu Dazai, The Setting Sun
H.D., Trilogy
Robert Duncan, Groundwork
Selected Poems
Eça de Queirós, The Maias
William Empson, 7 Types of Ambiguity
Shusaku Endo, Deep River
The Samurai

Jenny Erpenbeck, The Old Child
Visitation
Lawrence Ferlinghetti
A Coney Island of the Mind
A Far Rockaway of the Heart
Thalia Field, Bird Lovers, Backyard
F. Scott Fitzgerald, The Crack-Up
On Booze
Forrest Gander, As a Friend
Core Samples From the World
Romain Gary, The Life Before Us (Mme. Rosa)
William Gerhardie, Futility
Henry Green, Pack My Bag
Allen Grossman, Descartes' Loneliness
John Hawkes, The Lime Twig
Second Skin
Felisberto Hernández, Lands of Memory
Hermann Hesse, Siddhartha
Takashi Hiraide
For the Fighting Spirit of the Walnut*
Yoel Hoffman, The Christ of Fish
Susan Howe, My Emily Dickinson
That This
Bohumil Hrabal, I Served the King of England
Ihara Saikaku, The Life of an Amorous Woman
Christopher Isherwood, The Berlin Stories
Fleur Jaeggy, Sweet Days of Discipline
Gustav Janouch, Conversations With Kafka
Alfred Jarry, Ubu Roi
B. S. Johnson, House Mother Normal
Franz Kafka, Amerika: The Man Who Disappeared
Bob Kaufman, Solitudes Crowded With Loneliness
Heinrich von Kleist, Prince Friedrich of Homburg
Laszlo Krasznahorkai
The Melancholy of Resistance
War & War
Mme. de Lafayette, The Princess of Clèves
Lautréamont, Maldoror
Denise Levertov, Selected Poems
Tesserae
Li Po, Selected Poems
Clarice Lispector, The Hour of the Star
Soulstorm
Luljeta Lleshanaku, Child of Nature
Federico García Lorca, Selected Poems*
Three Tragedies
Nathaniel Mackey, Splay Anthem
Stéphane Mallarmé, Selected Poetry and Prose*

Javier Marías, All Souls
  A Heart So White
  Your Face Tomorrow (3 volumes)
Thomas Merton, New Seeds of Contemplation
  The Way of Chuang Tzu
Henri Michaux, Selected Writings
Dunya Mikhail, Diary of a Wave Outside the Sea
Henry Miller, The Air-Conditioned Nightmare
  Big Sur & The Oranges of Hieronymus Bosch
  The Colossus of Maroussi
Yukio Mishima, Confessions of a Mask
  Death in Midsummer
Teru Miyamoto, Kinshu: Autumn Brocade
Eugenio Montale, Selected Poems*
Vladimir Nabokov, Laughter in the Dark
  Nikolai Gogol
  The Real Life of Sebastian Knight
Pablo Neruda, The Captain's Verses*
  Love Poems*
  Residence on Earth*
Charles Olson, Selected Writings
George Oppen, New Collected Poems (with CD)
Wilfred Owen, Collected Poems
Michael Palmer, Thread
Nicanor Parra, Antipoems*
Boris Pasternak, Safe Conduct
Kenneth Patchen, The Walking-Away World
Octavio Paz, The Collected Poems 1957–1987*
  A Tale of Two Gardens
Victor Pelevin, Omon Ra
Saint-John Perse, Selected Poems
Ezra Pound, The Cantos
  New Selected Poems and Translations
  Personae
Raymond Queneau, Exercises in Style
Qian Zhongshu, Fortress Besieged
Raja Rao, Kanthapura
Herbert Read, The Green Child
Kenneth Rexroth, Songs of Love, Moon & Wind
  Written on the Sky: Poems from the Japanese
Rainer Maria Rilke
  Poems from the Book of Hours
  The Possibility of Being
Arthur Rimbaud, Illuminations*
  A Season in Hell and The Drunken Boat*
Guillermo Rosales, The Halfway House
Evilio Rosero, The Armies
  Good Offices
Joseph Roth, The Leviathan

Jerome Rothenberg, Triptych
William Saroyan
  The Daring Young Man on the Flying Trapeze
Jean-Paul Sartre, Nausea
  The Wall
Delmore Schwartz
  In Dreams Begin Responsibilities
W. G. Sebald, The Emigrants
  The Rings of Saturn
  Vertigo
Aharon Shabtai, J'accuse
Hasan Shah, The Dancing Girl
C. H. Sisson, Selected Poems
Gary Snyder, Turtle Island
Muriel Spark, The Ballad of Peckham Rye
  A Far Cry From Kensington
  Memento Mori
George Steiner, At the New Yorker
Antonio Tabucchi, Indian Nocturne
  Pereira Declares
Yoko Tawada, The Naked Eye
Dylan Thomas, A Child's Christmas in Wales
  Collected Poems
  Under Milk Wood
Uwe Timm, The Invention of Curried Sausage
Charles Tomlinson, Selected Poems
Tomas Tranströmer
  The Great Enigma: New Collected Poems
Leonid Tsypkin, Summer in Baden-Baden
Tu Fu, Selected Poems
Frederic Tuten, The Adventures of Mao
Paul Valéry, Selected Writings
Enrique Vila-Matas, Bartleby & Co.
Elio Vittorini, Conversations in Sicily
Rosmarie Waldrop, Driven to Abstraction
Robert Walser, The Assistant
  The Tanners
Eliot Weinberger, An Elemental Thing
  Oranges and Peanuts for Sale
Nathanael West
  Miss Lonelyhearts & The Day of the Locust
Tennessee Williams, Cat on a Hot Tin Roof
  The Glass Menagerie
  A Streetcar Named Desire
William Carlos Williams, In the American Grain
  Paterson
  Selected Poems
  Spring and All
Louis Zukofsky, "A"
  Anew

*BILINGUAL EDITION

For a complete listing, request a free catalog from New Directions, 80 8th Avenue, NY NY 10011
or visit us online at www.ndpublishing.com